Diamond River Man

DIAMOND RIVER MAN

EUGENE CUNNINGHAM

THORNDIKE
CHIVERS

This Large Print edition is published by Thorndike Press, Waterville, Maine, USA and by AudioGO Ltd, Bath, England.
Thorndike Press, a part of Gale, Cengage Learning.
Copyright © 1934 by Eugene Cunningham. Copyright © renewed 1961 by Mary Caroline Cunningham.
The moral right of the author has been asserted.

The text of this Large Print edition is unabridged.
Other aspects of the book may vary from the original edition.
Set in 16 pt. Plantin.

LIBRARY OF CONGRESS CATALOGING-IN-PUBLICATION DATA

Cunningham, Eugene, 1896-1957.
   Diamond river man / by Eugene Cunningham. — Large print ed.
     p. cm. — (Thorndike Press large print western)
   ISBN-13: 978-1-4104-4317-5 (hardcover)
   ISBN-10: 1-4104-4317-5 (hardcover)
   1. Large type books. I. Title.
PS3505.U428D53 2011
813'.52—dc23   2011033350

BRITISH LIBRARY CATALOGUING-IN-PUBLICATION DATA AVAILABLE

Published in 2011 in the U.S. by arrangement with Golden West Literary Agency.
Published in 2012 in the U.K. by arrangement with Golden West Literary Agency.

U.K. Hardcover: 978 1 445 88132 4 (Chivers Large Print)
U.K. Softcover: 978 1 445 88133 1 (Camden Large Print)

Printed in the United States of America
1 2 3 4 5 6 7 15 14 13 12 11

To Jean
This Book is "Decorated"

Chapter I
"How Are the Old Folks Betting?"

The plaza was the only busy part of Tom's Bluff when young Lit Taylor came along the Diamond River's bank from Ike Menter's saloon. There was to be a race of unusual sort — a man against a horse. The lithe, carefree young buckaroos of the Bar-B, the XLA, the L-in-a-Box, the Ladder-M, the Three-Prod, and other outfits big and little, had gathered to watch the race and lay some bets — chiefly on the horse, of course!

Lit was not much interested in the race. Today, he had a decision to make. And he was pulled two ways — pulled by loyalty to Old Man Barbee, his foster-father, pulled by restlessness that burned in him and made him weary of everything he knew, made him itch to swing up on his black horse and go riding to meet the line where the blue Texas sky came down to touch the flat lands.

He went slowly across the dusty width of the plaza, six feet tall, wolfishly lean in blue flannel shirt and green wool trousers that were rammed hit-or-miss into bootlegs. His floppy black hat was pushed back on dark hair. Ordinarily pleasant face was a mask of sulky bronze.

He loafed up to the men massed about the starting line. "Slippery" Elms, like Lit a Bar-B rider, cocked tousled towhead up at the taller man. He was more than a little drunk, Slippery. He always stayed that way when the Bar-B outfit played in Tom's Bluff.

"It ain't in reason no man can outrun a quarter hawse — not fifty yard to that post an' fifty yard back!" he said belligerently, as if Lit had held the contrary. "Is it, boy?"

"Don't know," Lit shrugged, without interest.

"If I had me some *dinero* I'd certainly bet," Slippery grunted. "But I spent my last *sou* on a bottle — drink, Lit?"

Lit hesitated, then nodded. He took the flask and lifted it to his mouth. He didn't *want* another drink, but he was not yet twenty-one and correspondingly anxious to show that he could do anything, at any time, that anyone else could do. He let the flaming home-made whiskey run down his throat, choked back a sputter and returned the bottle. As he watched the odd, imperturbable figure of the man who would run

8

Jick Rogers's sorrel horse, a slight haze wavered between his eyes and the broad, long-legged stranger. For he had downed several tincupfuls of Ike Menter's liquor since breakfast and it was not yet eleven of the morning.

"Yon' comes Frenchy an' his gang," Slippery grinned. "I bet you Frenchy an' them other Rowdy River boys'll bet."

Lit turned a little. Dark eyes narrowed. It was the boy-gunman who had given him his problem. One by one, he sized for the hundredth time the quartet crossing the plaza toward him. But with more thought of Frenchy Leonard than of the others, who were merely the followers of the handsome, deadly youngster.

Good sports, all, were Frenchy, Art Brand, big "Irish Tim" Fenelon and "Hognose" Ott. Tom's Bluff said so, in a majority of its voices. Good fellows, for all that three of them were, each in his own right, figures of blazing notoriety throughout a wide scope of country, and much wanted by the authorities of certain counties in the neighboring Territory.

During the winter, like the dozens of other cowboys who made Tom's Bluff their rendezvous or place-of-call, to drink and gamble at poker and monte, to dance at the *bailes* down in "Hogtown," the Mexican quarter, and make wild love to the slim, pretty, ready-mouthed girls, Lit Taylor had fraternized with the four outlaws. He had eaten with them, drunk with them.

Their records meant nothing at all to the Diamond River buckaroos. It was a long way from this little cow-town on the Diamond's bank over to the Territory. Rewards on their heads, even, were nothing more than appealing marks of saltiness. The happy-go-lucky riders in and about this lusty little community scorned blood money.

So Frenchy Leonard's gang, which had ridden like a band of raiding Arabs up and down the Territory, was greeted in Tom's Bluff precisely like any other quartet of floating cowboys.

"Hell!" the cowboys said. "They never dabbed a loop on any of our stuff. And they put none of our bunch in Boot Hill. If that bunch of star-toters over in the Territory want Frenchy and his outfit so bad, why don't they come get 'em? It's not up to Diamond River men to do their work for 'em!"

Even now, Lit saw how, as usual, Frenchy and the others had Diamond River men with them. The slender, dark, cat-graceful,

10

cat-quick boy owned an odd magnetism that drew most men irresistibly. Lit had fallen under the spell during the winter. Now, it was for him to decide whether he would throw in with Frenchy, ride west with the four, or stick on the Bar-B to go through all the hard, tiresome work of spring round-up and ensuing routine. He found it a troublesome decision.

Not that he bothered much about the legal features of Frenchy's troubles. He was at the age to look at the adventurous side of things. Too, Frenchy had several times told him how the price had been put upon his head. As Frenchy related the story, it was so reasonable, so familiar, that Lit or any other could say:

"Off the old chunk! Big cowmen are always up to something like that. It could happen to you, or me, or anybody!"

Everybody had heard of the Territory. Everybody knew how jumbled things were across the Rowdy River. Quite often, it was the honest man who found himself outside the law, while cowthieves and murderers sat in the saddle, riding roughshod, buying and selling county offices as suited them, issuing warrants for their rivals and competitors, shooting them down very legally on the pretense that they had resisted arrest.

It was old Barbee who checked Lit's quick acceptance of Frenchy Leonard's offer. Years before, back in Tennessee, he and Lit's father had been the closest of friends. When Lit had been orphaned, eight years before, it was Barbee who had heard of it and made the journey back to get Lit and bring him to his house and in every way stand in place of Lit's father.

Barbee was like the rest of the big cowmen. As men of property, they were naturally more analytical of strangers than were their wild young hands. Old Barbee had in no degree fallen under the spell of this always-smiling master gunman who, despite his scant twenty years, was said to have no equal at handling the Colts, and who was acknowledged leader of men almost twice his age. He did not like Frenchy. He said so, very plainly.

They came on across to Lit and Slippery. Frenchy stopped at Lit's elbow:

"Hi, boy!" he cried cheerfully. "How you bettin'?"

"Don't know," Lit shrugged. "Likely, neither way."

"He aims to git his growth, an' not crowd his luck none, before he steps out an' bucks growed-up men," a voice drawled.

Lit turned slowly, to stare into the long,

jade-green eyes of a man whom he had hated at first sight, hated without asking himself why he should know instantly that here was an enemy — the first man he had ever hated.

This was a newcomer to Tom's Bluff, known only as "Bisbee." The cowboys had nicknamed him promptly after their fashion, when he *said* that he was up from Arizona and named a camp without too much of hesitation. He was as tall as Lit, but forty pounds heavier. Wide of shoulders, thick of chest, there was something bearish about his bigness and the way he moved, shambling, yet sure of himself, among the wild, touchy young riders using the cow-town on the Diamond.

He had long, sleek, black hair and a large, strangely pallid face. Slippery Elms, looking for the first time upon this "Bisbee" after several shots of Ike Menter's scorching whiskey, had remarked confidentially to Lit that Bisbee's face reminded *him* of a ham.

"If, you understand," Slippery had hedged, "a ham was to be whitewashed an' put in a black wig, an' had two ears an' one ear was to be gotched by somebody's bowie."

Bisbee's strange, long green eyes, his gash of a mouth, his habit of sitting statue-still

13

by the hour in a saloon's corner, staring straight ahead; the shrill, spine-rasping cackle of his infrequent laughter — all these things had effect upon Tom's Bluff in general, as upon Lit Taylor in particular. Though he had hooked up with the Three-Prod and proved himself a Hand in every department of the puncher's work, not even to fellow riders had he ever thawed in the least degree. Now, with heavy, doughy face contemptuous, he grinned at Lit.

"How" — Lit spoke in gentlest drawl, copying as nearly as possible old Barbee's war voice — "are the Old Folks betting?"

Bisbee's cackling laugh rasped his nerves, as always. But he kept his flaming temper under control. Above everything, he wanted to avoid acting like a yapping kid.

"Sonny!" Bisbee grinned. "Us grown folks, we feel like puttin' up some *oro* on the hawse. 'Course, mebbe we don't know. Mebbe it's the Orphan Asylum'll show us up."

"Looks like 'put up, or shut up' to me," Frenchy grinned.

Lit's eyes shuttled almost irritably to Frenchy. He had a hundred dollars, but that was spotted for a saddle. Left alone, he would have "experted" just as Bisbee was doing — in favor of Jick Rogers's horse against the runner. He came very near to disliking Frenchy at that moment. But he kept his face blank.

"Maybe a hundred dollars on the man will help you think, the next time you start picking a winner," he said evenly.

"Hold the stakes, Frenchy!" Bisbee grinned. "This is the nearest to money from home that I had in years!"

"They're about ready," Slippery Elms called excitedly. "Linin' up, now! Ever see laigs like that stranger's got!"

Lit held himself relaxed as he turned to watch the start. He was impressed by the indifference of the runner. The man's thoughts seemed to be miles away. Either he was beaten before he began, or supremely confident that he would win against that famous dun of Rogers's; win as he had won against the punchers who esteemed themselves afoot.

He had spoken merest truth, when he said that heretofore the race had not interested him. But, now that his money was up and what amounted to an issue existed, between him and Bisbee, he found himself staring grimly at his hope, appraising those long, knobby-kneed legs that must outpace the fastest thing in horseflesh that the Diamond River boasted.

As he stared, with brown face hardened, toward the curious ones at the starting line, he thought that he would cheerfully waive all claim to the hundred if he could only win. He wanted to look Bisbee up and down and laugh gently — the way old Barbee would do it, or Long Al Kendrick the Bar-B wagon boss, or any other of the salty, seasoned figures to whom the young buckaroos looked for Model and Manners.

The mass of men about runner and horse thickened, then gave back. Lit could better see the start, now. He frowned.

"Not going to give the man a start," he thought. "That looks funny. Any man running against that little dun devil ought to have *some* lead!"

He saw an arm come up above the wide hats of the cowboys. An arm that raised a long-barreled Colt. Over the murmur of voices, there sounded abruptly the heavy bellow of a .45 shot.

The runner was gone. Almost, it seemed, he "beat the gun." For he was crossing the plaza with those knobby knees lifting, falling, lifting, falling, while yet the dun seemed to be gathering himself together. He ran as Lit had never seen a man run before; ran as he had hardly dreamed a man could run. The dun, though, was moving now.

"Yaaaiiiaaah!" Lit yelled — nor knew that his voice was drowned by the other yells of the triumphant, or startled, cowboys about him. *"Yaaaiiiaaah!"*

The incredibly long legs were flashing like — like the pistons of an engine, Lit thought. The dun, though, was crawling up on the runner. He reached him, then for an instant as the cottonwood post on the plaza's far side was near, the runner was blanketed by the horse's streaking body, twinkling legs.

Bisbee spoke drawlingly, all but in Lit's ear:

"Aw, now! *Ain't* that hell! An' for a minute you could almost count that money! Well — live an' learn! ought to be a kid's motto, I say. An' nothin' like losin' money to learn 'em!"

"That so?" Lit inquired gently, narrowed, furious eyes on the confusion about that cottonwood post which the racers must round. "You ——" He stiffened incredulously, then whirled triumphantly back to Bisbee. "Looky!" he bellowed. "Just looky!"

For the runner had the inside on the way to the post. He slapped hand upon it, came around it in a snaky twist and was pounding down the homestretch while still the dun swung wide. Those knobby knees, those long legs, seemed merely something hazy,

17

fluttering, suspended from the runner's waist.

If he had seemed to run like a machine on the way to the post, Lit had no words to describe the speed with which he hurtled toward the starting point. When he came closer, with the dun now pounding in his wake, Lit saw that the indifference was vanished from the man's face. It was twisted, now, strained; he was concentrated on manufacturing the utmost in speed to beat that dun flash behind him.

Lit, at least, now had little doubt of the outcome. The light rider on the dun jerked arm aloft. His quirt descended, rose, descended . . . He was quirting his mount furiously — quirting him withers and haunches. But it was too late — the man was too far ahead to be more than caught at the line.

Pandemonium was all about Lit. Even those cowboys who had not felt like betting — or had not been able to place a bet on the horse, were infected by the thrill of this unexpected finish that overturned their every idea of values. The more excited sent hats sailing into the air — and popped away at them with six shooters. Lit leaned this way and that, to see through the confusion over there at the line what had happened. The dun was little behind the runner now.

Then ——

A terrific roar went up, from the crowd there. Lit sent his own hat zooming up and yelled savagely. Suddenly, he caught himself, wiped expression from his face as with a sponge. He relaxed in every muscle of long body and turned with slitted, indifferent eyes to Bisbee.

The big man's doughy face was whiter than Lit had ever seen it before. The gash-thin mouth was lipless and lifted at one side. Slowly, as if drawn by Lit's stare, Bisbee turned to face the Bar-B's "baby." Long, jade-green eyes were very bright. They made Lit think of the eyes of a sidewinder rattle-snake he had killed. But whatever Bisbee might have said or done was interrupted by Frenchy Leonard.

The grinning boy whirled and smacked a hand hard between Bisbee's shoulder blades. There was an impishness about Frenchy that Lit had noted before this — he was always finding a way to plague the men about him, egging one against another. He seemed to be laughing at Bisbee, now, as before the race he had seemed to laugh at Lit:

"Well, sir!" he cried. "If my eyes don't deceive me, the unpossible has happened. An' all this-here *dinero* I got in my paw, it's

Lit's. You see her like that, Bisbee?"

Bisbee swallowed, seemed about to speak, but only nodded.

"Looks like Bisbee experted the wrong way!"

This was Hognose Ott, junior of the Leonard gang, a weak youngster whose great ambition was to be thought a gunman.

"Shut your goddam mouth!" Bisbee almost whispered to Hognose. And the very repression of his tone made it the more deadly. He leaned a little toward Hognose and Ott slid a step backward, with mouth sagging.

"Yeh," Hognose said vaguely, eyes on Bisbee. "Yeh."

"Well," Lit said in the easiest, most careless, voice he could manage — a tolerable copy of old Barbee's in moments of strain, "I think I'll split my winnings with the runner."

CHAPTER II
THE TIN TYPE GIRL

Coming down the river bank, rounding the curve on which Boot Hill sprawled with its dozen of raw graves, Lit met Old Man Barbee. The wizened little cowman stopped and fumbled in the pockets of ancient, button-less vest for tobacco and papers.

"Well," he drawled, "looks like you kind o' shut Bisbee up — for the time bein'. But that won't end things, sonny. He will be to kill, yet! Don't you think he won't."

"He don't like losing," Lit nodded.

Barbee worked with brown "saddle blanket" paper, rolling a match-thin cigarette. He thrust it in his mouth under straggling gray mustache, reached to hat band for a match, flicked head on thumbnail. Over the tiny flame his shrewd, narrow old eyes were carelessly steady on the young face opposite.

"Reckon that Frenchy an' his bunch'll be hittin' out, today. Back to the Rowdy, huh?"

Lit's eyes shuttled suspiciously to the blank, wise old face. Barbee stared without expression down the street.

"Well," Barbee said after a moment of silence. "What do you 'low, Lit? You have been right thick with 'em."

Lit shrugged. His face was sulky. Barbee waited, but when it was plain that Lit did not intend to reply, he took the cigarette from his mouth. He was watching Lit, now. The roll of hard fingers that reduced cigarette to shreds of paper and tobacco, floating on the little wind, seemed unconsciously done.

"Sonny," he said very slowly, "I hope you

don't listen too much to Frenchy Leonard. He's a bad egg. I know it. You will know the same, some day. Swingin' a wide loop is one thing — lots of us have done that, then settled down to decent livin'. But Frenchy an' them gun-fightin' thieves with him, *they* are throwin' the long rope, dabbin' the hungry loop onto other folks' stuff. An' you can't talk around plain rustlin'! No, sir!

"The time is bound to come when this-here country will have to draw the line between straight shootin' an' shady dealin'. When that time comes — well! Frenchy an' his likes'll be took out an' used up for decoratin' the handiest cottonwood!"

He made a small motion of his shoulders. Lit, staring at dusty boots, still made no answer.

"I — think a lot of you, sonny. You *sabe* how I feel. For your father's sake an' for your own. You got the makin' of a fine man in you. I don't want to see you get off on the wrong foot. You know, Mother always figured like you was her own. If she was still with us, it'd about bust her heart to see you go ridin' off with the worthless likes of Frenchy Leonard an' them other no-accounts. No matter what Frenchy says he's aimin' to do, no matter if he does claim he's just handlin' wet stuff from across the Rio

22

Grande, it's a bad racket!"

Lit felt forced to say something. And there was very little that he thought of, nothing at all which would contradict Barbee's opinion. He nodded vaguely.

"I know," he nodded. "I know all that. I have been thinking things over a lot."

"You have got a good head on you," Barbee nodded, then added with the ghost of a grin hovering in the wrinkles of his weathered face, "even if to date you haven't used it much!"

He turned away. Lit looked after him. Sulkiness lightened. There was real affection in his expression. Then he lifted one shoulder uncertainly, went on around the loop of the Diamond that plucked with wet, greedy fingers at Boot Hill graves. Before he came to Ike Menter's weathered store-saloon, he heard the sounds of celebration. When he reached the door, on impulse he did not go in, but stopped in the doorway.

His lean six feet were all too many for the door. So he put back against one facing and stretched long legs comfortably. He stared out fixedly, unseeingly, upon the single dusty street of Tom's Bluff.

His position made it necessary for thirsty warriors of the various outfits to step over him. Several did so enter the saloon. They made goodhumored, if profane, comment, as they cleared the barrier. Lit hardly heard them. He was concentrating on the problem that worried him.

It seemed to him that old Barbee's voice was trying to drown the goodnatured voices at the bar. Lit identified some of the voices and sulkiness came again to his face, with thought of those men with whom Frenchy Leonard had asked him to ride and raid. He liked Frenchy, he told himself. He liked the huge, fearless, goodhumored Irish Tim Fenelon. Art Brand, the rat-eyed little first lieutenant of the gang, and that weak cowboy, Hognose, he liked not so much.

"But they're all right, when you come down to it," he told himself. "Anyway, there's a lot more fun to sliding across the Rio Grande into Mexico, swooping down on some *ranchero*'s herds and cutting out a bunch, fighting off the *vaqueros* and pushing the wet stuff back into Texas, than to sticking here. What'll I get, on the Bar-B? Hard work, that's what!"

He moved his shoulders impatiently, at last. He shifted the hang of his cartridge belt with a twitch that slightly moved the long-barreled, single-action .44 Colt in its open-topped holster, brought the butt under his hand. He straightened, with a single sinuous movement like the stretching of a young timber wolf.

As he stood erect, turning a little, he found himself staring Bisbee straight in the face. And Bisbee's long green eyes were narrow . . .

Lit wondered how Bisbee intended to greet him. It was the first meeting since the race. Into Lit's mind flashed abruptly the words of old Barbee — "he'll be to kill, yet!" So he strained to keep his face blank, his manner careless.

"You got a lease on that dam' door, maybe?" Bisbee inquired snarlingly. "If you ain't, then get to hell out o' my way!"

Lit's flaming temper, never very far from the surface, surged up instantly. Apparently, Bisbee had been drinking. But Lit guessed that it was the loss of his bet, and the "hur-rahing" that Bisbee had suffered from Frenchy and the Diamond River cowboys, which made him, now, obviously "on the prod."

But he gave little thought to that. He was stiffened by that instinctive hostility he had always known for this one-eared, green-eyed man. Deliberately, he let right hand sag a little more, until it was all but about the Colt's handle. He had only to close his fingers, to grip the curving black butt.

25

"There's a quick way of getting me out of here!" he told Bisbee, in the slow drawl that was copy of old Barbee's. "That is, of course, if you've got no grudge against hanging out in Boot Hill!"

The tension made the back of his neck seem to burn. He was nervous, strained, to the point of shaking — and he knew it and the realization made him more furious still. He was not afraid of Bisbee. He was merely afraid that he might not get through the mechanical part of a row with Bisbee in a way that would make him pleased with himself. He had seen the mechanics of a gun-fight three or four times, operating in battles between other men. He was horribly afraid that he would show the nervousness he felt. *That* was the deadly sin!

"Boot Hill, sonny," Bisbee replied in unworried-seeming sneer, "is a place I might use for a garden. But it won't be no mouthy damned kid makes me use it for a bunkin' place!"

With that grim boast, he came straight at Lit, who waited stiffly, sucking breath in swiftly between hard-clenched teeth, his gun-hand like a claw that *ached* for sheer rigidness of tendons. Over the way, in Hogan's dive, some dance-hall floozie was hammering tinnily on a dilapidated piano.

26

From the saloon at his back came the sound of cheerful voices with, for undertone, the high drone of that incorrigible liar "Double Ananias" Willeford, relating some incredible — but of course plausible — tale of his single-handed combats.

But all this was far and far away! Lit felt as if he were standing high up above everything, in a sort of cold isolation. In a split-second, he was either going to kill a man or himself be killed. It was his first experience of the kind and he had plenty of imagination which leaped ahead of this moment, painted the details in vividest colorings. He was much like a thoroughbred colt at the first barrier. Then ——

Bisbee brushed past him, went on inside without a sidewise or backward look.

Lit wheeled mechanically, to watch the big figure shamble down the length of the unpainted pine bar. He watched Bisbee halt beside Frenchy Leonard. Bisbee leaned to the slim boy and pressed great shoulder against Frenchy's. He seemed to be whispering and Frenchy listened intently, head on one side, staring up into Bisbee's tallowy face. At the end, when Bisbee straightened, waited, Frenchy seemed to consider for seconds. Then he grinned, shrugged and shoved a whiskey bottle toward Bisbee, who made a long arm and got a tin cup, poured himself a drink.

Now that the strain was past, Lit found himself shaking violently. He wondered why Bisbee had backed down. He wondered if he had comported himself properly. Should he have made Bisbee stand up to his threats? It bothered him very much. He tried to think it out, recalling what he knew of men who were looked up to as models in this rough world.

But he had not made any decision when the throng inside came surging out to the street. Lit stepped back to watch them pass. He hoped that they would simply swing into the saddles and go on, taking it for granted that he was not joining them. That would simplify his problem. Rather, it would wipe out the problem. He would always regret not going, but if he went, he knew that he would be uncomfortable every time he thought of old Barbee's wise, wrinkled face, his shrewd, kindly eyes.

Frenchy passed, looking toward the horses, missing Lit. Art Brand, Hognose, the huge Tim Fenelon, went past Lit without noticing him. Then Frenchy, catching up trailing reins, turned. His amber-flecked black eyes found Lit, who leaned gloomily against the building's front wall.

The little outlaw's prominent teeth — that showed always in the semblance of a grin, whether he danced or drank or fought — flashed now in widening of the grin. He lifted a hand.

"Lit! Oh, Lit!" he called. "Come here a minute, boy."

Unwillingly, Lit went over to stand and look down at Frenchy. Brand and Fenelon and Ott mounted, then sat watching the two, the tall youngster and the short.

"Aw, come on with us," Frenchy urged Lit, in confidential tone. Grudgingly, Lit admitted that it still had influence over him, in spite of the way Frenchy had seemed to play Bisbee against him, at the race. "You're too good a man to stick here!"

"I don't know what to do," Lit shrugged. "I swear — I just don't. I think one way, then think the other."

"Think this way, then!" Frenchy grinned. "We're headin' for a hot time, a sweet time. I'd like to cut you in on it. I need another good boy I can depend on. An' his name's — Lit Taylor! Listen!"

He leaned toward Lit, lowered his ingratiating voice:

"I got a hacienda picked out for a lick. Old Gonzalez's *rancho* across the river. It's lousy with stuff for us. Fat, sassy steers!

Horses that *is* horses! An' them *vaqueros* o' Gonzalez's — hell! They'll hightail it the minute they sight *me!* We will clean Gonzalez like he never dreamed o' bein' cleaned!"

He waited, but when Lit made no reply, only moved his shoulders sullenly and stared at his feet, Frenchy shook his head:

"You dam' fool!" he cried, half in good humor, half in exasperation. "What does a man have to offer you, to make you look halfway interested? Well, then — the cows ain't all! Nor the *caballos.* Gonzalez has got three-four gals . . . I seen 'em! They're just the kind to look the sweetest, ridin' behind our saddles when we head back for the Bravo. Lookers! Why, these cow-camp battle-axes — hell! They ain't one-two on a ten count, alongside them Gonzalez gals. Come on, Lit! What's here? Twenty-five a month — an' sweat your backbone out! Boy, you ride with me an' I'll weight down your hat with gold pieces! Dam' it! If I hadn't cottoned to you, I wouldn't be askin' you to come!"

Lit's shifting eyes found a face, grim, weathered to the red-brown color of an old saddle, blank of all expression, in the background of the men outside the store. Old Man Barbee watched without making any sign whatever. But mere sight of him was enough to make Lit uncomfortable.

Frenchy scooped up his reins, swung into the saddle. He looked down at Lit.

"We'll do more'n bulge your pockets," he grinned. "We'll make a Man out o' you, sonny!"

The cowboys laughed, staring from Frenchy to Lit and back again. Lit stiffened and glared at Frenchy. Standing an even six feet in bootless feet, muscled like a jaguar, flashingly deft of movement as a big cat — to have Frenchy Leonard, a year his junior, insinuate that he was no more than a kid, infuriated him as almost nothing else could have done.

Under the smooth tan of his face the blood surged up. He could break Frenchy across his knee, throw Art Brand or Hognose Ott over his shoulder, even match the huge Fenelon at rough-and-tumble fighting. He lowered at them, where Fenelon and Brand leaned across saddle horns, grinning at him and Ott — after a quick glance around for cue — began to laugh.

"Say!" he cried furiously. "Any time I —— You — none of you —— Make a man out of me, hell! Why ——"

"Hightail!" Frenchy yelled. "We'll come hear him preach, some day. I bet you, he's a Babtis'!"

31

He roweled the long-legged buckskin he rode, went up the sandy track like something shot from a gun. The others hurtled after him. Back to the crowd before Menter's came Frenchy's gay yell:

"Yaaaiiaaah! Leavin' town!"

Lit stared after the riders, now vanishing in the dust cloud. Leaning there against the Cottonwood hitch rack, he found himself disgusted with everything he knew. Found himself, too, faced by a new puzzle.

"Maybe I ought've dragged him out of that hull," he thought. "I could've held both of those slick, quick gunhands he's so proud of, with one of mine, then slammed him up against the wall and shook some manners into him. But, if I had touched him, one of the others, or all of the others, they would have drilled me before a man could say *Robinson* — or a lot shorter name than that! And be damned if *that's* Spanish!"

His wandering eyes found something in the sand at his feet, something that glinted from the spot where Frenchy Leonard had been standing. Lit moved a step forward, bent, picked up an oval locket of yellow gold that dangled, now, from a bit of thin chain. He stared.

"I wonder! Did Frenchy drop this?" he asked himself. Certainly, he had found it in a spot which had been all but under the buckskin's hoofs.

He turned the locket over and over, saw a tiny catch button and pressed it. There was a picture inside. He stared and his eyes went narrow as he looked at the girl's face.

She was young — very young, he decided. And the fluffy hair was yellow. He knew it, somehow. So, naturally, the wide, frank eyes must be blue. She had a forehead low and broad, a pert little nose, well-shaped mouth that matched determined chin. All in all —

"By Gemini!" he breathed amazedly. "I didn't know they raised 'em like that, in this part of the country or over in the Territory! In all *my* ramblings and tramblings, I've never come onto anything like her match. Wonder who she can be? And how the devil did that little killer-rustler get hold of this?"

He regarded the face with head on one side, put up a hand to move his hat over one eye. Critically, he inspected the face once more, feature by feature. He smiled at her.

"Glad to meet you!" he said softly. "And damned if *that's* Spanish! You pretty thing! Oh — you pretty, *pretty* thing!"

A soft scuffing of feet behind him, that stopped suddenly, stiffened Lit. Instinctively, he slid the locket into a shirt pocket, then turned, fumbling with the strings of tobacco sack.

It was Bisbee, a yard away. The doughy face was expressionless, but the green eyes were narrow, very bright, as he stared fixedly at Lit's lifted hand. Lit took out his tobacco, met the stare stonily. Bisbee rid himself of cigarette stub by the simple expedient of blowing it from his lips.

"What was that you picked up, sonny?" he demanded flatly.

Lit drew a long, slow breath, trying to rid himself of the tension that this one-eared man could rouse in him. Then, holding his voice very low, very even: "And how does that happen to be any of *your* damned business?" he asked.

He was standing now with the hand that held tobacco sack against the black butt of his Colt. It seemed to him that Bisbee's green eyes flashed down to find Lit's gunhand, then up.

"I can easy *make* it some o' my business, sonny," Bisbee nodded meaningly, after a lengthy moment.

"Oh," Lit nodded in his turn. "You've got a wolf, then. Well, untie him! Let him howl! And you listen to one thing, Mister: Don't make any more of your 'sonny' breaks!

34

Around me, they'll average up just about one to a killing!"

"I see," Bisbee said mockingly. "It's got its li'l' popgun — just like real folks. It might even think it *was* real folks. But I ain't easy bluffed! Now, about whatever it was that you picked up ——"

Lit could hold the copy of Barbee's drawl no longer.

"What's the matter?" he jeered. "Where's that great, big wolf that was going to bite me? Hell's bells! Mean to say I'm not dead, yet? I must be! After all your big talk. Oh, you want to know about what I picked up, do you? Well, I'll tell you about that: Whatever it was, you can have a look at it — when you get big enough to take it away from me! Put up or — shut up!"

"You got a lot to find out, yet," Bisbee grunted. But if his voice were contemptuous drawl, he could not keep balked fury out of his eyes. Lit saw — and wondered — and was suddenly triumphant. He grinned one-sidedly at the elder man.

"Don't you think for a minute that this'll settle a thing!" Bisbee warned him and turned away, back toward the saloon door.

Lit frowned after him. Suddenly, he was not so pleased with himself as he had been. Watching the broad, retreating back, he

asked himself once again what a seasoned
man would have done. He wondered if he
should have forced a showdown then and
there, matching his speed on the draw
against whatever Bisbee could do.

"Looks like making up my mind is the one
thing I can't do without somebody helping
me," he thought sulkily.

Then he grinned faintly. It had been
amazingly easier to face the prospect of gun-
play, here, this time! That much he could
mark down on the credit side of the affair.

CHAPTER III
"WHAT'D YOU PICK UP —
SONNY?"

Toward supper time, Lit wandered back to
Ike Menter's. He was in bad humor. For, as
he had expected, everywhere that he had
gone he had been greeted by Frenchy's
taunt. The gunman's sneer at his callowness
had been recalled with huge enjoyment by
the cowboys in town. The fact that they
were all his very good friends made their
grinning remarks the more aggravating, for
it limited the steps he could take to show
his resentment. So he was scowling when
he stalked into Menter's and pushed in

36

between drinkers to demand whiskey.

"That's right — sonny!" someone yelled from the bar's end. "Make a Man out of you!"

Before Lit could whirl to locate the jester, Bisbee's flat drawl sounded, all but behind him:

"What'd you pick up — sonny? Off the ground a while ago?"

Something seemed to click in Lit's brain, warning him not to make a sudden turn. So it was slowly — very slowly! — that he wheeled, letting his right hand slide most naturally toward his side as he turned. He faced Bisbee, who stood with feet wide apart, both thumbs hooked in the crossed shell belts that sagged on his thighs. Bisbee's hands were almost upon the wicked white butts of the heavy Colts that he wore in tied-down holsters.

"This," Lit thought with odd surprise, "is showdown."

But when he stood watching Bisbee, he could manage — if with immense effort — to control his face, to look with surprise at the green-eyed man, even to shake his head bewilderedly.

"Why, it seems to me" — he was pleasantly surprised to hear the steadiness of his voice — "that I spoke to you about it, then.

Let's see — what was it I told you? Oh, yes! I remember, now! I told you it was none of your damned business!"

"An' I told you that I could easy make it some o' my business — sonny!"

Bisbee's tone was flat, as always; his heavy, white face was without expression. But in the long, green eyes now burned a light that Lit, young as he was and comparatively inexperienced, knew as the killing lust shining through.

Beyond Bisbee, in the forefront of the now silent cowboys, Lit saw Old Man Barbee, rigid of body and features. There was nothing that the old man could do. By the code of the day and place, Lit was a man grown and this was his battle. No matter how much that old man might want to interfere, take this fight upon his gnarled, experienced hands, he could not do it. If he stepped in between the two, he would make Lit the laughing stock of this wide country. He could only watch, fearing the tragedy that must come, but helpless to do anything.

For Lit, the day had brought the first real crises of his life. He felt like two persons — one his old self, looking at a stranger. He kept his eyes almost blankly trained upon the gunman's changeless face. His lips were oddly dry. Mechanically, he licked them.

"I was comin' upstreet a while back," Bisbee told the company. But he watched Lit, and Lit only. "I lost a couple twenties. When I went back to hunt 'em, I seen this kid pickin' 'em up out o' the sand."

He leaned suddenly, a little:

"I aim to have them gold pieces — sonny!"

"You're a goddam liar!" Lit cried furiously.

He saw Bisbee's hand twitch. His own fingers moved as if automatically. They curled about his Colt's familiar butt. He was conscious of its jerk from the open-topped holster, conscious of leveling it — hammer back — upon the big man so close to him, conscious of letting the big hammer drop.

In his ears the heavy report crashed deafeningly. Almost blending with it, but the thinnest of split-seconds later, he heard in the still bar-room the roar of Bisbee's shot. But he had no time to consider noises. Twice more he thumbed back the .44's hammer, let it go. He glared at Bisbee, marked almost incredulously the big figure stagger, turn half about and drop. He leaned forward, staring down.

Old Barbee's rigid pose shifted flashingly. The assumed deliberation of movement that marked him, usually, was gone, as well. He

39

lunged forward, stooped over Bisbee, clawed the fallen gun aside, jerked the left hand Colt from its holster. He turned the still figure over easily — much as he might have flanked a big calf on the range. His hand went to Bisbee's chest. His wrinkled face was tense.

Suddenly, he came to his feet and glared furiously at Lit:

"A hell of a shot *you* turned out to be! You never did a thing but snag his gun-arm. Ah — hell!"

Then he stooped again. He began to shake Bisbee viciously.

"Get off that floor! Get off it before I boot you from hell to breakfast! You dam' four-flusher! You ain't hurt! You just turned yellow!"

Bisbee sat up slowly and stared around. His left hand came up to grip the forearm from which blood ran, now. He found Lit, glared at him.

"By God! It was lucky for you — my gun stickin'!" he cried grimly. "But it'll be plenty different — next time!"

Nervousness was gone entirely from Lit, now. In its place red fury such as he had never known gripped him, shook him. He had the savage impulse to leap forward, to stamp that heavy, white face into the floor;

stamp it until there was no semblance of features left.

"Next time!" he said thinly — and was surprised to hear his own voice sound like a stranger's. "Next time! Why — damn your sneaking soul! You pick up that gun and we'll have our next time right now. Pick it up — you lying, four-flushing bluff! *You* lost two twenties! You did nothing of the sort. I called you a liar once and I'm calling you a liar again — now! You're trying to run some kind of sandy. I don't know what it is, yet — but I'm beginning to have a notion about it. And I'm *begging* you to pick up that gun! Pick it up and I'll fill you so full of holes you'd drown in an inch of water!"

"I'll pick it up in my own good time!" Bisbee said in a flat, oddly expressionless voice. "An' when I do — you'll wish plenty that I hadn't. I ain't shootin' today, with a hole in my gun-arm. I ——"

"Gun-arm?" Old Barbee yelled. He checked with lifted hand Lit's tirade. "Gun-arm? You never used the left hand, yet! What's the matter with that hand? You pack two guns, don't you? Well — does that other gun maybe belong to some of your relations or somethin'? You have to write a letter home an' collect permission to use it, maybe? Gun-arm! Hell! For a big talkin' hairpin, you calm down the quickest I ever see! A kid makes you calm down, too! A kid that you picked because you figured he was easy; that you could build up a rep' by downin' him without really bein' in danger! Now, I'll tell you somethin'!"

He leaned forward, rather like an enraged terrier. And the cowboys and townsmen there in Menter's, reckless, hardbitten men, the pick of quick-shooting, hard-riding warriors from far and wide, they watched fascinatedly this old, gray wolf of the pack, who had seen trouble and plenty of trouble, through the smoke.

"You climb onto the Three-Prod *caballo* that suffers from a tinhorn in the saddle! You get to hell out o' Tom's Bluff an' you raise dust doin' it! I never butted in on the row until Lit had had his chance — I knew well enough he'd settle you! But, now! Now, she's plumb different! I'm the boss o' the Bar-B an' he's a hand o' mine! I'm tellin' you, now — drag it before one o' us comes lookin' for you! With a Winchester!"

"I'll suit myself," Bisbee told him. Lit was puzzled by the green-eyed man. In Bisbee's place, he thought, he would have been furiously ashamed. Bisbee showed no embarrassment, no worry. His face was without expression. He looked straight at old Barbee. "I don't aim to do no more shootin' today. But I am tellin' you, flat: There's goin' to be a next time an' when I come, that time, I'll come smokin' it!"

"Maybe you'll be able to use that other gun," Lit drawled, and the cowboys laughed. "And get the glue out of the holster. You had better!"

He stared narrowly at Bisbee. He had a grip on himself, now. He thought that he would never lose it again. Already, he was beginning to piece together certain odds and ends of incidents, to make a pattern of them that had some meaning. Bisbee *knew* that he had picked up the locket. He was not guessing about it, not guessing about the picture it held. He knew! For, otherwise, there was no reason strong enough, for this tale of dropped gold pieces, this forced row.

"You come shooting — any time," he invited Bisbee, very quietly. "Better glom a Winchester and start the shooting a long way off, too. For the next time I throw down — on you, or anybody else — I am not going to be surprised. I'm going to plug you straight center and deadly. And be damned if *that's* Spanish!"

In the instant of stillness, Slippery Elms' voice rose:

"*Por dios!* Did *he* grow up all in a minute,

I ask you!"

Lit waited only until Bisbee had lurched out of Menter's, before he, too, elbowed his way to the front door, shaking off Slippery Elms and other grinning cowboys. Behind him, Old Barbee followed quickly. Lit, noticing him, grinned a little. Barbee, he knew, was thinking of a practice not uncommon — the lying in wait for a man by a vanquished gladiator. But he was not worried much, about Bisbee dry-gulching him. He had seen the big figure pass the door, mounted.

Barbee caught up with Lit a few steps beyond the door. He went silently and alertly beside him for a little while. Then he made a rasping sound deep in his throat which Lit knew indicated deep disgust.

"A hell of a shot you are!" Barbee grunted. "You ought've plugged him! Dam' polecat! Now, you got to be lookin' forty ways at once until he's cashed in!"

"Do you think, maybe, that I didn't try?" Lit cried bitterly. "I was shaky! I'm not telling you otherwise."

"I know! I know!" Barbee admitted, in softer tone. "Bein' your first shootin' scrape, naturally you'd be shaky. But — I certainly do wish you'd killed him! Save a lot o' trouble . . ."

Lit said nothing. They moved on down the street toward "Hogtown" where 'dobe houses held rough saloons, gambling places, dance-joints with blowzy girls.

"What *did* you pick up, Lit, that Bisbee see — an' wanted?"

"A —— Oh, I reckon Bisbee watched me lean down and naturally he thought I'd found money or something valuable. He thought he could scare me into handing over whatever it was."

"Yeh?" Barbee drawled, and let the word hang.

Lit tried to stare through the dark at the old man.

"Yeh!" he said with a great deal of conviction.

They walked on quietly for a minute, then:

"I'm sendin' Long Al out, tomorrow, to comb the Rowdy River country for our stuff," Barbee said with apparent irrelevance.

Lit was fumbling for tobacco and papers. He grunted without interest. He had expected the start to be made any time now. It was the season. Then a thought came to him. He stopped the movement of fingers. His eyes were lifted, to stare in the direction in which Frenchy and the gang had disappeared. Slowly, a grin twisted his mouth.

He nodded shadowily.

"Who's going with Long Al?" he asked, in careless tone. "I reckon there's a lot of our stuff down in the breaks — always is after a hard winter like last."

"Oh — Slippery Elms, Ed Sanders an' — Charley Burdette — an' you better trail along, too. Long Al Kendrick's the best wagon boss, best all-around cowman, too, between This an' That. I like to have you out with him, Lit. You can't help pickin' up heaps an' heaps. Yeh. You'll go with him."

"Good enough!" said Lit, still staring down the street.

"Oh!" Barbee said in what Slippery Elms always called his "tone of voice." He seemed to hesitate, then: "Oh!" he said again.

"Well, I want to be getting my stuff together. See you some more."

Lit moved off whistling. He told himself that Frenchy must have had the locket when he came to Tom's Bluff the December before. So ——

"He came in from west of the Rowdy, then. So! Chances are, that he got it over in the Territory, somewhere. And if he and Bisbee didn't know each other, from somewhere else — But they did! That stuck out, plain. So he guessed that I'd picked up the locket and either wanted to know what was in it, or he knew and just wanted it! Now, what's the joker? What would Bisbee want with her picture, if he knew it was her picture? Well! What do *I* want it for?"

He grinned vacantly. He knew very well why he wanted it!

"If we ride Rowdy-way, Long Al's bunch, there's maybe a chance of seeing her — this Tin Type Girl . . ."

His grin widened as he went on down the street.

"Sam Bass was born in Indiany,
It was his native home!
At the age of seventeen
Young Sam began to roam.
He first come out to Texas
A cowboy for to be,
A kinder hearted fellow
You seldom ever see!"

Thus Lit, with right hand mechanically close to Colt's butt — just in case Bisbee might lurk somewhere ahead — but with left hand in trouser pocket gripping that oval locket.

CHAPTER IV
"STRAYED OR — STOLEN?"

"By — Gemini!" Lit grunted very thoughtfully. "I wonder! I do that. If this is not the funniest thing that I ever came on, it'll do until something really funny comes past! And be damned if *that's* Spanish!"

He sat Midnight, the chunky black that was favorite of his string, at the rim of one of those shallow cañons that sliced the Rowdy River country. Below his out-thrust boot toes, where he slouched comfortably in the saddle, the green brush on the cañon's floor stretched to right and left, all undisturbed by life, or movement.

And it was this absence of all trace of Bar-B cattle which puzzled Lit, on the third day of his cow-hunting. He scowled and fished out tobacco and papers. He built a cigarette and got match from hat band. As he flicked the head upon his thumbnail and put the tiny flame to cigarette end, his narrowed eyes were searching the greenery down below. He drew in smoke, blew it out. As if the puff were signal, out of the brush into a tiny clearing came a black cow with the Bar-B iron on her side.

But such a cow! By every rule of place and season, there should have been bunches

48

of Bar-B stuff all through the Rowdy River breaks. Thin, to be sure, for the winter had been both hard and long. But never such dogified creatures as this walking bag o' bones which came so slowly, dragging one hindleg pitifully behind her. Lit leaned a little forward, waiting expectantly. But there came no second to the crippled cow. Lit shook his head, scowl deepening.

"It's funny! It's dam' funny!" he commented grimly.

Three days of cow-hunting, combing the breaks in this section allotted him by Long Al Kendrick, had been all but useless. The Bar-B strays which from time immemorial collected in these little cañons and were gathered each Spring were simply non-existent this year.

"By Gemini!" Lit grunted with sudden conviction. "It's no use playing around any more, boy. You're heading back for the wagon, Midnight! We're going back to see what the rest of 'em found. Three days riding for nine-ten dogified critters means nothing much. Unless —" he amended the statement very slowly, very thoughtfully "— it just happens to mean a whole lot . . ."

He touched the black softly, affectionately, with spur rowel. Midnight walked along the cañon's rim with wise eyes looking right and left. He came to the narrow game trail that angled down to the cañon's floor. There, he shoved his feet out before him, all but sat down on stub tail and fairly slid to the bottom. Lit had no need to turn him. The black had seen the cow picking weakly at the new grass. He broke into a trot of his own accord. Lit pulled him in to look at the gaunt creature.

After a moment of staring, Lit lifted one shoulder and put hand on pistol.

"Hate to do it, old lady," he told the black cow. "But a lobo'll collect you, anyhow. I reckon a .44 through your head will be a lot easier than getting chewed up by wolf tushes."

He shot the cow through the head, then rode on across the cañon. There was a zigzagging and precipitous path up the other wall, matching that they had just descended. When Midnight had scaled it and they topped out, Lit turned the black north, toward the camp on the Long Fork of the Rowdy, where Charley Burdette, the cook, should be, and perhaps Ed Sanders, Slippery Elms, and Long Al himself.

Midnight smelled smoke before the pleasant tang drifted to Lit's nostrils. He slowed his running walk and pushed out slender head with ears pricked forward.

"Now, who might *that* be?" Lit puzzled aloud. "It's too close for Long Al and the camp. He didn't aim to move it —"

"Ever try findin' out things you was wonderin' about?" a mocking boyish voice desired to know, calling from somewhere upon Lit's left.

He whirled, searching the brush on that side. After a moment, he made out the darkish bulk of a horse. Apparently, the animal had simply been backed into the bushes, for there was no sign of a trail.

"Who's there?" he challenged sharply. "Come out here where I can take a look at you. Come on, quick!"

"Say!" snapped the boyish voice. "Who the hell do you think *you* are, anyway? Quit wavin' that gun around! You might shoot yourself, you know. An' if it interests you — *I* been a-holdin' down on you for quite some while, anyway, fella! *Put it up* — unless you want a hunk o' lead to chew on!"

Lit jammed his gun back into the holster and waited, in curiosity rather than alarm. Both hands were in plain sight upon his saddle horn. There was silence in the thicket for a long minute.

"Now, I'm comin' out because I'm dam' good an' ready to come!" the voice announced defiantly. A scrubby sorrel sprang

51

into the trail, to stop within arm's length of Midnight. At sight of the rider, Lit's jaw went slack.

She was a slim girl of seventeen or so, as dark of hair and eyes — almost as dark of skin — as Lit himself. She was dressed in rough men's clothing, a good deal too large for her — an ancient, wide-rimmed Stetson, blue flannel shirt with several rents in voluminous sleeves, faded jeans trousers jammed into high-heeled boots of dimensions generous even for a man. About her slim waist sagged a heavy cartridge belt, well filled, from which hung an open-topped holster. The holster was empty now, for the tenant-Colt was in its owner's hand, trained with disconcerting steadiness and directness upon Lit's belt buckle.

"Now, who might you be?" Lit inquired amazedly.

"The Queen o' Spades!" she retorted promptly. "But, o' course, I ain't. An' who might *you* be?"

"The King of Spades," Lit grinned. "But — of course — I'm not!"

"Can you prove you ain't the — *joker,* fella?"

There was something menacing about the way she drawled the question. Lit watched her curiously, without making reply.

"You deef, or somethin'?" she snapped. "*I'm* holdin' down on you, fella. It's certainly yo' move to speak yo' piece — *pronto!*"

"Why, so you are!" nodded Lit pleasantly. "So you are! Nice of you to let me know about it."

He nodded vigorously, grinning at her, while he reached into a shirt pocket for the Durham that solves perplexities, passes idle moment. The girl's mouth tightened ominously. Spots of color shone through the tan of her smooth cheeks. Lit shook tobacco into a paper and unobtrusively his left spur rowel, that on the side farthest from her, tickled Midnight. The little black danced upon the trail and with left hand Lit hauled violently at the reins.

"Cut it out, you blame' gopher!" he reproved Midnight. "What's chewing your fool ear, anyhow?" Again he tickled the sensitive side and Midnight's ears went back as his head went down.

He was almost alongside the girl's sorrel now, and, with a flirt of the wrist, Lit sent the loose tobacco into the snapping black eyes, plunging home both rowels even as his hand moved. The girl's bullet sang through the space behind him, which he had just left. Then he was twisting the Colt from her hand and reining back to watch with grave and scientific attention her varied and violent gestures.

"Child! Child!" he chided, after a moment of blazing mule skinner comment. "You're making me blush! Honest to grandma! I don't remember hearing anything like it since — well, not since the boys slipped a wad of prickly pear into Long Al Kendrick's bed roll. Cut the bawling! You sound like a scared calf. Here! Wipe it out of your eyes with my handkerchief!"

She took the proffered neckerchief blindly, dabbed at streaming eyes with the silk until she could look at him once more. Lit, comfortable with long leg hooked around the saddle horn, regarded her with indulgent smile that brought a glare from her. But she was caught by a paroxysm of coughing — excellent preventive of effective glaring.

"You'll be all right, pretty soon," he said tolerantly. "And think how much more you'll know! That's an old one, that tobacco stunt. It oughtn't to fool anybody over ten years old. But, then, you're really nothing but a baby, now that I look at you again. Naturally, you wouldn't know it. But I certainly would like to get hold of the nitwit that let you out with that gun! Kids have got no business playing with pistols!"

"Playin'! Playin'!"

Her voice lifted to a furious shrillness:

"You — you —— You're pretty dam' smart, ain't you! You think I play with guns, do you? You gi' me back that hogleg an' I'll show you a few! You ——"

"Cut it out!" Lit bellowed as she drew breath. "You'll talk like a lady around here, or — by Gemini! I'll turn you over my knee and you'll collect the spanking of the year. The idea! A kid like you helling and damning around the way you do!"

She stared at him uncertainly and he kept his face grimly threatening.

"Now, if it's not a secret," he drawled, "what's the idea of all this bushwhacking? Who handed you a license to sit back in the brush and point a pistol at peaceful folk?"

"Well, what you doin' in the country?" she countered sullenly. "How do I know what you're up to?"

"How do you know? How-come you *have* to know, anyway? Is this your range? I've combed these Rowdy breaks a-many's the time, Spring after Spring. This is the first dry gulching ever *I* ran into."

He shook his head sadly, made a disgusted noise.

"I swear! I don't know what the Territory's coming to! Kids that ought to be home sewing on their dollrags, squatting in the bushes with their papas' guns . . ."

"You quit callin' me a kid, Mister! I'm
sixteen years old. Old enough to maybe
show you a few! An' I got some friends, too.
You wait! I'll sick Frenchy Leonard onto
you an' don't you think for a minute *he*
won't clean yo' plow! Dollrags, is it? All
right! Frenchy'll shoot you into dollrags."

Lit's face went blank. He stared at her
with eyes narrowed.

"Oh," he said very softly. "Oh! Frenchy.
Leonard . . ."

"Yeh, Frenchy Leonard! I'll make Pap kill
a horse, but what he'll catch up with
Frenchy. I ——"

"He's that close?" Lit cried, putting
surprise in his voice.

"He's that close! An' him an' the boys
ain't travelin' so fast but Pap can catch up
with 'em. They ——"

Lit lifted restraining hand. He found this
very interesting. Something like instinct told
him to be careful.

"You wouldn't hoorah me? About Frenchy
being a friend of yours? Is he, really? A —
particular friend?"

Under his watchful stare she seemed to
swell and over the hard, angry — and yet
boyishly pretty — brown face came an
expression of immense pride. She lifted her

chin a little.

"A friend o' mine!" she said contemptuously. "He's a sight more'n just a friend. Me an' Frenchy, we're goin' to be married!"

"Right away?"

"Well" — she stared at the ground, seemed to hesitate — "no. But — some time."

"How long have you known him?" Lit asked carefully.

"Ever since I can remember! Him an' Pap, they knowed each other down in Old Mexico, years back. So" — she glared at him again — "don't you never think he won't stop yo' clock!"

Lit grinned and nodded.

"Sounds bad," he admitted. "But why send for Frenchy? If your Pap can ride, why can't he get out his great, big gun and shoot me?"

"Ah, Pap, he wouldn't shoot a fly!" she said with vast disgust. "Pap's a — ah! he's just measlin', Ma always said. But Frenchy, *he's* a Man!"

"He is that," Lit nodded. "You see, I happen to know him, too. I wintered with him over at Tom's Bluff. In fact, he wanted me to ride with him, this trip. He said he had a hen on, across the Rio."

"Hell!" she cried, staring. "Why — you must be all right, then, if Frenchy wanted you in the gang. I never guessed that, Mister, else I never would've throwed down on you like I done. I was afraid you was just some long-nosed meddler, come a-messin' into Frenchy's affairs. Didn't Frenchy tell you anything about me — Kate Quinn?"

"I don't remember it, if he did. But there was no reason for him to talk about you."

He was thinking of Frenchy, rather than of this queer, wild creature who was so obviously one of the gunman's conquests.

"Well! That certainly does change things! But — why didn't you take Frenchy up? Or — are you ridin' to catch up with him?"

Lit studied her frowningly, hesitated, then shrugged.

"I didn't take him up," he said slowly, "because I had a notion that maybe Frenchy wasn't telling me everything."

"O' course he wasn't!" she cried — and laughed. "Frenchy never does. That's why he's boss o' the spread. He's always a guess ahead o' anybody else. He told you it was Old Mexico he was headin' for? That's the way he does! He aimed to head for the Rowdy, all the time."

"Looks that way," Lit nodded. "But he began to look off-colored to me, in Tom's Bluff. So I stuck to the Bar-B and — here I am! Hunting our strays."

"Bar-B," she said, eyeing him intently from under sagging lids. "Bar-B . . ."

There was shrewdness in her face, now, out of all keeping with her avowed sixteen years. "Didn't you ever hear of that iron? It's Old Man Barbee's outfit, over on the Diamond. Our stuff always drifts this way."

"Oh, sure! I've heard o' the Bar-B," she nodded quickly. "Pap, I bet he knows every iron from here to Canada. We're livin' over yonder a piece. Got a dugout. Been here since fall."

"I've been out of camp for three days, now," Lit told her. "Have you seen any Bar-B stuff? I haven't found a dozen head. All I saw today was one black cow and she had her leg broke. I shot her a while ago, down in the cañon. Unless the other boys have rounded up a lot, I don't know what to think."

It came to him that she watched his face with an intentness almost strained. Again, instinct warned him. So he grinned at her, lifted a shoulder in small gesture:

"Funny about our stuff, this year. Mostly, by this time of spring, they're scattered from hell to breakfast in these breaks. But not this time. I was even wondering, a while back, if somebody mightn't have run 'em off. Your Pap hasn't been riding with a

59

sticky loop, has he?"

She matched his mechanical grin with one that seemed to him just as mechanical. Nor was her laugh natural.

"Pap? *Amor de dios!* That man's too lazy to go farther 'n across the table for his beef! You'll find the other boys ridin' herd on yo' strays — o' course! How many of 'em are there?"

"Three boys and the wagon boss. Camp's on the Long Fork of the Rowdy. I took the south end of the breaks. Well — if you haven't seen a lot of Bar-B strays, they must be north."

"Must be," she nodded. "They're funny critters — cows. Likely, they drifted north this time. When you hit camp, likely you'll find the others rounded 'em all up."

"Maybe," Lit admitted. "Well, Kate — in spite of your playful little ways with a hog-leg, I'm glad I met you. Since we've decided not to shoot each other, reckon I'll be high-tailing for camp."

He gathered up his reins. She pushed forward, smiling.

"Better gi' me back my cutter, before you go!"

"Oh! That's right. I did forget, didn't I?"

He stared down at the worn Colt in his hand. Looking up suddenly, he caught on her face an expression of such malevolence that it startled him. He stared and she twisted her hard mouth quickly, into the smile she had held before.

Lit was not quite a fool. He had expected no danger, here, in the Rowdy's breaks. Even her claim to friendship with Frenchy had not alarmed him, peculiar as he might think Frenchy's change of plans. But that sixth sense which had twice before warned him to be careful, in dealing with this fierce little nester's child, jogged his caution again. So ——

"You'll get the gun back, of course!" he said heartily. "But — not right now! Tell you what: I'm heading straight for the Long Fork. Somewhere along the Rowdy bank I'll find a rock or stump in plain sight. I'll put the gun down there where you can't help finding it."

She protested bitterly. Lit hardly listened. More and more, he was sure that something was queer here. In fact, there were two or three puzzling matters that he wanted leisure to mull over. With a caution quite new to him, he guarded his tongue almost without knowing that he did it. At last, he picked up the reins again. Then he said slowly, after a moment of staring:

"Frenchy is — quite a fellow . . ."

"He's just — *wonderful!*" she said softly, and this time her smile was unforced.

Lit looked long at her, then hurriedly he looked away. He was quite untutored in reading women but, as he pushed Midnight off for the Rowdy he shook his head pityingly at memory at what he had surprised in her face.

"That poor kid! That poor *damn'* kid," he said to himself.

And then and there it was that he began to dislike Frenchy Leonard. Actively to dislike him. The magnetic something about the outlaw which had drawn him during the winter had quite lost its hold. Lit began to see Frenchy more as Old Man Barbee had seen him. Not altogether, for there was much about that daredevil young outlaw that he must secretly admire. But for the first time Lit could sit as critic — upon certain of Frenchy's ways, at least.

"I wonder how he came to turn this way?" he asked himself after a long time of riding. "He *said* that the bunch was headed for Old Mexico. Headed for that Gonzalez hacienda. I — wonder! If he talked so much about that because he wasn't even thinking about it. That was Kate Quinn's notion . . . Funny!"

The more he mulled it over, as he rode on

toward the Rowdy's Long Fork, the "funnier" it seemed to him. Particularly as he recalled the several oddities of Kate Quinn's manner, and his three days of cow-hunting which had produced so few Bar-B strays.

"Well!" he told himself at last. "Long Al can settle it, pretty quick. If they have rounded up everything, that's that! And if they haven't — that'll prove a lot!"

Chapter V
"It Was Frenchy and His Bunch"

He could hear voices before the brush gave him a view of the wagon. Loudest of them was the snarling bellow of Long Al Kendrick and Lit, listening with head on one side, nodded. One corner of his mouth lifted unpleasantly. He thought that he did not need to speak to the old wagon boss to know what had roused Long Al. He rode on, came up to the wagon, stopped.

They were all standing about the fire — Slippery Elms and Ed Sanders and Charley Burdette and Long Al. The wagon boss stared frowningly. Before Lit could speak, he nodded viciously.

"An' the same with Lit!" he roared.

"Abs'lutely the same! *He* never found no strays, neither!"

"Nine-ten dogies. One black cow with her hindleg busted," Lit reported, swinging down. "Same with the rest of you?"

"More so!" Slippery Elms said judicially. "More so!"

Lit stripped the hull from Midnight and led him to the rope corral. When he came back with headstall over his arm, supper was ready. He got tin plate and cup and sat down. And Long Al, already eating, spoke with full mouth:

"Nine-ten dogies for y' tally, huh, Lit?"

Lit nodded. He was busy, marshalling his thoughts.

"That's the tally. For three days up-and-down the cañons."

"Did you go clean to Pillar Rock?"

"Yeh," Lit grunted. "I'll swear not a Bar-B hoof or horn's there."

Long Al waved his coffee cup angrily: "There's no two ways about it," he told them. "Twenty-thirty head o' Bar-B stuff in all this scope o' country! Nobody's goin' to make *me* believe that them critters growed wings an' flew out o' here. They was run off, an', by God! I bet that Frenchy Leonard an' his bunch o' rustlers done the runnin'!"

"Aw, Frenchy, he wouldn't run off Bar-B stuff like that," objected Charley Burdette, a lank, melancholy man with pendulous mustaches. "Now would he, Slippery? You know he wouldn't!"

"No? Well, I say: Like hell he wouldn't!" Kendrick growled. "I know mighty well that, if we could locate Frenchy an' the others, tonight, we would find 'em wrapped up in Bar-B stuff all-same as in a blanket."

Lit made a cigarette and said nothing. He had not spoken of his encounter with the girl, nor of the several suspicions he had been nursing.

Charley Burdette looked at Lit, now, for support of his defense of Frenchy. "Frenchy wouldn't do it, *would* he, Lit?"

"He would!" Lit said, between his teeth, with much grimness. "Long Al's right: It was Frenchy and his bunch that cleaned the breaks ahead of us."

He looked around at them all, looked at Long Al's seamed, hard face, looked at Slippery Elms, at happy-go-lucky Ed Sanders, at sad-faced Charley Burdette.

"But, I tell you —" Charley Burdette began again.

"Aw, shut up!" grunted Slippery Elms. "Lit has got something on his li'l' old mind. Can't you see how his hat's wigglin'?"

"How come *you* figured Frenchy?" Lit demanded of Long Al, curiously.

"It wasn't so awful hard! I've been on the Bar-B, it's a good while, now. An' I made this clean-up plenty times. So, when we'd rode a couple days without findin' much but cow-tracks — an' some hawse-tracks — I begun to think about them Territory hawses that Frenchy's gang brought up to the Diamond — an' how Frenchy was *so* careful to let ever'body know how his outfit was hittin' the trail for Old Mexico. You know! When I added that to the big, wide hole where our strays ought to be an' wasn't, why I tallied me up an answer!"

"That was the right answer," Lit said quietly. "Frenchy was making it just a little bit *too* plain that they didn't even think of coming toward the Rowdy. But I found out today that they had come over this way."

"So did I," the wagon boss nodded grimly. "You boys happen to remember that spotted hair rope that Irish Tim Fenelon was so stuck on? Well ——"

From his pants pocket he pulled a piece of hair rope, marked with alternate diamonds and circles in the strands. Every man there recognized it. They stared at it, then stared expectantly at Long Al Kendrick. He looked around grimly from face to face.

"I found this tassel in the brush, right beside a lot o' cow-tracks. An' a little piece from there, in soft ground, there was hawse-tracks. Any dude could have told that the fellow on that hawse was pushin' them cows. An' that hawse was a big one — twelve hundred pounds, anyhow. An' it was rode by a heavy man."

"Irish Tim Fenelon rode a big bay." This was Ed Sanders, nodding like a mechanical doll.

"An' Tim is more'n six feet high an' he weighs around two hund'd pounds!" Slippery Elms added.

Long Al Kendrick nodded, looked sideways at Lit. "Well, Lit?" he said. "How did *you* find out that Frenchy had been up this way?"

"Well ——" Lit stared at the ground, hunting the way to tell about the girl. "Frenchy said that they were heading for Old Mexico when they pulled out of Tom's Bluff. But the bunch must have turned west, instead of south, as soon as they were out of town. For I ran into a — a nester down the Rowdy. Uh — he said Frenchy and the bunch had been through here last week. Naturally, nothing was said about our stuff."

Long Al brought down a hard palm upon his thigh with a resounding smack.

"That settles it!" he bellowed. "That gang run off our stuff an' the bunch of 'em will decorate the cottonwoods high, wide an' handsome before I quit."

He jerked tobacco and papers from vest pocket.

"Mexico! Mexico — *hell!* They knew all about these strays of ours over here. They rounded 'em up an' they shoved 'em over into the Territory. They'll sell those critters to some of the big ranchers, maybe to the soldiers at Fort Lowe. They have got plenty start of us too.

"So, here's what we'll do: One o' you'll hightail it back to the Old Man, to give him the lowdown. Me an' Charley an' one other, we'll git the wagon rollin' an' start the measlin' li'l' bunch o' stuff we gathered, back for home. But — I want one man to start down into the Territory, to keep his eyes peeled for the trail o' our stuff — peeled for Frenchy, too!"

"That last will be Yours Truly," Lit said very quietly.

Long Al stared long and hard at the youngest member of the bunch. Lit met the calculating eye of the range boss very steadily.

"Well," said Long Al. "I figured to send Ed back to the Bar-B. Charley stays with

68

me, so — I reckon it's between you an' Slippery, Lit, who makes the ride of the Territory."

"Well," Slippery grunted belligerently, "an' why not me?"

Something like a smile flickered under the wagon boss's mustache.

"Well, Slippery," he drawled, "maybe the same reason that I ain't thinkin' about sendin' Ed over. Both o' you are top hands an' mighty handy with guns, but I do remember the time when you boys was ridin' for the Three-Prod, an' the two o' you was sent ahead o' the chuck wagon to buy grub, an' how you both fell from grace in a monte game an' lost the grub money an' the whole outfit had to eat off the country for weeks. An' how you boys worked six months free until you made up the money you gambled off."

"Aw!" Slippery said uncomfortably. "I reckon we never will hear the last o' that story!"

"Well," Long Al grinned, "it does kind o' give Lit the edge, here. Maybe *he* would have gambled off the money too, if he'd been along. But, he didn't! An' he *has* got a pretty level head on him."

He looked at Lit again.

"Think you can handle it?" he asked. "No

tellin' what you'll run into before you land where y' goin'."

"I don't know," Lit said, quite calmly. "Could *you* say that you could handle anything that might come up, Al — not knowing, as you say, what *is* ahead? You'd just do your damnedest, wouldn't you?"

Long Al grinned. "Fair enough! All right — come mornin', you head south. You'll hit for Porto. Stick around Slim Hewes's store a spell. Find out if Frenchy has been through Porto. But he has! I'll bet on that! There's too many there, though, that'd think it funny if he showed up with a bunch o' Bar-B stuff. So he likely never showed our strays in the neighborhood. He'd come in on his lone or with one or two o' the gang, leavin' the stuff off a piece. But — you'll maybe pick up somethin'. If you find the man that'll talk."

Long Al looked at the fire for a time, smoking silently.

"You go on down to Gurney. Hunt up Smoky Cole — he's sheriff there, now, an' he's an old side-kick o' me an' the Old Man. You can put all y' cards on the table with Smoky, for he's a straight shooter. He'll tell you exactly what's what.

"Now, one thing more, Lit: This-here Territory, it's mighty nigh split two ways —

70

you're either a big rancher's man, or you're sidin' with the little fellow, the squatter. You got to remember that, when you talk to a man. For he'll be on one side *or* the other. So, the *best* way is not to talk a-tall, unless you done found out, sure, from Smoky, where the fellow you're talkin' to is sittin' in the argument. Got that?"

Lit nodded. Somehow, he felt quite old tonight, able to handle anything that might come up. "Sure, I *sabe*," he replied, "and I'll hightail it, come morning."

Slippery Elms looked at Ed Sanders very gravely, then turned solemn face to Lit.

"All that is mighty good advice!" he said heartily. "But that ain't all there is to tell. You have been into the Territory as far as Porto, all right. But you *ain't* been — like Ed an' me — clean down into where the which o' the Territory is the whichest. There's just heaps an' heaps that Ed an' me could tell you about it."

"About monte games, maybe?" Lit grinned.

Slippery nodded even more gravely than before.

"Yeh, about monte games — but about lots o' other things, too. Now, you take yo' manners, Lit. They ain't *bad* for a boy raised in Tennessee, but they ain't what you'd call

71

first class. Not for a high-up place like the Territory."

Lit looked suspiciously sidelong at the solemn face. Slippery sighed, shook his head. Ed, too, made a mournful head motion.

"That's right, Lit!" he said gloomily. "Slippery is plumb right. The Territory is hell on manners."

"But, bad manners, mostly!" Long Al contributed.

"So," Slippery went on, "when you come to a saloon in the Territory, you don't want to hesitate a bit. You just amble right straight up to the bar-tender. You tell him you're from the Bar-B over on the Diamond an' what you want there is ——"

He hesitated. Ed nodded, but Lit's fingers, going as by instinct to his pants pocket, found there the oval shape of that locket picked up in Tom's Bluff.

"You tell him" — Slippery's voice came as from across a great space — "that you want — *milk!*"

The roar of laughter in which even Long Al joined meant nothing to Lit. He stared at the fire, fingering the locket.

"He's deef!" Slippery cried sadly, "plumb deef!"

Lit roused himself from thoughts of wide,

72

blue eyes, golden hair, and determined, yet pretty, mouth . . .

"Oh, no I'm not!" he denied. "I am to go into any saloon in the Territory and, when the bar-tender asks what I want, I'm to say milk. When he says 'Why milk?' then I say it's because behind me on the trail is a pore old stove-up cowboy without any teeth, and I have got to have milk for him. And if they want to know his name all I say is: 'Slippery Elms.' "

" 'At a boy, Lit!" Long Al bellowed. " 'At a boy!"

The night was not altogether quiet, for Lit was not too engrossed by thoughts of the yellow-haired girl in the locket to overlook three smallish, sharp rocks. He stumbled upon them near the wagon. Then, catching Ed Sanders' eye, he made a significant gesture.

Ed nodded understanding. He led Slippery Elms to one side and engaged him in talk while Lit busied himself at the bed rolls with the rocks.

There was a great deal of noise and excitement when young Mr. Elms got into his bed. Ed Sanders and Charley Burdette joined Lit in demanding the reason for the noise. There was even more noise when Mr. Sanders and Mr. Burdette fell across their own beds and discovered the second and third rocks. Slippery Elms and Lit were as one, in inquiring the reason for the howlings that alarmed the Rowdy breaks.

"Well!" Lit said, yawning. "I think I'd better get some sleep. And I do hope you tender backs'll get used to this rough life in time to let me get it. You boys ought to get toughened up, so you won't have to send a rep' ahead to order your milk. You, specially, Slippery — and if you chunk that boot at me, I'll sink it in the Rowdy!"

"Oh, that's all right," Slippery grunted drowsily. "Go ahead. It's Ed's boot."

Chapter VI
Porto — And a Dead Man's Saddle

"We'll get in touch with you, when the Old Man decides what to do," Long Al told Lit. "All you need to do is let Smoky Cole know where you are, most o' the time."

Lit, sitting Midnight at the wagon, nodded. He was ready to go. Behind the cantle was his blanket and slicker, wrapping biscuit and fried beef and coffee can.

Ed Sanders was already gone — riding fast back toward the Diamond to carry

Long Al's message to Barbee on the home range. Lit jerked his hand up in farewell to Charley Burdette, Slippery Elms and Long Al.

"See you some more!" he said.

"Stay single!" Slippery called gravely and Lit grinned.

"Not if I can help it!" he grunted cheerfully.

As he forded the Rowdy's Long Fork and rode west with mechanical alertness, he found himself entirely pleased with life. This virgin country was, in Spring, a very lovely land to ride across. There seemed to be a mocking bird singing deliriously on every other twig. Within an hour he had flushed a half-dozen deer.

Looking back, he knew that he was glad that he had not listened to Frenchy Leonard. Even if the little outlaw's trail had really led to Mexico, Lit knew that he would not change his present status for that other. Not even a wild raid over the border, a swoop down on the Gonzalez herd, could be so good as this. Not only was he free of the hard work of the ranch and occupying the virtual position of Bar-B detective, but this trail he rode led vaguely toward the girl of the locket. It *had* to lead toward her — he would see that it did!

So, he sat very contentedly in the big saddle, watching the country about him. And as he rode a smile lifted his mouth corners.

"She's waiting for us, Midnight," he told his chunky little black. "She may not know it — in fact, she *can't* know it! But she's waiting, all the same."

He fingered the locket tenderly:

"Oh, foot in the stirrup, hand on the horn,
Best dam' cowboy ever was born."

Then, presently, he began to consider what might be before him in the way of business. It might be a very noble idea to look around the Territory a little, before paying his call on Sheriff Smoky Cole at Gurney.

"Can't tell what we might run across. As is, all we can tell this Smoky jigger is, the Bar-B has misplaced some stuff. Yes, sir, Midnight, we're due to take us a *pasear* all around to see what we can see."

He considered his job in the light of what he knew of Frenchy, and what he had heard of conditions in the Territory. As Long Al had warned him, the country west of the Rowdy was split into pretty equal halves.

As far as Frenchy was concerned, it was

pretty well split, too. Those who were for him were loyal to the last ditch. Those who were against him sat up nights to hate him. Which meant that either he would get no information at all — might even collect a slug of lead between his eyes! — or he would get complete reports on the outlaw's movements, whereabouts. As the day wore on, he thought a good deal about what he might find in that little cow-town on the edge of the Territory's settled section.

He knew Porto very well. Spring after Spring, the Bar-B and other cowboys made the drowsy village to break the monotony of rounding up the Diamond River's scattered stock in the breaks of the Rowdy. Except for the visit of the Bar-B men and their like, Porto saw few visitors. But, usually, there were a few hard-faced, watchful-eyed gentlemen, using around Slim Hewes's store-saloon.

Not the same men, week by week. But they were very much alike in their reticence about the back trail which they had used. Men who would be especially troublesome now, to Lit, because he would have no way of knowing upon what side of the Territorial fence they might stand.

"And here I come," he told himself, "straight from where our stuff was stolen.

With Midnight wearing a Bar-B iron — Not so good! Frenchy has probably got somebody in Porto to do nothing but watch this back trail. Not so good!"

But he could think of no alternative to riding straight into town. He could not have brought himself to part with the black, even if a substitute horse had been available.

"Anyway," he consoled himself, "my face is pretty well known in Porto. Just changing horses wouldn't fool anybody!"

So he rode on and in the middle of the afternoon swung down before the hitch rack in front of Slim Hewes's place. Hewes came to the door and leaned against the facing. When Lit ducked under the rack and walked toward him, Hewes showed yellow teeth in black stubble of beard, in what might have passed for a smile.

"Howdy, Lit," he said tonelessly. "Where's the rest o' the Bar-B? Ain't draggin' it by yourself?"

"That's me!" Lit nodded. "I'm what you might call a pore little orphan. Well, it had to come sooner or later. Fellow said, one time, that the world's a bodaciously big, wide place, but, hell! you can't take stock in chuck wagon yarns. So, I've come out to check up on that fellow's story for myself. How's the horse feed? Midnight is right starved."

Slim Hewes straightened the six feet four inches of him, let Lit go by. Then he came in and passed the shorter man. Lit was impressed, as always, by the enormous height of the store-keeper. As Hewes's head was outlined against the line of tinware that dangled from roof rafters, Lit noticed something that for the moment drove thought of Slim's height from his mind.

All that tinware was unsalable, now. For each pot or pan had been punctured raggedly from two to ten times. The cottonwood saplings of the ceiling were pocked in a manner easily understood by any cowboy who had ever witnessed a pay-day celebration.

It puzzled Lit. Slim Hewes was nobody's shrinking violet! Slim could — and would! — whang away with Winchester or Colt just as freely as any man Lit knew. So, those gentlemen who had held pistol practice upon Slim's dangling row of tinware were no ordinary riders of the range. Had they been (Lit glanced down surreptitiously), the rough pine floor would now be thoroughly stained with red. And it was not.

Slim went on around the end of the rough counter which served as bar. "Drink?" he grunted, and pulled the Jordan from under the bar. "I'll git you some ear corn for your billy goat, after while."

"Well, I don't mind if I do, seeing that you ask *so* sweetly."

Lit accepted the filled tin cup and bowed to Slim: "To your long, red nose!" he said smilingly. "Keep your liquor old, your women young, and die happy!"

He lifted the cup, tipped his head back, set the cup down empty. He fished in chaps pocket, got out a quarter, rolled it across the counter. He was wondering if, and how, he might extract any information from the notoriously close-mouthed store-keeper.

"Anybody I know in Porto?" he inquired blandly. "Anybody been through lately?"

"Depends," Slim grunted. "Depends on who you know."

After a moment of staring, Lit gave the store-keeper up. If Frenchy Leonard and the others of the gang had been the gentlemen shooting at Slim's tinware, it was quite plain that Slim had no intention of publishing that fact.

So he took his sack of corn out to Midnight and came back. He demanded food for himself and in the back room of the place stowed away fried beef and black beans brought him by Slim's youngest Mex' woman.

80

Then he wandered out to make cautious inquiries about the town, concerning recent wayfarers. But he had to be so careful as he talked that he had no success in prompting from the blacksmith and the other year-round residents of Porto any information. If Frenchy or any other of the bunch had been in the town, the same hesitance that held Slim Hewes seemed to grip these others.

Lit gave them up after a while. He went to sit on the bench before Hewes's store. As he sat there, smoking, trying to decide upon a plan of action, there came around the store a tall, slender and handsome Mexican riding a big bay gelding. He looked sidelong at Lit, then turned his eyes front again. He tickled the bay into a swift running walk.

Lit stared after him curiously. He had not been able to see the brand on the bay, but there was something vaguely familiar about both horse and headstall. Suddenly, he snapped his fingers and stood up like a spring uncoiling. Back into the store he went. From Hewes he ordered coffee and cooked food and "air-tights." It seemed to Lit that there was something strained about the store-keeper's face as he went about filling the order. Something evasive, also. He watched Slim curiously, wondering how best to frame his question.

"That Mex'," he said diplomatically, "he certainly was riding a good horse and saddle. Who is he, Slim?"

The store-keeper laid the groceries on the counter.

"What Mex'?" he asked, turning back to the shelf. "I never seen him!"

"You didn't *see* him!" Lit burst out unguardedly. "Hell's bells, Slim! He came right around the store."

"I said — I never seen him!" Slim's drawl was frosty. "Why I never, might be due to some several things."

"Yes," Lit nodded, narrow-eyed. "Now that I think about it, it certainly might."

Slim turned slowly before the shelf. His face was very still: "Meanin'?" he said.

The drawl was frostier than before, and the lean, freckled hands were hidden beneath the counter.

Lit saw the danger signals — saw them very plainly.

"Well, just to begin — meaning that if you don't fish your paws out into the open, on top that counter, I *will* begin to think that something is wrong in here! And when I get my hoglegs out, *I* won't make holes in your tinware, Slim!"

"By God! You're gettin' to be a wise kid, now ain't you!" the store-keeper snarled.

But the hands came hurriedly from beneath the counter, for Lit had drawn his Colt half out.

"Maybe," Lit nodded. "But I wouldn't have to be *terribly* smart, Slim, to tell you one thing: You can't run with the rabbits, and the dogs, both. And, say! Arch Holmes had something else beside a big white-faced horse and a silver-trimmed headstall and saddle. Something a lot more important. He had a lot of good friends on the Upper Diamond. You and the Mex' both can think that over!"

Having delivered these vital statistics, Lit backed to the door. He had pistol clear out, now. He slipped through the door very quickly. He jumped behind Midnight and swung into the saddle before he threw off the hitch. Then, mindful of the lovely target afforded by a man's broad back, to an unusually tall store-keeper shooting straight up the street, he jumped the black around the corner of the store and left Porto.

When he had time to think, he was sorry that he had betrayed any suspicions to Slim Hewes.

"But," he told himself, "Slim is siding with Frenchy, you can bet. Frenchy stole our stuff and pushed the herd south over back trails. Then he and some of the others left the herd bedded down somewhere nearby and they rode into Porto for a drink. Or, maybe they rode in just to tell Slim to keep his eyes skinned for inquisitive Bar-B riders! That Mex' riding Arch Holmes' bay — either Slim sent him out to tell Frenchy about me, or the Mex' is working for Frenchy on his own. Well! it's beginning to look like the Bar-B's young detective had better head for Gurney without much more delay, to hunt up this Smoky Cole!"

When darkness came, he made camp beside a tiny wet weather spring. It was chilly when the sun had gone and he was glad to hug his fire. As he sat thoughtfully beside the red embers with his tin cup of coffee, there came the *whang!* of a Winchester. There followed instantly the smack of a bullet striking a nearby rock. Before Lit could move the Winchester *whanged!* again and the tin cup left his hand with a little whining yelp.

Lit dived into the safer darkness. He was clawing at his pistol-handle with a gun-hand that tingled. He crawled away from the fire, which now was being methodically sprayed with lead.

"I'd say that *gunie* out there was serious!" he grunted. "And my Winchester in the saddle scabbard right by the fire, of course!"

He waited and presently the firing ceased. He edged back to the scattered, pounded fire. It had been so lead-whipped that it gave off very little light, but what there was shone upon the saddle.

As he hesitated to expose himself, Midnight nickered from behind him. Lit grinned. He went over to the little black and from his neck took the lariat which staked him. It was easy to build a loop and flip it out over the saddle horn, then drag the hull into the darkness. Instantly, a splatter of bullets came, all around the fire. Lit flung himself down, now armed with his Winchester. He opened up — firing at random in the direction of his assailant. When carbine was empty, he stood up.

"Hell's bells! He — or they — seem to be getting closer! Here is where the Bar-B's detective leaves a man-sized hole in the air behind him. I don't know who that hairpin's boss is, but he came mightily near to getting his money's worth out of his hired help tonight!"

Five minutes later, he was spurring Midnight generally south and west. Through the night he rode steadily and, near dawn, pulled up in the bushes on the bank of a deep arroyo, to make his bed in the brush, with Midnight staked close to him.

Chapter VII
"I'm Miss You! W'at the Hell!"

When he awakened near noon he made breakfast of cooked food and canned stuff and rode on. He kept his Winchester stock conveniently close at hand.

But, as careful as he was to inspect the country ahead from the crest of every hogback, he was surprised when on a long, clear slope a Winchester *whanged!* and a bullet glanced off his saddle horn.

There was a shallow arroyo paralleling the trail. On that arroyo's lip, Lit threw Midnight with magnificent horsemanship. He threw him flashingly, then dived out of the saddle and into the shallow water course. There was no opportunity to retrieve his rifle, for Midnight rolled over, came to his feet, shook himself, then trotted off a few steps.

Lit, shaken by the hard jolt of landing, listened tensely. There was now silence down the slope, from the direction of the bullet's coming. But Lit knew all too well that the bushwhacker would hardly consider that shot a hit. For Midnight, not his rider, had fallen, and Midnight was now on his feet.

The arroyo ran vaguely down the hill. It was barely deep enough to hide Lit as he crawled on hands and knees down hill. Frequently he looked up over his shoulder and his spine crawled when he discovered that his arching back was almost level with the arroyo's edge. It was slow going and painful, over the little rocks of the arroyo bed.

At an acute angle in the wall he stopped. Then, around the elbow of the arroyo materialized a bare-headed, black-haired man who was on his hands and knees, a man with thin, brown face and twinkling sea-blue eyes. He all but ran into Lit and sprang to his feet with a grunted oath. He had been carrying a Winchester in one hand. Now, he tried to jerk it down to cover Lit.

"*Stick 'em up!*" Lit grunted mechanically. "You dam' bushwhacker!"

Slowly the black-haired man's hands went climbing toward his ears. He shook black head in a gesture that seemed one of surprise.

"*Válgame dios!*" he said. "I'm *miss* you! W'at the hell!"

Lit studied him with curiosity. He was

87

very much the dandy. His blue shirt was of fine flannel, his trousers were of hand-woven blue wool, his boots of alligator hide were expensive looking. There was a pearl-handled Colt hanging in holster of hand-stamped leather upon a shell belt of the same beautifully tooled workmanship.

"I ought to just put a hole in you!" Lit told him angrily. "Trying to bushwhack me, the way you did!"

"*Pues,* w'en you're bushw'ack me, will you be surprise' w'en *I'm* bushw'ack you?" cried the black-haired man, very calmly.

One sinewy brown hand came down to the spike point of his little mustache. He twirled it with an air, shrugged.

"Last night, you're bushw'ack me. Today, I'm see you ride like the dam' fool over these hogback, an' crack down with the Weenchestair. *Por dios!* An' I'm wonder, now, how I'm miss you. I'm not miss much times!"

Lit glared at him.

"Last night! Bushwhack you! Why — why ____"

It was too much for him, recalling as he did that tin cup leaping from his hand. He glared at his captive. Then anger slowly gave way to bewilderment. For the man's face was quite sincere.

"Look here!" Lit cried. "Where *were* you, last night?"

"Me? Why I'm mabbe ten mile back north. Me, I am Carlos José de Guerra y Morales, *señor.* I'm w'at the fellow in this dam' Territory they're call 'Chihuahua Joe.' Last night, I'm make camp all ni–ice. I'm eat, then I'm sit an' smoke an' drink the w'iskey — one drink only! — then, w'ile I'm look with love at the bottle — bang! the Weenchestair's pop at me, Chihuahua Joe! I'm jump like the hell! An' — I'm bust them bottle! *Señor!* she's one funny, funny thing — I'm ride slow all the night. I'm ride all the morning. An' I'm see *nobody* until I'm see *you* on those hogback."

"Hell! *I* never shot at you! Why, somebody shot a cup of coffee out of *my* hand last night. Hell's bells! What kind of country is this, anyhow!"

The tall man lifted his shoulders in a shrug typically Latin: "*Señor,* she's — I have them permission to put down my hand? — *Gracias!* — She's a place w'at you do not mistake to call one hell of a country. I'm live here thirty year. My father — she's them Spaniard, of Madrid. My mother, she's them Navajo. An', w'at this Territory is, I'm *know!* Here! These line I'm make, she's them Rowdy River. These dot — she's Gurney, w'ere Smoky Cole, she's sheriff — until somebody's kill him dead. These dot, she's Los Alamos Rancho. *Señor,* you're know these 'King' Connell?"

Lit had reholstered his gun. He lifted his eyes from study of the rough map that Chihuahua Joe had made, nodded slowly.

"Of course," he said. "Everybody has heard of King Connell and Los Alamos. He's a — pretty big rancher?"

"*Por dios!* W'en King Connell, she's just w'isper in Los Alamos, them fellas they're jump down in Arno. *Pues,* this dam' Territory, she's one war all time. King Connell, she's fight them squatter. Them squatter, she's fight King Connell. This whole dam' Territory, she's take one side or take those other."

"Which side are *you* taking?" Lit shot at him suddenly.

"Hah! Chihuahua, she's not *take* side — yet. In Gurney, Smoky Cole, she's one fine man. Work like the hell for those law an' those order. Me, I'm like to see Smoky win."

"How about rustling?" Lit asked cautiously. "How about — Frenchy Leonard?"

Chihuahua was making a cigarette of corn husk and inky-black tobacco. He finished rolling the thin cylinder, lit it with a match from Lit's hatband. Then he cocked a bright blue eye at Lit.

"Señor," he said softly, "in this dam' Territory, she's only those dam' fool w'at will ask them question to one stranger!"

Lit flushed. Chihuahua studied him keenly for an instant, then grinned.

"But this time, she's all right. You are not here for those health an' me — hah! Me, *I'm* Chihuahua Joe an' not give one dam' for anybody. . . . Rus'lin'? W'y, she's go on all time. King Connell, she's rus'le them cow from Wolf Montague an' them Howard Boy. An' they're rus'le them cow from King Connell. Me, I'm work for King Connell, two year ago. Work five-six month. But me, w'en I'm take them poor man's cow, my stomach, she's get sick. I'm quit."

Shrewdly, he grinned sidelong at Lit:

"Me, I'm ride for Gurney. You're ride those way? *Bueno!* We will ride together an' if we're see those bushw'acker *we're* help him to git sick. An' w'ile we're ride, mabbe you're like to tell Chihuahua w'at you're want over here in this dam' Territory."

There was something steady, dependable, about the halfbreed. So, as they rode stirrup-to-stirrup, Lit told his story, or all but his secret hope of finding a certain golden-haired girl. Chihuahua nodded thoughtfully at the end.

"*Pues,* me, if I'm lose them cow, an' think Frenchy, she's rus'le him, I will go to Los Alamos an' have the look around. Frenchy, she's rus'le lots o' cow from Wolf Montague an' those Howard Boy. King Connell, she's buy 'em. I —— *Válgame dios!* She's more bushw'acker!"

A steady rattle of shots burst upon them as they rounded a shoulder of the low hill. Down below and to their left, in a sort of natural amphitheatre, was a knot of horses. On the ground, wriggling toward a pile of boulders, from which puffs came rapidly, were men who stopped to fire at the boulders, then wriggled forward again.

Chihuahua's sinewy fingers played a tattoo on the stock of his Winchester. Suddenly he snatched out a pair of field glasses from his saddle bags and trained them, first on the attackers, then on the men behind the boulders.

"She's them stranger be'in' those rock. Two of him. Them other fellas, I'm see in Gurney. Mabbe they're work for King Connell. Mabbe for them Howard Boy. Mabbe for Wolf Montague. In this dam' Territory — *quién sabe?*"

Lit took the glasses and studied the battle. From man to man of the attackers he turned the lenses, then stiffened suddenly:

92

"I don't give a dam' who those fellows in the open are working for," he gritted. "I'm siding in with the ones in the rocks. Come on! We can ride around the rim here and open up on 'em from above the rocks. Are you on?"

"*Pues,* two an' six, she's *not* so good as four an' six!" grinned the halfbreed. "I'm figure, Lit, that them fella in the open is mabbe those one that bust my w'iskey. Hah! Me, *I* will help them to git sick!"

They put spurs to the horses and went scrambling around the rim, until they could throw themselves down upon the crest of the slope, almost over the two attacked ones. Chihuahua rested his Winchester upon a low rock. With the whiplike crack of the report Lit saw a man upon the ground jump convulsively, then rise, take two amazingly long steps, turn around and crash prone.

The two men in the rocks were gazing upward. Lit waved at them and, as if heartened by the reinforcement, they took up their firing again. The attackers were now concentrating their fire on the rim where Lit and Chihuahua were alternating shots.

The shooting was a continuous tattoo, now. Lit almost forgot his original intention to get Bisbee, whom he had seen through

Chihuahua's glasses. He fired mechanically whenever a man exposed himself, but he was far from a deadshot with the rifle. He was so engrossed in the work that he failed to note the slackening of fire from the rocks. It was only when a thud of hoofs sounded behind him that he turned. There were the two men whose cause he and Chihuahua had espoused.

"Let's git while the gittin's good!" a squat, bearded man was yelling. "Yander's two more murderers a-comin'!"

Lit peeped over the rim again. There were two new riders, flinging themselves off their horses to join the battle. He yelled at Chihuahua:

"Our fellows are here! Let's go!"

Chihuahua nodded with a wide grin.

"*Pues,* my w'iskey, she's one drink they will remember! *Bueno!* We're go."

They caught the horses, swung up, set in the spurs and were gone at a pounding gallop across the slopes. Hell-for-leather they raced for miles before slackening pace to take stock of each other.

The two men they had rescued were efficient-looking individuals. The squat one who had warned Lit of new attackers appeared the leader, for his companion, lean, walrus-mustached, seemed always to wait for him to speak.

"Well, partners, yuh certainly wandered up real providential!" grinned the squat spokesman. "Jake an' me, we're prospectors. We'd been a-standin' off them dam' cowboys for half an hour an' we seen the pearly gates openin' up for us, too! But, by God! They never would've stretched us!"

"Why would they want to stretch you?" asked Lit.

"Do'no'. But they waved a lass-rope at us right understandable, while they was a-doggin' us into that valley. Me an' Jake, we're peaceful men, we are. But no dam' cow's-chambermaid's goin' to run a sandy on us while we got a ca'tridge left!"

"She's this dam' Territory!" sighed Chihuahua. "Them fella, they're work for somebody, like I'm say, Lit. They're ride out for to find them other fella's cowboy. *Sí!* An' w'en they're find some stranger, they're hang 'em. An' *then* they're ask them question."

"Well, me an' Jake, we owe yuh-all one," grinned the squat prospector. "Mebbe we can hand her back to yuh sometime. We was headin' over toward The Points, to have a look-see."

"Five-six mile, now, an' she's them trail for your Point," Chihuahua told him. "We have one pleasure, Lit an' me, to shake them old load from the Weenchestair for two dam' good fella — hey, Lit?"

When the prospectors had turned off upon the trail to that roaring mining camp, The Points, Chihuahua grinned affectionately at Lit.

"*Por dios!* She's one ni–ice place, this dam' Territory, no? Now, you an' me, we're have them fine fight w'en we're meet them cowboy again. One fella, she's have them glass, same as me. *They* will know us!"

"I'm going to Los Alamos, Chihuahua," Lit returned unworriedly. "If King Connell is buying rustled stock from Frenchy, like as not he bought the Bar-B's strays. Can you come along? Will you?"

"No, I'm ride for Gurney. There is one dam' good reason, w'y I'm never ride for Los Alamos, any more. But, in Gurney I'm see you! Me an' you, Lit, we're not lose them other — no!"

Chapter VIII
A Student of Brands

Lit found himself strangely lonely, with parting from "Chihuahua." He wondered why the smiling breed had made so much impression upon him. He had not missed

Slippery Elms and Ed Sanders particularly. And he had worked and spreed with the two ever since old Barbee had brought him, a shy, gawky kid, to the big rambling Bar-B house on the Diamond.

"I'll bet there's a lot on his back trail a man'd like to know about!" he thought, as he rode the miles of the trail to Los Alamos. "He's plenty salty — it sticks out all over him."

He grinned with a sudden, surprising, thought: "*Por dios!* I outfoxed him in that arroyo! Partly, of course, it was dumb luck — that I didn't go hunting him, but let him come to me. But life's a good deal just getting the breaks or not getting 'em. And my getting that break set me up in Chihuahua's opinion."

He grinned a shade self-consciously. For he sensed that the good opinion of Chihuahua was not to be easily had. He mulled what Chihuahua had told him, of Territorial affairs and conditions. For it was beginning to dawn on young Mr. Taylor that what had seemed no more than a pleasant ride down into the Territory, an investigation of Frenchy's doings, was perhaps more of a detail than he had thought when Long Al had talked about it.

He watched the land's lie ahead. He

wondered where the boundaries of this great Los Alamos range might be. Wondered, also, when he would come upon a Connell rider. Then a thought came to him, born of memory of those two prospectors whom he and Chihuahua had rescued . . .

"How'll I know 'em for the King's hands?" he asked himself sardonically. "Unless, maybe, I get a look-see at their horses' brands!"

So he came to the top of a hogback. To right and left he looked, into a shallow valley between this hogback he was on and the next rise. Dark brows climbed.

"Well!" he said softly, as if the stooping one down in the low ground might hear him. "It looks like a committee of one to pass on brands and earmarks!"

The puncher below him had thrown a steer. A rangy yellow horse held the lariat taut while its master bent over the creature and seemed to study the brand.

"My business being what it is this week," Lit thought, "a fellow curious about a brand on Los Alamos range — and I reckon this *is* Connell's range — is out of the same rock with me. Be damned if *that's* Spanish, either!"

So he watched the engrossed one; watched him — Suddenly, he lifted himself to see more clearly. There came to him an odd excitement. The slender one down there was dressed like a puncher, but — there was something about the way of moving, that told Lit he watched a woman, or a girl. And, being a woman, a girl, might it not possibly, just possibly, be —

He slipped back down to Midnight, swung into the saddle and rode off toward an arroyo that promised to lead down the slope and arrive somewhere nearabout the student of brands. Very cautiously, he followed the rocky bed of the dry stream around a flank of the hogback.

When he came in sight of the yellow horse's owner, she had got her rope off the steer and it was standing, shaking head angrily. But she was at the horse's side, now. As the steer made up its mind to charge her, she went into the hull easily and the horse danced out of the steer's path. She slapped the steer with her rope and sent it galloping, then began to coil the lariat.

Before Lit could ride out into view, she was moving off. Lit trailed her, grinning. Then, out of a cross-arroyo, two riders came. They were between Lit and the girl in the hundred yards that separated them. Each had a Winchester across his arm. As Lit stared, one man lifted his long gun. His intention was plain.

The girl had just begun to turn. Lit made a flashing draw of his own carbine from saddle scabbard. He lined the sights on that one who was going to fire, and cocked and fired the Winchester.

The man in the lead dropped his gun and swayed in the kak. He clawed desperately at the saddle horn, pulled himself straight.

His companion had spun his horse about with the shot. Lit shifted aim with a twitch of the carbine's muzzle. Firing fast, he shot high. The man's hat went off. But it altered his thought of firing. Instead, he kneed his buckskin around and rammed in the hooks. The buckskin went back into the arroyo like something shot from a gun. Lit tickled Midnight with the rowel and tore down upon the arroyo's mouth.

The man he had shot now jerked his horse toward the arroyo. Lit had a queer feeling with sight of the red stain that spread on the back of this one's gray shirt.

Neither rider stopped in the arroyo. Lit had a glimpse of them vanishing around the first curve of it. He took it for granted that they had enough of the war and rode with just a trace of swagger toward the girl on the yellow horse. She had ridden hard for another hundred yards but now, with disappearance of the two men, she had reined in.

With his first full view of her face, Lit's heart began to pound. He had hoped that when he found a girl over here in the Territory she would be the girl he hunted. But that this one, whom he had saved from pretty certain death at the hands of that bushwhacker, should be that one whose face was in the locket ——

He was grinning broadly when he loped Midnight up to her. She stared long and fixedly at him. The eyes so wide and frank in the tin type were narrowed, now, calculating. But he had already decided that the tin type was all but slanderous. This girl was so much more than the picture had indicated that he must draw a long breath before he was able to speak with controlled voice.

"I reckon they're gone for good," he told her.

"If they are, then it's the first good for them!" she said. When Lit, hardly hearing her, still sat staring at her, impatience came to the clear face. "What's the matter? Haven't you ever seen a girl, before?"

"Not like you!" Lit answered solemnly, very truthfully. "In fact, I would have argued not so long ago that they didn't make 'em along those lines."

"What?" she cried, flushing. "What are

you talking about?"

"You!" he said. Then he caught himself, smiled.

"Never mind all that," she told him stiffly. "I haven't thanked you for saving me that bullet in the back. The Howard Boys aren't much on missing, with short or long guns. You certainly were the answer to a maiden's prayer, about then!"

"Now, if I can only be that, all the time!" Lit sighed. "But, I suppose that's asking a lot?"

She shook her head reprovingly at him — as if she were much older, wiser, than he.

"I thanked you for snagging him, but, just the same, it was a foolish thing to do. For you, a stranger . . ."

"Foolish! Then, let me be foolish all the time! The Howard Boys didn't seem to me to be more than ten-eleven feet high. Any time I can help you ———"

"That's the thing!" she nodded. She was very grave. "You didn't know which side you were taking. It might have been the other way 'round: It might have been one of the Howards getting smoked by a couple of Los Alamos *vaqueros.*"

"Oh, I see," Lit nodded vaguely. "In that case, it would have been all right for a couple of sneaks to pour lead into a man's back. So long as the sneaks wore the Los Alamos brand."

"Sneaks!" she cried. "You ——"

"Wait a minute," he said quickly. It had not occurred to him that what he said would infuriate her so. "That is an ugly word. But I don't like to see two *gunies* — no matter *what* outfit they're riding for — jump a lone man and start pumping lead into his system without giving him a chance. And that's what our friends the Howards were at. It riled me."

"Strangers aren't wise if they get themselves riled too easily — in the Territory," she warned him.

"I never had any use for a man who didn't let himself get riled when he had good reason. Anyway, I don't reckon myself a stranger. Your Territory certainly hasn't let me stay one! It's dragged me right into the house and up to the table, so to say! As for being wise — didn't I tell you in the beginning that I never had seen a girl like you? Well! If that's not proof of my good sense — ! No . . . I reckon I'm just in the habit of saying what I please. Anyway — I did happen to hit on the right side, didn't I? I did join Los Alamos against the Howard Boys. I take it you wear the Los Alamos brand."

"In a way," she said very dryly. "I'm

Sudie-May Connell."

"Kin to King Connell?" Lit asked innocently. But behind his smile he was telling himself to be careful. For he was a spy on Los Alamos range. He must not let his feeling for this girl betray him to the enemy.

"In a way," she said again, more dryly than before. "He's my father. And you?"

"You can call me Rose," he grinned. "Of the famous Four Roses. Youngest and handsomest of the bunch."

"Mr. Rose," she nodded. She looked at the neat job of hair branding that he had done on Midnight's hip. "Of the Box-Eight. I don't seem to recall that iron . . ."

"Why, that's funny!" he cried. "For a lot of our stuff's been run off, one time or another . . ."

"Is that supposed to be funny? We don't like that kind of jokes, on Los Alamos. And we run a good School for Manners . . . This Box-Eight outfit — where might it be?"

"On the Sarsaparilla River, just above the Gumdrop Mountains," Lit said thoughtfully. "I had a map, but it must have melted. No matter! Probably I'll never go back. The folks over there are all too honest. So I headed for the Territory where a wide loop's appreciated. I was making for Los Alamos when the Howards came."

"Let's go, then. It's eight miles to the house."

But when they had ridden stirrup-to-stirrup for a silent mile, she turned her face sidelong. Lit grinned at sight of the small frown with which she eyed him. She was wondering about him, he thought, and that was precisely what he wanted. "Are you job-hunting?" she asked slowly. "My father's not at home, now."

"He's not?" Lit said in tone of bitterest disappointment. "Ah! That's too bad! But he'll be home pretty soon, won't he?"

"I don't know. He may come back tomorrow. He may not come home for a month. Nobody ever prophesies about King Connell — except strangers . . ."

"Well, I'll have to wait for him, I reckon," Lit decided aloud. Inwardly, he was much pleased. He had not hesitated to admit to himself that thought of bearding the formidable monarch of Los Alamos had not been pleasant. If the King were gone, he could make certain quiet investigations much more easily.

"I'll be relieved of some lying," he thought whimsically. "Not all, of course. But some of the most complicated lying can be done without, if I don't have to try to fool *that* hairpin!"

"What" — Sudie-May broke in upon his thoughts abruptly — "was that Box-Eight brand before you — ah — hair-branded it?"

"Ah, you oughtn't to have thoughts like that. Hair-branding! The very idea! That you should suspect a pore cowboy like me of such practices!"

Again, she looked at him as when she had reproved his blind mixing in affairs of the Territory — as if, cowboys of his like were the irresponsible charges of the Connells, father and daughter.

"You're a nice boy," she said tolerantly, with an edge of superiority in her voice. "I think I'll have Dad hire you and assign you to me. The first thing you'll need to learn is not to try being clever with me. What was the brand?"

"Well," he shrugged. "It was the Ladder-H on the right hip, with the Fencerail under-sloped in the right ear. Then the Galloping-XYZ on one forehoof and Twin Diamond in the dewlap. We didn't have much to do, the day we branded him, so we practiced our geography lesson on his outsides."

She was furious. Little as he knew of girls, instinct warned him that if any of the rosy daydreams he had been nursing since Tom's Bluff were to become reality, meekness and good temper would never achieve the transformation.

"Let her treat me like a sort of lightish Mex' to hold her stirrup and pick up her rope, and that's what I'll be forever," was the way he phrased it.

So he whistled cheerfully and looked with bright, interested — but wholly unimpressed! — eyes upon this section of the vast Los Alamos range.

Apparently, curiosity burned behind her stiff, red face. She rode for a mile or so with stare straight front, then: "So your name is Rose, is it?"

"Rose? Who said it was? It's Lily. W. Lily. We're a big family, too! Long on water. That's why I left the ivy-hung walls of the ancient castle. I got so tired of hearing about water that when I heard about cowboys washing in the winter time once for the whole year, I came straight for the Range of the Buffalo. And I certainly do like it — now."

They topped the crest of a rise and below them, on the flat where a little creek ran, he saw a red tile roof all but hidden in the green foliage of cottonwoods.

"That headquarters ranch?" he asked, nodding toward the long white house. "Nice little place, it looks like!"

She turned clear around in the saddle and

eyed him very levelly. He met the stare with unchanged grin.

"I said that you seem like a nice boy. And I'm under obligations to you for stopping that chunk of Howard lead. But, even if we don't forget our obligations on Los Alamos, we *can* be rubbed the wrong way! Especially by — strangers!"

"I wish you wouldn't keep harping on that string!" he protested. "I might have known you all your life, since I was just a boy, the way I feel! I *hope* that the liking is mutual . . ."

"I'm afraid it's not!" she said irritably. "In fact, if you hadn't stepped between me and the Howards, I'd be ready to have a couple of the boys deliver a good, thorough chapping to you!"

"Two that you wouldn't mind doing without, of course!" Lit nodded, serenely. "For you'd certainly *do* without 'em, after they waved a pair of chaps at me the first time and I understood!"

"Ye-es? Per-haps! It's just possible that the kind of men who use around the Territory are a little bit harder than the ones you're used to . . . You see that buckskin horse down by the corral? It's own-brother to this one of mine. Its owner is pretty well-known in the Territory. He is —"

"Frenchy Leonard," Lit said calmly. But he was thinking desperately fast. "Shoo! Did you think that I didn't recognize his *caballo,* in the very beginning?"

She stared at him, then caught herself and shut her mouth hard. She was silent while they rode toward King Connell's 'dobe palace that was set in the huge cottonwoods that gave his ranch its name — Los Alamos — The Cottonwoods.

Lit, too, was quiet. He had not expected to meet Frenchy so soon. He was bracing himself for the time of meeting.

CHAPTER IX
"HAVE YOU THOUGHT ABOUT FRENCHY?"

When they pulled in before the horse corral, Lit swung down and was moving toward her side when Frenchy Leonard came loafing from the corner of the house. Sudie-May turned in the saddle. Lit, watching without seeming to stare, saw how she smiled in reply to the little outlaw's habitual grin.

Frenchy stared at Lit. He lifted a careless hand, waved.

"Hi, Lit!" he cried. "What you do, boy?

Change your mind?"

He did not wait for answer, but came on at his catlike gait, to stop at the girl's stirrup. He put up his hands and she, clearing a foot from the off-stirrup, swayed to him. So he swung her out, held her for an instant off the ground and they smiled at each other, then lightly set her down. For some reason, the small business infuriated Lit. Frenchy grinned at him.

"Change your mind, boy?" he said again. It was more statement than question. Lit forced grin to match Frenchy's.

"No-o. Not exactly," he said carelessly. "That is, not as to riding with you. Anyway, I'd have hit for the Bravo if I'd thought about catching up with the bunch. I didn't think about you heading back for the Rowdy. But I did change my mind about sticking on the Bar-B. Lord! a man could chouse cows around the Diamond until he sprouted a beard. I want to see a few things before I pass in my chips for cashing."

" 'Course!" Frenchy nodded, still grinning. But the shrewd eyes were very watchful. "Way I feel, too."

His eyes shuttled to Sudie-May. But if he expected her to help him out, with information about Lit, he was disappointed. She merely watched Lit without expression.

"Ridin' by yourself?" Frenchy asked.

"Yeh. There was nobody on the Diamond that I cared a lot about siding. Too, the Old Man was making up his bunch for a Spring cow-work in the Rowdy breaks. He'd hobbled everybody for one job or other. Nobody else felt the way I did."

It seemed to Lit that the alertness went out of Frenchy's eyes. The gunman's smile seemed friendly.

"Well, if you want to throw in with me, *'sta bueno!*"

"Thanks!" Lit nodded colorlessly, then turned to look curiously around him.

The headquarters ranch of Los Alamos was the usual collection of 'dobe buildings typical of the Territory. There were picket corrals, storerooms, a row of low houses for the *vaqueros* with families, and a long log-and-'dobe bunkhouse for the other Los Alamos riders.

Lit stripped the hull from Midnight and led him into the horse corral. When he came back, Sudie-May and Frenchy had disappeared. So he went across to the bunkhouse. Three or four cowboys were lounging there. They invited him to "sit and look shorter." He grinned his thanks and sat down on an unoccupied bunk. Quite openly, he and they studied each other.

"Chuckline-ridin'?" one asked him.

Lit nodded. Before he could repeat the tale he had given Frenchy, a rasping voice was lifted from the doorway.

"You the fella just rode in with Sudie-May?"

Before he twisted on the bunk to face the door, Lit disliked the owner of that voice. And he noticed that the cowboys seemed to tense at the sound of it. So he made a point of turning very deliberately, keeping his expression uninterested, replying carelessly.

"Meaning me?" he inquired blandly, facing the tall, slender, too-handsome young man in the doorway.

"Well — I did kind o' figger I was, yeh! Far's I can see, you're the only stranger in here!"

"Well, I wouldn't know that!" Lit said in bored tone. "But if I'm the only stranger here and you know a stranger rode in with Sudie-May, why would you ask me what you already know? If there's anything in the world that tires me worse than a winter's work, it's dam' fool questions."

The tall man came on into the room. Lit saw that he was yellow-haired — like Sudie-May — and that his blue eyes were cold and savage. He observed, also, that the man wore two guns, in holsters the toes of which were tied down to his thighs by raw-hide whangs — the sign of the gunfighter — sometimes; one sign of the gunman, the real quill or — the imitation.

"Oh," he said stiffly. "Don't like questions, huh? Well, on Los Alamos, fella, a stranger's apt to be ask' a good many questions. The stranger's a dam' fool if he don't answer up right quick an' mighty straight! But, happens I already know all about you. You want a job on Los Alamos, huh?"

"Why, yes — but likewise, no!" Lit frowned. "Yes, if I like what's offered. But, hell, no! if I don't. I thought I'd come by and maybe talk turkey to King Connell!"

"You don't have to do no talkin' to Connell. I do the most o' the hirin' an' the firin' on Los Alamos. I'm Jed Connell. I'm King's second cousin an' the foreman."

"Well, I wouldn't know all that, just by looking at you."

"Well! What about it? You want a job, or not?"

Apparently, he could not make up his mind to be offended. Lit studied the making of his cigarette.

"Yes and no. Right now, no! I'll just sleep here, tonight. Tomorrow, I'll mosey on toward Gurney. You see, foreman is the least job I'd want on Los Alamos. And since you're the King's cousin, I'd have a fat chance getting an even break — no matter how much better man I was. So, I'll take my foot in my hand, come morning, and go on."

Jed Connell glared at him steadily. Lit faced him serenely as he put cigarette in mouth and fumbled for a match.

"Likely, it's just as well you're not wantin' a job," Jed told him meaningly, then turned and stalked out.

Lit shivered ostentatiously and grinned at the staring cowboys. Then he got up and said that he would wander around and get the saddle-stiffness out of his joints.

Apparently, none watched him as he loafed about. Presently, behind the row of 'dobes tenanted by the married *vaqueros,* he found two yellow curs snarling over a green cowhide that they must have pulled down from where it hung. Lit watched with amusement while the tug of war went on. Then a jerk of it revealed a certain peculiarity.

He moved over, kicked off the gaunt curs and stared at the ragged hole where a brand had been cut out of the hip. Upon the margin of the hole was a hairless mark, the end of a brand-scar that told him nothing. It *might* have been the end of the horizontal line that was the "bar" of "Bar-B."

He picked it up and went to the door of the nearest house. A fat and slatternly *mujer* came to the door. To her, in rapid Spanish, Lit explained how he had found the dogs with the hide. She asked him to toss it up to the dirt roof of the house. But when Lit grinned at her, she settled herself comfortably against the door frame, to eye him coquettishly and giggle at his suggestive talk. He knew very well how to make himself *simpático* with her kind. Presently, he felt safe to mention the brand cut from the hide.

"Somebody has been killing a cow very quietly," he told her. "Somebody who did not wish the *patron* to know that an animal of Los Alamos had been slaughtered . . ."

"*Pues,* that has been," she said — and met his knowing grin with one as knowing. "But I do not think that it was so with that cow. As you would know, if you thought of the Los Alamos iron: For *we* brand LA of a size to cover half the cow. No . . . This was a cow of the herd bought by the King somewhere beyond our line. Only a few of the fat cows were driven here for beef. Most of the others were sold to the agent of the Indians on the reservation at Rio Lobos."

Lit nodded, almost holding his breath for fear that he would betray the interest, the burning interest, he felt.

"Matters," he said sententiously, "are not always as they are usually. I brought the hide to you for fear that someone might meet trouble —"

"I thank you," she said. "I can see that you are not only handsome but — one of kind heart, *simpático* . . . I — could like one such — very much. And it pays to be watchful on Los Alamos. The *patron* is one who likes a tight mouth. For he buys many cattle. Some of them ——"

She grinned and lifted a shoulder eloquently.

"What're you spyin' an' sneakin' around about?" Jed Connell snarled from the house corner. "I'm tellin' you —"

"Well!" Lit drawled mockingly, "if it's not Bitter Creek, himself, again. What are *you* sneaking around behind me, about? Afraid I'll show you up and get your foreman's job? Or did you just want to know what a real hand looks like?"

He watched the tall man closely. How dangerous Jed might be, he had no idea. But he fancied that he was more "on the talk" than "on the shoot." But, even if Jed were as dangerous as Bisbee had seemed, Lit knew that he felt no such nervousness as had gripped him in Tom's Bluff. He was in control of himself. As Jed's hands seemed to slide closer to gun-butts ——

"Don't you!" he said coldly. "Don't start for those plow-handles unless you mean it! Any time you wave 'em at me, you'd better be ready to go the whole hog. Else you'll wake up trying to tell St. Peter's right hand round-up angel what a mistake you made!"

Jed's big hands twitched — but seemed to get no closer to the Colts' butts. Lit watched him very grimly.

"Now, is he just a plain bluff, or does he need a push to get him into a war?" Lit wondered. "Those cowboys in the bunk-house acted like he was a whole bottle of wolf poison with the stopper pulled out. But —"

"Jed!" Sudie-May cried sharply, from the house corner.

Both men turned to face her. Jed's manner blended defiance and unease. Lit looked at her with calm interest.

"Let this man alone," the girl said in flat, emphatic tone. "He saved my back from a Howard bullet today. The least we can do, on Los Alamos, is to let him do as he pleases."

"He was snoopin' around, talkin' to the *vaqueros'* women," Jed said. "That don't go on Los Alamos."

"Why, what are you hiding, that you're afraid somebody'll find out?" Lit asked innocently.

Jed seemed to have no answer for the question. But the girl stared hard at him, then spoke to Jed without turning.

"Trot, Jed! I'll talk to Taylor."

Lit watched him stalk away. When he looked at Sudie-May, he grinned. "Is he really poison? Or did somebody tell him so, once?"

"He's salty enough," she said almost absently. "So are — some others around here. I think it might pay you to remember that — just as a sort of general thing."

"I'll try," Lit promised meekly. "But I don't expect to have much time for thinking about Jed and Company. You see, I will be thinking about you so much —"

"Never mind that! What *were* you doing — when Jed caught you?"

"Just snooping around. Trying to find the place where he buries his thousands of victims. But, since you like me what does Jed matter!"

"You think I like you?" she said angrily. "I have to keep remembering that I owe you a debt, when my natural impulse is to slap your face!"

"Oh, you'll get used to that!" Lit assured

her cheerfully. "In time, you'll probably come to like it, wonder how you got along before I came. But — in spite of the fact that the place will never seem the same to you — and to Cousin Jed! — I have to leave you. Come morning I'll have to get into Midnight's middle. But it's not 'adiós!' that I'll say! Not — any! It's *'hasta la vista!'* Until I see you again. For I certainly will see you again!"

He moved a step nearer. All trace of banter was gone and the seriousness of his expression seemed to check what she intended to say.

"You don't know as much as I do — about you and me," he told her. "I know I'm just a harum-scarum *vaquero,* to you. That's natural. I rode up to you, out of Nowhere. You had to get used to me without warning. But, if I told you how it is that I happen to be here, today — Well, no matter. But you can take this for gospel:

"When a man finds a girl who can make him say: She's every last thing that I ever dreamed of looking for — Well, what kind of hairpin would he be, who didn't have the nerve to declare himself to the girl?"

He put out a hand quickly, caught hers, held her.

"So — I'm telling you *hasta la vista!*"

She stared up at him frowningly. But there was more of surprise than irritation in her face, her eyes. Even a trace of — alarm! Lit saw, and smiled down at her.

Then she pulled her hand free, stepped back quickly.

"Wonderful!" she cried. "He just rides into the Territory, onto Los Alamos, swings down and tells the girl. And that settles everything!"

"What else is there that you'd like to have me settle?"

"Oh — there's Frenchy Leonard! Have you thought about Frenchy? Some folk think he matters, a little."

There came to Lit memory of Kate Quinn, the nester's girl. "He's just — *wonderful!*" she had breathed, in her boyish brown face abjectest worship . . .

Red fury rose in him. Not even toward Bisbee, in Ike Menter's saloon at Tom's Bluff, had he felt such hatred. He was no innocent, no "preacher." But he was like most of his kind, in that a "decent" woman brought his hat to his knee. And thought of Frenchy and the girl Kate, thought of Frenchy and this level-eyed girl who was queen of Los Alamos set him shaking with rage.

Partly, he knew, it was jealousy. He had

built up a pretty plan, with first sight of Sudie-May's face in the locket. And she was so much more than a pretty girl, merely, that the dream had altered form to take on almost a definite shape. He knew exactly what he intended to do. He had already told himself that, come hell or high water, here was the woman he would have.

His fury wrestled with the faint pull of cold common-sense that warned him to wait. That told him this was neither time nor place for facing Frenchy Leonard. He knew that he had not the slightest hope of matching gun-speed with the grinning boy.

Sudie-May retreated another step, staring fascinatedly into his face. Slowly Lit got hold of himself. "Why, yes," he drawled. "I have sort of thought about him."

CHAPTER X
No Law West of the Rowdy

"So I told the agent I was riding for the M-in-a-Box over Four Rivers way and we'd been missing cows. Said I'd heard he'd just bought some beef and I'd like to have a look at the hides, if he didn't mind. Figured, you see, that if he *was* buying stolen stuff, he'd be tickled to show me that this bunch *wasn't* what I was hunting."

Lit grinned ruefully at the memory. Smoky Cole, tall, gaunt, grizzled, watched him steadily from his post in a chair tilted back against the wall of the sheriff's office in Gurney, without change in his seamed saddle-brown face.

"He busted out laughing," Lit went on. "He's a fat, red-faced *hombre,* you know, and he like to died a-laughing. Finally, he got both his hands to his sides and sort of held in for a minute.

" 'Sonny!' he says. 'Ever see an Indian eat a beef? Uh-huh, I thought you hadn't. For he just pulls a couple of hairs out of the tail and ties his ears back with them. Then he starts eating. And when he's done — there isn't hide nor hair left of the critter!' He was still rolling around the agency floor, a-whooping, when I rode off."

" 'S truth," nodded Smoky. "They just boil 'em, hide on. So yuh never seen nothing o' hides, then?"

"Not a thing. You might believe that two-three hundred of Bar-B stuff just left the Rowdy breaks and the lot was swallowed whole by this dam' Territory."

"Son," grunted Smoky very dryly, still with tiny, squinting blue eyes upon Lit, "that ain't nothin' to some o' the things this Territory's swallowed in her time. The' ain't

122

a Chink's chance o' yuh findin' them cows. But if yuh can plant the deadwood on King Connell, an' if we can catch him off from his boys, we can mebbe git the money fer 'em. I'll think it over."

Lit took this as his dismissal and went out to seek Chihuahua Joe. He asked up and down the street of everyone he met where he might locate the halfbreed. And he began to have brought home to him the plain truth of Long Al's lecture about warring halves. For as he ranged the dusty street, men eyed him suspiciously and replied with non-committal grunts to his questions.

But at last he encountered Halliday, one of the town's store-keepers. Halliday looked Lit over shrewdly.

"Chihuahua? Why, he's prob'ly wroppin' himself around the Jordan. Just listen as yuh go, till yuh hear what sounds like a whole dern' band. That'll be 'Brownie' with his mouth harp an' bones. Some'r's right around, yuh'll find Chihuahua, a-pattin' his foot."

But there was no sound as of "a whole dern' band." Lit stopped finally in the Antelope Saloon and was standing at the bar, glass in hand, when a noisy group entered, high heels clicking upon the rough floor, spur chains jingling, talking loudly.

"Wolf Montague's gang," muttered the bartender nervously. *"Oh, Lord!"*

They were a hard-looking quartet. But Lit had seen too many of their like to share the drink-dispenser's emotions. So he but kept an eye on them in the bar-mirror while he admired the color of his drink. Then entered Bisbee. He and Lit recognized each other instantly.

"Hey!" shouted Bisbee, to the four men already at the bar. "Here's one o' our rustlers! By God! I seen him through the glasses, other day! Fella! You're sure goin' to stretch a rope tonight!"

"Don't you reach for those guns unless you mean it, Bisbee," Lit advised him. "How's the arm I burned for you? And your crippled left arm that you can't shoot with? Too bad you can't sell that other gun to somebody that could use it! Shame to let a good Colt get rusty."

Bisbee snarled wolfishly and took a half-step forward. But a burly warrior came shouldering past him, to stand with arms akimbo and glare at Lit, who now leaned lightly against the bar with folded arms.

"So yuh're one of them dam' rustlers that got away from us, huh? Well, yuh're goin' to trot along of us right peaceful, an' when we come to a cottonwood that's just your proper fit, we're goin' to take a new rope an' tie a cute little knot in one end of it — for your collar, see? Then —"

"*Pues,*" remarked a plaintive voice from the saloon's rear door, "w'at is it you do, I'm wish it you're start him. I'm git so *dam'* tired to hold this Weenchestair . . ."

Lit dropped his hand to the butt of his Colt and grinned. As for the others, they kept their hands conspicuously clear of contact with their weapons. It began to dawn upon Lit that Chihuahua Joe was not without a certain reputation in the locality.

"Well!" grunted Chihuahua, inquiringly. "Is it not to be, then? This hanging? *Dios mio!* I am disappoint' like the hell. *Pues,* if those hanging, she's just as fine some other time, p'raps you will go now? It will be much better. For if my frien's in town an' me — you're know poor ol' Chihuahua! — we're find you ——"

"Mebbe we'll go," snarled Bisbee truculently, "but don't you never think we won't come back. An' when we come, we'll come a-shootin'!"

"Said the bold, bad Bisbee, one time in Tom's Bluff," nodded Lit. "I recollect, now. Couldn't figure, for a minute, where I'd heard that before . . ."

"An' as for you ——"

"And as for me" — Lit moved over to stare into Bisbee's long, green eyes "— you can't come shooting too soon to suit. Tell you what! We'll step out into the street right now. Stand back to back. Walk ten steps and turn and let go! That suit you? Come on!"

"I shoot when an' where I'm good an' ready!" Bisbee met Lit's eyes steadily enough and Lit was forced to concede that the big, tallowy-faced man was not bluffed. He began to understand that Bisbee was merely a "sure-thing" gambler. He would shoot — when he thought he had the edge.

"Mabbe you're *shoot* w'en you're ready," Chihuahua reminded him, "but you're high-tail it w'en me, I'm good an' ready! *Pues,* me, I'm ready now . . ."

The muttering group swaggered it outside and to the hitch rack. Like a great cat, Chihuahua flitted to the door after them. He crouched there with Winchester thrust outside, a lean, deadly figure. Presently, he straightened and came loafing back to the bar.

"Hah! I'm tell you, Lit, that me an' you, we're not lose the other, w'at?"

He flung an arm about Lit's shoulders, then shouted for drinks.

"W'ere's them Brownie?" Chihuahua roared suddenly. "W'at the hell! She's

126

s'pose' to play with them mouth-harp w'ile I'm dance them *cachucha.* We will drink the w'iskey; we will dance. We will put them town marshal in them water trough! *Yaaaii-iiah!*"

Entered two familiar figures, Irish Tim Fenelon and Hognose Ott. Tim greeted Lit with a wolf-howl and he, warmed by the Jordan to friendliness with all the world, replied in kind. Dimly, there came to him the memory of Irish Tim's hair rope, found by Long Al beside cattle-tracks upon the Rowdy. But, after all, Frenchy was to blame for the rustling, thought Lit blurrily. Tim had always been a good fellow, in Tom's Bluff. As for Hognose, he was never taken seriously by anyone. His aspiration was to be known as a man and a hard one, but his attempts to achieve the status were always either squelched promptly or ignored.

Brownie appeared presently, a shambling, grinning creature, the town's ne'er-do-well. He sat himself down, and played frantically while Chihuahua danced the *cachucha.*

It was a large night and it spoke loudly for their constitutions that all but Hognose were upon their feet when the dawn came to them in Mig' Garcia's dance-place at the end of town. They left Garcia's for the Antelope Saloon. Now, as they came picking up their feet carefully and setting them down in what each considered to be the straight line of progress, appeared to them a sight which made each rub his eyes.

The Widow Duncan owned, amazing in that dry land, twelve snowy Pekin ducks and a drake. They were the pride of her sour heart — as certain duck-hungry Mexicans could prove by rock-salt scars from the widow's shotgun — and regular residents of Gurney would have given them a wide berth. But to these bold warriors the file of thirteen quack-quacking ducks appeared first as a warning and then as a provocation.

"I'm bettin'," Irish Tim swayed where he stood, fishing for elusive Colt-butt, "that I'll be snappin' off the head av wan wit' me firrst shot."

Out came Tim's gun. The Colt wavered to three points of the compass, then down it came and with the report the lordly drake at the head of the procession leaped into the air with squawk and came down running. Followed a second report — but not from Tim's gun. This one was far louder and had its origin on the opposite side of the street, where the Widow Duncan stood at her paling-gate with a double-barreled shotgun quite accustomedly at her shoulder.

With the sting of the rock-salt on their nether-sections, the four leaped high into the air and, like the drake, came down running. Near the watering-trough by the smithy they met the marshal, who invited them to halt and be arrested for discharging firearms "within the business-district." They came meekly up to him and wrapped long arms about him and with as many hands as could grip him, gripping him, he was borne to the watering-trough and ducked triumphantly.

"If we're not get them duck," grinned Chihuahua, "is not the reason w'y these marshal, *she's* not be give the duck!"

Sometime after noon, Lit waked in the corral behind Halliday's store, to stare blearily up at the store-keeper.

"Marshal's a-lookin' for yuh," Halliday told him solemnly. "He's plumb scandalized about the way yuh-all scarred up the honor an' dignity o' his high office. Yes, sir! He's goin' to shoot yuh on sight."

"I wish he would!" groaned Lit. "I wish he'd already done it!"

"Sho! Yuh just feel thataway now. Come on inside an' Sary-Ann, she'll shake yuh up some cawffee. Here! Couple o' hairs off'n the dog that bit yuh won't hurt nothin'. Come on, son. Smoky Cole, he wants that

129

yuh should come down to see him right away."

When he had eaten the meal served him by the buxom Mrs. Halliday, Lit's interest in life was much revived. He thanked his hostess and went through to the store, where Halliday waited.

"About this marshal," Lit said penitently. "I reckon we ought not to have ducked him . . ."

"Well, the's two opinions about that, o' course," the storekeeper nodded. "Yours an' the marshal's. Yuh better see Smoky. Kind o' dodge the marshal, if yuh can. Yuh see, he come to be rulin' the roost here in an odd way: We figgered that since we was a-goin' to have him with us, anyhow, he might's well have a star fer his excuse!"

Lit grinned weakly and went out. The street was vacant of sign of the marshal so he drifted down to Smoky Cole's, where the sheriff sat with his chair tilted against the wall, hatbrim slid down his nose.

"S'pose yuh found all your cows, last night?" Thus Smoky, very dryly. "Understand yuh was lookin' around right smart."

"We didn't do any harm," Lit shrugged, reddening under the cold blue scrutiny from beneath the hatbrim.

"No? Well, if I was boss o' the Bar-B iron

130

an' one o' my hands was carousin' around with the very jiggers he says rustled my stuff, I'd shore think some funny thoughts."

Lit shrugged again. Viewed in the uninspired light of afternoon, the complicity of Irish Tim Fenelon and Hognose in the rustling of Bar-B strays had a more serious appearance than at the time of their entry into the Antelope the night before.

"I'd had a drink or two," he acknowledged. "Guess I got to blaming Frenchy for everything and —— Oh! I knew Tim and Hognose real well back in Tom's Bluff."

"I've knowed a good many *gunies* real well — an' then pumped lead at 'em. But what I'm drivin' at, young fella, is what yuh figger to do, now. Goin' to just hell around the Territory, or d' yuh really figger to find them cows?"

"I'm going to find the cows, no matter how long it takes," Lit told him hotly. "If my own brother — if I had one — was in on this deal, I'd hang the deadwood on him, regardless."

"Yeh," Smoky nodded, without sign of impressment. "Yeh — mebbe. Yuh certainly made a good start towards standin' in with decent folks, last night: Shootin' a defenseless widder's ducks!"

"Defenseless!" cried Lit. Involuntarily, his

hand went to the tender, rock-salted section of his anatomy. "Defenseless!"

"Well — ne' mind the ducks," Smoky conceded solemnly. "When I took this sheriffin' job I told everybody that I aimed to *be* the sheriff; an' do all one man could do, towards cleanin' up the mess in this neighborhood. I play no favorytes. I'm not for nor ag'inst the big fella; not for nor ag'inst the li'l' fella. They all collect a square deal — no matter if it was King Connell that begged me to pin on this star."

He flipped a soiled envelope across to Lit, with the deft air of a stage magician, producing the letter from nowhere.

Lit opened it. It was from Barbee. Lit was to carry out Long Al Kendrick's original instructions. He would either find the Bar-B strays, or find the rustlers. When he had news, Smoky Cole would relay it for him and the Bar-B would move as seemed best. He was to play a lone hand in the detective-work.

"When did this come?" Lit asked the old man.

"A while ago. Ne' mind who brung it. Them that does the work for me, they don't want to be knowed. For if they was, they not only wouldn't never do another job for me — they wouldn't never do another job

132

for anybody else!"

Lit nodded, understanding perfectly.

"Big thing is," Smoky drawled, "yuh got Barbee's powders. An' I got a letter along with that. Now, son, I told yuh plain, I don't play favorytes. Can yuh do the same, for me, if I help out all I can towards findin' them Bar-B strays?"

Lit nodded slowly, somewhat puzzled.

"Then stick up yo' paw! I'm appointin' yuh a dep'ty sheriff under me. Here's a star. Pin it on an' — remember yuh' wearin' it."

Lit turned the nickeled badge over and over in his hand. At last he looked narrowly at the gray sheriff.

"According to you, King Connell gets the same deal from us as, say, the Howard Boys, or Wolf Montague?"

"Other things bein' even, yeh!"

"But," Lit said slowly, "does King Connell think that?"

For the first time there showed a change of expression in the grizzled brown face. It was a flicker that might have become, with growth, a tiny grin.

"Son," Smoky grunted, "bein' sheriff here is a job that keeps me right busy. A lot o' inter-est-in' things I just don't have time to bother about. An' one o' them things is — what Connell thinks!"

Lit, pinning the star on, found himself very proud of the glint of it, on his button-less vest.

"Yuh can tell folks I made yuh a dep'ty because o' friendship for Barbee," Smoky said tonelessly. "It'll cover things."

Lit lifted narrowing eyes to the inscrutable face. It was probably the truth! He had not been chosen for special abilities. The letter from Barbee to Smoky had put this star on him. So he nodded respectfully and went out of the office.

The badge might have weighed pounds, for its effect upon Lit as he went upstreet, heading for Halliday's store.

"*Por dios!* You're walk like the w'iskey, she's still with you yet, Lit!"

Lit halted before Chihuahua. The breed's quick blue eyes found the badge. Long and liquidly he whistled.

"*Amor de dios!* She's one dep'ty sheriff. Ah! those poor, poor boy! Just w'en I'm find me one good fella, she's fix himself up fi-ine for to git killed!"

"Maybe," Lit grinned. "Anyway, it's done. I'm Smoky Cole's deputy, whatever comes out of the bag."

They went silently on together. At the door of the Antelope Saloon, Chihuahua leaned toward Lit, pushing him toward its door.

"For to c'risten them fi-ine, new star!" he grinned.

Tim Fenelon and Hognose were at the bar. They turned, whooped joyously at sight of Lit. But when quickly the star's twinkle caught their eyes, Hognose gaped at it, then looked nervously at Tim for guidance. The huge Irishman leaned upon the bar. Into his daredevil blue eyes came a mocking, dancing light. "So ut's a real dip'ty sheriff, he'll be now . . . Well, well, well . . ."

Lit stiffened instantly under the mockery.

"A real deputy and be damned if that's Spanish, either! That goes as she lays with everything she means."

Ostentatiously, Irish Tim turned his back upon Lit and Chihuahua and devoted himself to his drink. Later, as Lit gathered his dunnage together in Halliday's corral, Irish Tim came swaggering up to him. It was dusk, now, and the outlaw showed a vast, dim bulk when he leaned against a corral post to stare at Lit.

"So ut's a dip'ty ye'll be now. An' ut's the Bar-B stuff ye'll be findin'. If ye'll be takin' a word o' good advice, ye'll saddle that hammerhead an' ride for the Diamond. Ye'll tell Barbee that his stuff has gone 'where the winds come from . . .' Tell him 'twas like to be too big a job for ye!"

"But that'd be a lie!" cried Lit, in pained accents. "You wouldn't want me to be lying, now would you?"

"Listen!" gritted Fenelon. "Whin meddlers come nosin' around the Territory, they'll be wise to come a-shootin'!"

"Sure!" nodded Lit pleasantly. "Sure, I *sabe that.*"

"For over this bank o' the Rowdy, there's but the li'l' bit o' law we're makin' to suit ourselves."

"Sure!" Lit nodded pleasantly again. "Sure! But did you ever figure, Tim, that the real law will soon be coming? You think about that for a while, Timmy-boy!"

When Tim had gone, Chihuahua rose from the shadows and came over, teeth flashing in the darkness.

"Jed Connell, she's just ride in," he grunted. "King Connell, she's still ridin' in the country, somew'ere. For to buy more rus'led cow, mabbe . . . Me, I have smell an' I have look an' I'm think those trail you hunt, she's lead back for Los Alamos again."

"I've got to go somewhere!" shrugged Lit. "I got a letter from the Old Man, today. He says for me to stick on the job and either find the cows or find out who got them.

He's pulled the other boys back to the ranch."

Mechanically he put hand to shirt-pocket, then swore.

"So *that's* how Irish Tim knew what I was here for! I lost that letter and he probably picked it up!"

"Well!" Chihuahua replied philosophically, "in this dam' Territory, me, I'm think a little more trouble is one small thing. Me an' you, Lit, we will ride out tonight for Los Alamos. No! No! No! You're *not* make them fight with Tim an' Jed. We're wait an', one day mabbe we're hang them both by one cottonwood!"

"You're going with me?" Lit asked in surprise. "Why, I thought you said ———"

"Sure! Me, I'm say those other things. But I'm know you better now, an' I'm think, tonight. Me, I'm got not one dam' thing for to do, an' mabbe forty year more for to finish him, so — w'at the hell?"

Chapter XI
"Come Shootin' — Sonny!"

"Pues, w'en we're git close by Los Alamos, we're turn in them west an' we're have one look by King Connell, his Little Pasture."

They jogged along side-by-side, Lit en-

137

grossed with a pocketful of pebbles and certain maneuvers: Upon his right wrist he placed a pebble, then extended his arm to shoulder-level and with a flip of the wrist let the pebble fall — while gun-hand flashed to Colt-butt, drew the empty gun and clicked the hammer as if firing at an opposing gunman. Then another pebble, another draw.

"Getting faster," he grunted finally. "Clicked her four times, then, before the rock hit the ground."

"*Pues,* w'en you're sit in them horse, you're one long way from them ground," Chihuahua reminded him, with flash of teeth. "Me, I'm think she's better w'en you're climb them tall mountain. Then, your pebble she's take more time for them fall."

He gathered in his reins and swayed, grinning as his sorrel bucked and squealed under the sting of the pebble Lit had flipped against its haunch.

"I want to find out where our cattle went!" Lit grunted suddenly. "We're both sure they came to Los Alamos, that some of them were sold. But we don't *know.* We don't know . . ."

"*Pues,* in Los Alamos, she's one man w'at *will* know! She's one funny fella w'at those cowboy, they're call 'McGregor them Handy

138

Man.' Dam' funny . . ."

"Funny? How?" Lit looked sidewise.

"*Sí*, most funny! So dam' honest. She's tell those cowboy how it is bad for to rus'le cow. She's talk all time about those law an' those order."

"McGregor . . . Scotchman, huh?"

"No-o. She's — w'at you call it? Presbyterian! If them Bar-B cows is in Los Alamos, she's know it."

"But even if he doesn't hold with rustling, he isn't going to tell us about King Connell's business. Not while he's working on Los Alamos, he won't."

"*Sí, es verdad,*" nodded Chihuahua. "She's one honest fella; so she's not talk about his boss."

Lit rode on silently for some miles. He could not put thought of McGregor out of mind, though in his mental pictures of a dourly-honest Scot was no scene where McGregor discussed with outsiders his employer's dishonesty. But there was one possibility, vague, and yet —

"How-come he sticks on Los Alamos if he knows there's rustling going on?"

"*Pues,* me, I'm think she's hope some day for to make King Connell one honest fella. Hah! She's all time tell King about them hell fire for rus'lers."

139

Lit grinned sourly. "And what does the King think about that?"

"Oh, she's lis'en — sometimes," Chihuahua shrugged, with answering grin. "Me, I'm think these McGregor, she's like King one fi-ine whole lot. But she's like King's girl more — much more."

Lit, jogged by the reference to thought of Sudie-May, had the vividest mental picture of those wide, steady eyes, the arrogant lift of square little chin. He could hear, as plainly as he heard Chihuahua's voice, what she had last said to him:

"Have you thought about Frenchy? Some folk think he matters, a little."

He nodded vaguely, barely noticing anything about him.

"Couldn't blame him!" he muttered. "For liking Sudie-May, I mean. Couldn't blame him a bit."

Then he pulled in short, to stare at a suddenly altered Chihuahua, who had spun his sorrel about into Midnight's path, and who stared at Lit with blue eyes very cold.

"What the hell ——" Lit began amazedly.

"My frien'," Chihuahua said very softly, "you're please to tell me how you're come to call them lady by her first name! Me, I'm interest' like the hell to know!"

"Well," Lit said with the beginning of irritation, "I don't know whether I'm pleased to tell you, or not! Why are *you* so interested in my calling her by her first name?"

"Me, I'm dam' interest' in everything w'at's to do with her! An' I'm ask for to find out!"

"*Por dios!* I ought to tell you to go straight to hell!" Lit grunted. "Well, if you're so interested, I met her the other day after I'd left you. I shot one of the Howards who was about to shoot her. I'm going to hang the hobbles onto our rustlers and as soon as that's straightened, I'm going to marry her!"

Chihuahua's tight mouth went tighter still. Lit watched the evidences of repressed emotion with very real curiosity.

"Well!" he demanded, belligerently. "What's so flabbergasting about her marrying me? Not that I really give a whoop! About your notions, I mean. I'm going to marry her and — be damned to you, and McGregor, and anybody else who doesn't happen to like it!"

Slowly, very slowly, Chihuahua's thin mouth twisted in a crooked grin.

"*Bien!* Then I'm wish for you those luck. For if Sudie-May, she's make for to marry with you — she's fix'. An' if she's make *not* for to marry with you — she's fix' just the same."

141

"I want to meet this McGregor. There's a little old idea rolling around under my John B. and she's going to bring home the bacon. Just you lead me to this Presbyterian-jigger!"

"*Pues,* she's easy for to find him," shrugged Chihuahua. "But for to make him talk w'en we're find him —"

Perhaps three hours later, Chihuahua pointed down from a hogback's crest to a long 'dobe upon a creek-bank, with a corral of cottonwood-logs behind it.

"She's those Little Pasture. We're wait here for those McGregor. She's all time ride around an' mabbe she's come here in two, three day."

They made themselves at home in the 'dobe. Here and there in the distance were scattered bunches of cattle, grazing slowly. There was no sign of any herder and with nightfall they cooked supper, lay beside the fire for a little while smoking, then rolled into their blankets.

The next day passed idly, except when Lit rode about cautiously, inspecting the varied brands on the lean cattle. Evidences of brand-blotting he found, enough to have hanged a smaller one than King Connell. But of all the cattle he found, none bore a brand that was indubitably an alteration of Bar-B.

"McGregor!" grunted Chihuahua, in mid-afternoon. He jerked a thumb toward a rider coming slowly across the Little Pasture toward the creek and the 'dobe.

"Howdy!" Lit greeted the raw-boned man on tall black, when McGregor had forded the creek. "We were waiting for you. Chihuahua figured you would be along today or tomorrow."

"Aye? And why wad ye wait for me?" The blue eyes were noncommittal, like the craggy face.

Lit hesitated. The old Scot was so forbidding that for an instant he wondered if it would not be wiser to find some other means of getting that information he must have. Then he decided to venture upon his original plan, and that required frankness.

"If you'll climb down and listen to me for a spell, I figure to keep you interested."

McGregor grunted and swung down.

"Ye'll be the laddie that rode in wi' Sudie-May," he accused Lit. "Weel?"

"But it isn't well!" protested Lit. "I've heard you put down as one of the two-three honest fellows in the dam' Territory."

"Dinnae sweer!" roared the old man rebukingly. "Vain oaths are the de'il's ain language that leads ye surely tae hell's fire!"

"Oh! Excuse *me!* I'm riding for the Bar-B over in the Diamond River country. Now, our strays were rustled by Frenchy Leonard this Spring and driven over here. King Connell, he bought all or most of them. I'm going to get them back or collect the price of them. I'm going to put Frenchy where the little dogs won't bite him for a while! Now, I'm asking *you* to help me put the deadwood where it belongs."

"Ye're an ambeetious laddie! Wad ye nae like a deed tae the Territory, as weel?"

"She's a big enough job," Lit agreed. "But I figure to do it and do it without getting killed off, either!

"Look here! I *sabe* how things are going in this Territory. I know the big fellows buy rustled stuff off the likes of Frenchy about as much to keep them off their own herds as because they like shady deals.

"I know how the big cowmen like King Connell crack down on the little fellows, the Wolf Montagues and the Howards. Each side figures to put the other clear out of business. I *sabe* that it isn't going to happen! There'll always be big and little. Big and little, they have got to stop this bushwhacking and rustling!"

"Sae I ha' said, mony's the tame!" McGregor's craggy face was still unreadable, but into the blue eyes had come enthusiasm as he stared at Lit.

"All right! I'm deputy under Smoky Cole. I'm going to hang this Bar-B rustling onto Frenchy's gang and make King Connell ante up our stuff or the cash for it. That's half of the ticket. The other half is — I'm going to help to bring law and order into this Territory. Now, are you game to side in with me? Or will you just sit on the fence and let the other fellow do it?"

"What wad ye want o' me?"

"King Connell bought our strays off Frenchy, didn't he?"

"Sae ye ha' said," fenced McGregor. Lit eyed him scornfully for an instant, then got up.

"Come on, Chihuahua! Let's catch up the horses and hightail it!"

He went inside the 'dobe and came out with saddle and bridle. Chihuahua went in and came out with his gear. His bright blue eyes went furtively to Lit in questioning glance. Chihuahua might have no idea of what moved in Lit's mind, but he backed his play to the limit.

"Laddie!" McGregor called. "A moment, laddie."

"Yeh?" Lit turned without appearance of

interest.

"Why wad ye expect *me* tae gi' ye evidence against Connell?"

"Well — wouldn't you rather see this one job pinned on him, and costing him nothing but a little cash, than to have him packed out some fine morning with holes enough in him to keep him from ever floating again? What I'm trying to do is make these *gunies* see that the day's past when they can raid another fellow's herd, kill off his hands, and then thumb their noses at the whole world. Take it or leave it!"

Old McGregor squatted rigidly, staring at the ground. Lit pitied the old man. It was violating the very first article of the Range Code to give evidence against one's employer. But he felt a quick leap of excitement when at last the old Scot raised his grim face.

"I'm takin' ye for an honest laddie. 'Tis sair against my conscience tae tell ye sae much. But mayhap guid'll come frae it."

He fumbled for plug tobacco, worried off a huge bite and worked it into beard-stubbled cheek.

"Aye! Connell bought the Bar-B strays frae Frenchy. He paid Frenchy a thousand for the lot — some twa hunder' an' feefty head."

Lit nodded, trying to keep eagerness out of his face.

"And a tolerable average price would be three times that, beef the way it is!" he said grimly.

"Aye!" McGregor nodded. "Weel — saxty head ha' gone tae the Injuns on the Rio Lobos. A hunder' head went to Fort Lowe. These ha' all been et. We ha' beefed a few for headquarters. Seventy-odd head are on the range at Vilas Creek. An' Connell will buy a' the rustled stuff Frenchy can bring him."

"Where's Connell, now?" Lit asked softly.

"Arno. For mair rustled stuff, I make na doot."

Lit drew in a long, slow breath, lifting his chin.

"Funny, Chihuahua," he said, "I just happened to think that we are heading that way — towards Arno . . ."

"Ye'll tell Connell ye ken he bought the Bar-B strays?"

Lit nodded: "I'll have to. For I'm going to demand payment for every dogie calf! But he'll never know where I got the figures on what he bought. I know that I'm bucking a tough game on this bank of the Rowdy. But if things go, the way I am going to try to make 'em go — you've done a good job for everybody, today. For King Connell as much as for anybody else."

He stared blankly, grimly, through the old Scot.

"No law west of the Rowdy," he said softly. "Well — maybe we can change that!"

They left McGregor still hunkered before the 'dobe staring after them. Chihuahua shook his head.

"Por dios!" he said marvelingly. "Me, I'm find it very hard for me to believe! She's ride to them Little Pasture an' she's meet them Handy Man. *Por dios!* She's have them fi-ine charm! To make them McGregor talk about King Connell. I'm swear she's them — impossibles!"

"Luck!" Lit shrugged. "I reckon we just hit him on his soft spot — the hope that King Connell can be booted into being honest."

He was busy with his thoughts for a long while. The saddle slipped a little on Midnight's back. Lit muttered and swung down to tighten the latigo. Chihuahua rode on slowly toward the crest of a rise. So it was that Lit was on the ground, when he heard the *clop-clop* of a horse's hoofs. He turned, stared . . .

"Hel-lo!" he greeted Sudie-May, who sat her buckskin in an arroyo's mouth, watching him. "You weren't — looking for me?"

"What is it, this time?" she inquired. "Just another snooping expedition, like the one Jed interrupted?"

"Oh, don't say that! Say scouting. How is Cousin Jed, by the way? Not so well, we trust!"

She pushed the buckskin closer. Lit, done with his girth, leaned against Midnight and looked at her. She faced him without expression.

"I wonder how far an obligation goes," she said. "If a man does you a big favor, do you have to go through life letting him spy on your own people, without doing anything?"

"Well ——" Lit began judicially. Then he decided to throw off the pretense of misunderstanding. He came over to the buckskin's side and looked up into her face.

"I wouldn't say so!" he told her very quietly. "In fact, since I know what you're talking about, I say — no! You can realize that I couldn't come to Los Alamos as a friend. Not that day! Los Alamos was enemy-country. I didn't pretend otherwise, did I?"

"Then, why did you stop that Howard bullet that was marked for my back? It won't do, Mr. Taylor! You were coming to

Los Alamos on a spying trip. When you saw me about to be jumped by the Howard Boys, you thought it was just what you'd have ordered. You opened up on them, counting on putting me in a hole. You put me under obligations, so I had to step in between you and Jed ———"

"Lucky for him that you did," Lit nodded amicably. "He never saw the day that he could do a good job of gunning a man. Not from the front, that is!"

His hand came up, closed over the slender hand that rested on the saddle horn.

"You know exactly why I smoked up the Howard Boys? *You don't know a thing about it!* I didn't give a whoop who they might be; they were bushwhacking one man without giving him a chance. That was the way it looked — way it would have looked, even if I hadn't known all the time that you were a girl."

"And *that* doesn't do! How could you know that I was a girl? You saw nothing but my back. And I wear pants and shirt on the range, all the time! So ———"

"Oh, but I had been watching you study that cow's brand. What were you doing? Trying to figure out what it was before they blotted it? I placed you for a girl, even if you had four-footed her as well as any man could do."

"You were watching me, then?"

Her tone puzzled Lit. She stared at him, not pulling against his hand, now. Her clear face was very red.

"For quite a while," he nodded. "So ——"

"But you *were* spying!"

She seemed to reach for that angle of the affair.

"Of course! And I was spying on Los Alamos, when the bold, bad man from the hard water fork of Bitter Creek jumped me. I'm glad you stepped in, then. I didn't want to kill him."

"You think you would have killed him?" she said unpleasantly. "That never occurred to me! You see, I hadn't put you down as a gunman, then. But, even if you are one, maybe you're not the only one in the Territory . . . There's Frenchy. Oh! I have a message for you. From Frenchy. You see, we'd heard about the pretty tin star and your — brave plans. Frenchy understands that you're coming after him, soon. He says:

" 'Come shooting — sonny!' "

"Now that's downright kind of Frenchy! It is that. But — I don't see how I can go easy on him, for all his thoughtfulness."

But, for all his air of pleasant unconcern, Lit boiled inwardly. He fumbled in shirt pocket for the Durham and brown papers. An oval object was caught in the strings of the tobacco sack. It dropped to the ground and the girl's eyes followed it, then shuttled to Lit's suddenly red face.

"My locket!" she cried. "That's my locket! Where did *you* get it? Give it to me!"

Deliberately, Lit stooped and picked it up. He pressed the spring, opened it, looked up at her.

"Where did I get it! Oh — back where the winds come from. It's a poor sort of thing, compared to the girl the picture is supposed to represent. I'll hang to it until I get her . . ."

"Give it to me! I'll not have you carrying it!"

"I will not! *I'll* not have Frenchy wearing your picture!"

"Frenchy? Are you trying to make me believe that *you* got that locket from Frenchy?"

Red mouth curled with sudden scorn.

"You would have to add picking pockets to spying, to get anything from Frenchy!"

"You don't mean that," he told her quietly. "You may not know much about me, but you're too much of a person not to know something about men. You know that I'd not bother to lie to you. He lost it, in Tom's

Bluff. I picked it up. And when I saw that picture, I made up my mind to something. When I came upon you, that day, if my plan needed any stiffening, it got all the necessary!"

He clicked the locket shut, dropped it into his pocket.

"I'm going to keep it. Until the day comes that I'll trade you something for it. You know what that'll be? A ring! Fight the rope all you want to! If I can't make you love me, that'll be my hard luck. But don't you think for a minute that I'm not going to put in my licks trying."

"Love you?" Her teeth were caught furiously in lower lip. Suddenly, she laughed, a high, thin sound. "Love you — with Jed and Frenchy both looking for you! I think, Mr. Taylor, that whatever you intend to do won't worry me for very long!"

"Of course not!" Lit grinned. "You may even come to enjoy it. It can't worry you any more, to love me, than it worries me to love you! And even while I'm worrying, I like it!"

CHAPTER XII
ARNO AND "AN ARRANGEMENT"

They jogged into Arno very quietly. Chihuahua squinted down the peaceful rows of one-story 'dobes, where cow-horses drowsed at the hitch racks and occasional figures loafed from door to door. He shook his head sadly at the last.

"She's so ni-ice an' quiet," he said. "But me, I'm see them nice, clean sand all red . . . an' wet . . ."

"Might turn red and wet again, too," Lit nodded, understanding perfectly. "Well — we'll see . . ."

They swung down before the Last Chance Saloon. Chihuahua looked about him, at the faces of the men under the mud-roofed awning of the drinking place. He seemed to know none of them. So he and Lit hitched their horses with the forethoughtful slipknot and clink-clumped up to the Last Chance's open door.

"By them bar's end," Chihuahua breathed in Lit's ear. Then he vanished. Lit went on in.

He thought that he would have identified Connell even without Chihuahua's word.

154

The King wore the ancient and floppy gray Stetson common to half the drinkers in the Last Chance, wore a dingy shirt that had once been blue, tucked carelessly into trousers of a check so violent that none but an English lord would have dared wear them on a city street.

His boots were sunburned wrecks, the heels so worn that his ankles turned ludicrously. But — Lit found nothing ludicrous about the King, himself . . .

He was at least three inches over six feet, and his back — now turned to Lit — had the width of a barn door. Lit moved toward him and when he edged in to the bar at the King's heels, Connell turned slowly from talk with a man beyond. He had a round, red face, the King and wide, steady blue eyes. He wore long mustaches of the same sorrel hue as his thinning hair.

Lit studied him quite openly and when he was done, nodded to himself. Connell put up a huge red-brown hand to twist his mustache.

"Ye seem interested?" he suggested.

"That's because I am interested," Lit nodded. "I'd heard a lot about you. I wanted to — sort of check up for myself."

"And now that ye've checked up?"

He had a booming voice, but softened by

the trace of a brogue. Connell — Lit knew his history very well — was a fox-hunting squire from the Ould Sod, but unlike most of the Old Country youngsters bringing pounds sterling into the American West, Connell had prospered amazingly. He had schemed and fought his way to vast holdings and power in the Territory. That unusual discretion growing in Lit counseled him to be very careful, in matching wits with this master-schemer.

"I heard you'd come to Arno," he said slowly. "So I rode down to talk to you. About — some cows."

Connell looked Lit up and down.

"I love to talk," he said.

"You won't love it, this time," Lit countered — and grinned. "For it's about Bar-B cows — that came to you Half-Box HBH . . ."

"Half of that I understand," Connell said easily. "The Half-Box HBH half. But the Bar-B half — it's news ye're giving me. Buying and selling in the numbers I do, it would be queer if occasionally a cow or two misbranded didn't figure. But ——"

"Two hundred and fifty-odd head of mixed Bar-B stuff, blotted to Half-Box HBH," Lit drawled. "I wanted to talk to you about collecting market price for the

bunch, on Barbee's account. I have got —
arguments in favor of paying the bill."

Connell dropped his air of tolerant amusement. He leaned to Lit with blue eyes cold
and hard.

"And did ye ever hear, my son, that the
young rooster should make a small crow?"

"I don't know that I ever did," Lit
shrugged indifferently. "But I'll tell you
what I've figured out all by myself. And that
is, a man as old as you ought to know better than to buy rustled stuff!"

"I don't know why I'm long suffering,
today," Connell said slowly. "I'll not worry
to argue. I'll just ask ye if ye've happened to
hear that, from Mountain View in the north,
to Alamito that's some several miles south
of this, my say-so is — not without some
small influence?"

"Small puddles, big frogs!" Lit returned
with contempt that was only outward. "I'm
a Diamond River man and what's what in
this one-horse Territory is nothing to me.
You may loom up like a brick church
steeple, on this bank of the Rowdy. On the
Diamond River, you look about the right
size to hide behind a greasewood bush!"

He faced the King grimly, in his turn.

"I've told you that I'm over here to collect
for our stuff that you bought. If you want to

be reasonable — fine! If you don't, it's your funeral. About a hundred Diamond River warriors would ask nothing better than a crack at the cow-thieves west of the Rowdy! Not an outfit on our side but has some debts to pay off."

Watching Connell, Lit saw the first flicker of uneasiness in the shrewd, red face. In Connell's domain thousands of cattle grazed over miles of range. In a guerilla war with the straight-shooting warriors of the Diamond, Connell stood to lose enormously, even if he won in the end. And against the Diamond River outfits, he had no assurance of winning.

"Hell!" he said at last. "Ye're going off half-cocked! Ye come to me with a wild tale of Bar-B stuff ye've lost. *I* bought the stuff, ye say. And if I don't pay, it's to be war. I ask ye what proof ye have. Now and again I buy a cow misbranded — how could it be different?"

"Not good enough!" Lit scoffed. "One or two misbranded strays is held against no man. But I *know* that you bought two hundred and fifty-odd head of mixed Bar-B stuff from Frenchy Leonard. You sold part of 'em to the Indian agent at Rio Lobos, part of 'em to the military at Fort Lowe. The rest are on your range at Vilas Creek,

158

right now. I want the market price for two hundred and fifty head of Bar-B stuff!"

"It's a dam' lie!" Connell cried furiously. "And I'll listen to no more impudence!"

" 'Sta bien!" Lit nodded, grimly. "You can have until tomorrow morning to make up your mind. You'll pay or you'll see the Diamond River through enough smoke to make it look like a prairie fire!"

"I'll not pay a penny! I'm telling ye, now!"

"Your hard luck!" Lit shrugged.

He turned, knowing that at the back door Chihuahua's Winchester covered the barroom. He swaggered back to the front door and out. At the corner, Chihuahua joined him. They left the horses at the rack and moved together along the lines of 'dobe stores and saloons and houses.

"My belly, she's yell Supper Time," Chihuahua grinned. He yawned. "Them Bar-B cow, she's bother Connell plenty, hah?"

"They're due to bother him some more," Lit said.

They turned into a Chinese eating house and found Art Brand at the counter. He was staring at them. Lit frowned, at sight of the thin-faced, shifty-eyed first lieutenant of Frenchy's gang. He wondered what Brand was doing, alone, in Arno.

Brand met his stare with malevolent eyes.

Lit shrugged contemptuously, and trailed Chihuahua down the counter to a place beyond Brand. The little outlaw finished his meal before they were half-done. He got up, paid and went out. Thereafter, Chihuahua ate hurriedly. Suddenly, he rose:

"She's dark, very soon," he said. "Me, I'm think mabbe Connell, she's git into them trouble, if nobody's watch . . ."

He went quickly out and Lit, leaning an elbow comfortably on the counter, with hat rim low over his eyes, kept mechanically alert watch upon the street door and considered his talk with King Connell.

He hardly knew what to do, now. His threat to bring down the hard-bitten Diamond River warriors on Los Alamos was mostly bluff. At this busy season, gathering a considerable number of men would be no slight task. Even if the cowmen decided to join Barbee in a raid over the Rowdy, much time would be needed. Barbee might very well decide to let the business rest until later in the year.

"If I send him word," Lit thought irritably, "the chances are he'll snake me back to go to work."

But more than that, there was Sudie-May to consider. If he rode against Los Alamos, that would be the end of his day-dreaming.

He thought that she was unquestioningly loyal to her father. She would not believe that he bought and sold stolen stock. To her, Lit would be an enemy, nothing more, nothing less.

But, if the Diamond River men rode to make war upon Connell, Lit knew that he would ride with them. He asked himself furiously why she could not have been someone else's daughter.

He decided that he had to send word to Barbee about the buying of the strays and their re-sale — and about the discussion here and what he had threatened. Then he saw Chihuahua, standing in the eating house door. Lit got up, paid his half-dollar and went outside. It was dark, now.

"Well?" he asked Chihuahua, when they fell into step.

"Well? My frien', she's not well! I have scout for King Connell. An' w'en I'm find him, she's in them corral an' she's talk to them Art Brand. Connell, she's tell Brand for to ride fast for Los Alamos. She's tell them Jed Connell she's move them Bar-B cow for them place Jed's know. Then, Brand, she's find Frenchy. She's say w'at you're tell about them Diamond River fellas w'at will come smokin' Los Alamos."

"Oh!" said Lit. "Like that, huh?"

"Like more! Brand, she's say: By God! somebody, she's better hand them kid one fi-ine fast kick for to help him go tall over them tin cup an' me, I'm just so soon to be them one!

"But Connell, she's say: Never mind! Them kid, she's figure for to stick in Arno one long time!"

" 'She's this dam' Territory!' " Lit quoted.

Mechanically, he hitched up his shell belt. At the slight sound of creaking leather, Chihuahua leaned closer.

"Me, I'm think we're ride out, now, hah? *Pues,* we're bushw'ack Brand: *We're* help him to git sick!"

"No . . . Not right now. Let's go down and let King Connell have a look at a couple of real warriors! Come on! He's probably in the Last Chance."

In the darkness, he made certain shifts in his belt. Then he led the way along the street until they came to the Last Chance door and stopped there to look inside.

There was no sign of Connell, so he stepped inside. Chihuahua did not follow. Lit crossed to the bar, bought a drink. Some there were in the place who were curious about him. Part of the discussion with Connell, he reflected, must have been audible to their neighbors at the bar. So he was marked as a Diamond River man.

He loafed over to watch the monte game going on in a corner. But as he looked on, he did not forget to watch everything about him. So, when a heavy, brutal face, almost masked by black stubble of beard, showed for a moment in the front door, he saw it. It vanished, but perhaps a minute later a squat man swaggered through the door and his face was that which had shuttled right and left as if hunting for someone in the Last Chance.

When the man moved toward the bar and ordered in a roaring voice, one or two of the other drinkers moved uneasily. One said:

"There's Crowe back again — that mean freighter, you know."

Lit watched the squat man narrowly. This fellow had looked over the bar-room so carefully before coming in that his roaring entrance seemed odd, afterward.

When Crowe had finished his drink, he looked at the monte players and the watchers of the game. He straightened, came swaggering over. A path was made among the men there. But Lit was not disposed to step aside for Crowe. So the freighter met a hard shoulder thrusting out, as one of his feet came down on Lit's toe. Upon his beard-stubbled face was an expression of surprise that was ludicrous.

Lit turned slowly to face him. He lowered at the freighter and Crowe gaped at him.

"You keep to hell off my feet," Lit counseled him grimly. "Don't come pushing and shoving around so free or you'll end up with your rump on a hook!"

Crowe seemed to catch himself.

"Say!" he yelled — and that yell gave him away, even to Lit. "Who y' think y' talkin' to, anyhow?"

"What has the 'who' to do with it?" Lit said unpleasantly. "I know *what* I'm talking to — a dam' bar-room gladiator that bellows around until a *man* changes his bellow to a howl!"

With every indication of indifference, Lit yawned. It occurred to him that he knew none of that nervousness which he had felt when facing Bisbee at Tom's Bluff.

"Is that so!" Crowe yelled furiously. He looked down at the holster sagging from the left side of Lit's shell belt, then at Lit's left hand, which now fumbled with tobacco sack strings.

"I'll show y'!" he cried triumphantly, and slapped hand to Colt-butt.

Lit's right hand — his gun-hand — had been all the while almost upon the butt of his second Colt, which he had tucked in the waistband of his trousers. He whipped it out and let the hammer drop. Crowe spun about as the heavy slug crashed into him. Then he seemed to fold, bending at neck, waist, knees. He fell face-down upon the saloon floor.

Lit scowled broodingly around the room. He thought that this might not be the only gladiator hired by Connell to see that he stayed in Arno "a long time." But if any there owned hostile intentions, a gay voice from the back door checked them:

"Everybody is *please* to look at me!" Chihuahua cried. "Me, I'm much handsomer as my partner!"

He was facing the bar-room with Winchester across his arm, bright blue eyes shuttling from face to face.

"You're come, now, Lit?" he asked. "If anybody's move, me, I'm ready for to show them circus-trick . . ."

But nobody seemed inclined to move, in the face of that Winchester. Crowe moved on the floor, groaned, put up a hand to the hole in his chest. Lit stepped over and scowled down at him.

"And I'll bet you don't die!" he said disgustedly. "But if you ever cross my trail again that won't hold! You think I didn't see you, peeking in the door, trying to locate me?"

He went over to Chihuahua. The Winchester twitched in the brown hands. Three shots sounded. There was the crash and jangle of oil lamps smashed and darkness engulfed the Last Chance.

"Me, I'm bring them horses back here," Chihuahua grunted.

They ran across can-littered ground, to swing into their saddles. But no one followed them as they loped out of Arno. Chihuahua laughed softly.

"She's very fi-ine, them little business. Well? W'ere will we go, now?"

"Gurney!" Lit said. "Do you know what for? We're going to Gurney to get warrants for King Connell and Frenchy, Art Brand, Tim Fenelon and Hognose Ott!"

Chihuahua made a choking sound and his sorrel jumped. "Goddam!" he cried. "I'm *hunt* for them word w'at's mean you? Warrants! *Por supuesto!* You're git them warrant w'en me, I'm git them religion!"

"You don't mean that!" Lit said. "Why, I've just set my heart on getting warrants for that bunch. You don't mean that the district attorney won't want to issue 'em?"

Chihuahua laughed. "Ah, them district attorney! She's one fi-ine, brave man, Lit.

She's tell anybody — tell King Connell — just w'at she's think. An' w'at she's think all time for King Connell is — *si! si! señor!* I'm do just w'at you're say!"

"How'd my draw stack up, against Crowe? Think I'd have a chance, slapping leather with Frenchy?"

"*Pues,* me, I'm afraid Frenchy, she's still pull faster. But she's good for you, Lit — them practice. W'en you're pull with Frenchy, you're better if you're shoot him in them gut. Crowe, she's not die."

"I'll try to do a clean job on Frenchy," Lit assured him. "Bisbee and Crowe, I'll call them *sighting* shots!"

Chapter XIII
"Flocks of Warrants"

"Who owns Gurney, anyway?" Lit wanted to know, as their jaded animals climbed the stark slopes of the Diablos and so approached the county seat.

"*Pues,* you're not make them long walk an' not find some of King Connell, his claim-stakes. But some fellas, they're take side with them squatter, too. Me, I'm not know w'en them fella w'at yell loud for King Connell an' Frenchy, they're like him or just dam' scared!"

They jogged on silently for a time, then over a hogback ahead appeared a lone rider. Chihuahua grinned. "She's them store-keeper, Halliday!"

Halliday pulled up short at sight of them, but made no move to retreat. Instead, his hand clung with a certain significance to the rifle-stock beneath his leg. They came on and, when he recognized them, he shoved his heavy Sharps rifle back into the scabbard.

"Yuh-all plumb crazy?" was his greeting.

"Probably," grinned Lit. "But what put it into your mind so prominently this evening?"

"Gurney's full up — both sides. Jed Connell an' some Alamos hands. Wolf Montague's crowd. Frenchy an' his gang was in town till yesterday. Smoky Cole'd rid out some'r's, so they just took the place apart. She's all your lives are worth to show up there in daylight, even now! Young fella, stars are shore unpop'lar in this neighborhood right now!"

"Yeh?" Lit's mouth set stubbornly. "Well, they're probably going to be a sight more unpopular in this neighborhood before all the smoke blows away. So Frenchy raised some hell, did he?"

"Killed Brownie, that pore, harmless

good-for-nothin'. If I'd been in town that day, I'd shore've handed him a Sharps' .50 if nary other man'd stood by me."

Chihuahua swore furiously. But Lit was deadly cold. That such a killing could occur with practically no hope of making the murderer pay gave him, suddenly, a clear perspective of the Territory. His original task of tracing the Bar-B strays seemed almost unimportant now, in the face of his larger duty as deputy of Smoky Cole, the Law-Bringer.

"How did it happen?" he inquired tonelessly.

"Why, Frenchy never did like Brownie none. That day, he was comin' around a corner, an' Brownie, he never seen Frenchy as *he* come around the other side. They bumped together. Pore little Brownie, he was grinnin' an' makin' excuses, all scared to death — just like a pore, friendly yaller pup.

"Frenchy, he grinned at him, they say, an' Brownie grinned back. Then Frenchy pulled his guns an' flipped 'em up into the air. They spun around an' he caught 'em as they come down an' shot Brownie dead.

" 'Hell!' he said. 'He never kicked as much as a Mex'.' An' he walked off. Nobody dared to touch Brownie, till Sary-Ann made a couple fellas carry him into the store while she bossed the job."

"You riding somewhere?" Lit inquired.

"Up to Faith. Now, young fella, yuh better take my advice an' stay out o' Gurney till Smoky, he gits back."

"See you some more!" nodded Lit non-committally.

The store-keeper shook his head forebodingly as they rode straight on up the road toward Gurney. But Lit had no idea of foolishly parading his arrival. Dusk was falling as they reached the outskirts of the town. They turned to the left and rode in among the scattering houses. Finally, Lit drew rein and Chihuahua waited expectantly. He seemed quite content now to await the younger man's lead.

"Can we sneak into the district attorney's place from the back?"

"*Pues,* w'ere she's those back window, she's easy!" shrugged Chihuahua. "Me, I'm know his house."

He did not follow Lit inside when the latter, raising a warped sash cautiously, slipped into the musty back room. Beneath a door showed a pale line of light, but there was no sound. Silence hung heavy upon all the house, so he opened the door, turning the knob slowly, soundlessly.

At a table in the adjoining room hunched a wisp of a man, his back to Lit. Evidently he had not heard the door open, for he sat with fingers moving among a sheaf of bills. Lit stole up behind him. There was a folded legal-looking paper upon the table. Lit glanced at it mechanically, then his own name leaped out at him. It was a warrant, bearing, as near as Lit knew it, that day's date.

"Territory vs. Murder," it read. The victim was called "Como Sellama."

Como se llama . . . "What-do-you-call-him?" would be the English approximation. Lit grinned and noiselessly pocketed the warrant. Then he coughed.

With a mouse-like squeak, up leaped the district attorney, clinging tight to his money. He stared transfixed at the low-held black muzzle of the Colt, until Lit had to cough again to distract his attention.

"Happen to know who I am?" Lit inquired. "You do! That's easy to see. You're not glad to see me — and if you say you are, that'll make me sick as hell. And when I get sick as hell, I cloud up and I rain all over the fellow makes me sick as hell. And I make *him* sick as hell! Now, what were you about to say?"

"Nothing!" the district attorney said with

feeling and conviction. "But — I suppose you come after somethin'? If — if you'll just tell me what it is you want —"

"Warrants!" Lit breathed. "A yard of warrants!"

"Warrants? Oh!"

The relief in the district attorney's voice was so patent that Lit grinned as he nodded vigorously.

"Oh, well! That's not up to me, you know, Taylor. Nah! You want to see Judge Klink if you got warrants to swear out. I ain't got any warrants ——"

"I know a dam' sight better. Now, let's don't argue about it. First, I want a warrant for King Connell. For aiding and abetting the rustling of two hundred and fifty-odd head of Bar-B strays out of the Rowdy breaks. Make the charge receiving stolen property. Then, let's see some more . . ."

Dramatically, he scowled at the ceiling, in imitation of steel engravings he had seen, of the Elder Statesmen.

"One for Frenchy Leonard, for possessing those Bar-B critters. Same for Art Brand, Tim Fenelon, and Hognose Ott. And — I suppose you got one out for his arrest, Frenchy's, for the murder of Brownie?"

The district attorney swallowed.

"No!" he said huskily. "No!"

"No?" Lit cried amazedly. "Well, let's have a warrant for that, too. I don't know what that poor devil Brownie's real name was, but we'll call him —" he grinned wickedly down at the little man "— Como Sellama! I promise you the warrant'll be served. And you'd better give me at least a half-dozen made out in blank — just signed, you know. Then I can fill in the names when I see who I'm after. Hop to it! I'm in a hurry."

"But, I told you ——"

"Shut up — and get to work! You've got a drawerful of blank warrants, all signed. And don't you try to tell *me* otherwise or I'll make you eat a dozen of 'em to teach you manners! I'm hell on manners — from you, to me!"

The district attorney's watery blue eyes strayed hopefully toward the front door of his office. He seemed to tense in the kitchen chair, as if he strained his ears for some sound. When he looked back again, Lit had inched closer to him and was leaning toward him smilingly. But it was not a pleasant smile. The district attorney shrank away from that lip-curling.

"I never have killed a district attorney — yet!" Lit drawled thoughtfully, twirling Colt on trigger guard. "About those warrants, now . . ."

Hurriedly, the little man inched his chair back to the table. He opened a table drawer and drew out a stack of documents which proved him a monumental, as well as a futile, liar. For each was a warrant, and each bore the signature of one Judge Klink. He counted off a dozen, put the others back in the drawer. He reached for the dusty ink-well across the table. He hunted for a pen, until Lit rolled it to him. He looked at the point, scraped it against the table.

Lit's eyes narrowed. Someone might come in to see the district attorney at any moment. He felt the outside of shirt pocket, trousers pockets.

"Do you have a watch?" he inquired anxiously. "Any kind of watch. No matter if it's not a whaling good one . . ."

The district attorney duplicated Lit's performance of slapping pockets. His smirk was set and stiff.

"Why, yes! I have a Waterbury. Here it is! Knew it was somewhere. It's now ——"

"Put it down where it can remind you of things. The value of time, just for instance. Some nights, you could sit here piddling with those warrants and no matter how long you piddled, it wouldn't make a bit of difference. Then, again, some other night, if you took — oh! just ten seconds too long, to fill out a bunch of warrants that I'd come after, you'd wake up to find St. Pete offering you the loan of an old gown, so that you wouldn't catch cold waiting around his courtroom. *This* is one of the *other* nights!"

He pinwheeled the Colt in air, caught it with resounding smack of butt against hard palm.

The district attorney snatched up his pen, dipped it in the ink. It began to race across a warrant. Suddenly, he set it down and smirked at Lit.

"Ah, hell!" he cried genially. "You got the drop on me an' it naturally made me hot under the collar. But I never was one to hold grudges. You'll find a bottle behind the papers on the safe yonder. Box of cigars, too. Help yourself!"

"Thanks," Lit said slowly, puzzling this sudden shift of manner. "But, you see, I don't ever sit, drink *or* smoke. And — I'm still waiting for those warrants . . ."

"Well, suit yourself," the district attorney shrugged.

His elbows were moving rapidly, but the speed of his pen across the paper was by no means proportionately swift. Lit, observing this, saw how the district attorney's eyes kept flickering to the front door. So, when the door opened suddenly Lit was alert. His gun covered the opening, while he dropped behind the table.

"Hey, Lit! She's me!" Chihuahua called. "Me, I'm think mabbe-so you're take the shot for them door. So I'm yell first — careful."

His blue eyes shifted to the district attorney. His face twisted and no hired mourner at a funeral could have expressed sorrow more lugubrious than did Chihuahua, sighing gustily:

"We're stay with you one w'ile an', if them w'iskey an' them cigar, she's good like you're say, we're accept them most kind invitation. For — them fella w'at you're expect to come, all time, she's not come, *now*."

Outside, ten minutes later, with the warrants in the blouse of Lit's shirt, Chihuahua laughed softly:

"Me, I'm wrong about them district attorney, w'at? She's good for somethin'! An' me, I'm have one dam' fi-ine scout: I'm go first an' I'm find one Mexican *hombre* I'm hear about in Arno. One time, Frenchy, she's take them pretty girl from them fella. Then I'm come back an' w'en Jed Connell, she's come up to see them district attorney, me, I'm — *touch* him on them head with my Colt. Then I'm tie him up an' I'm put

176

his neckerchief through his mouth."

"You found a Mex' who's sore at Frenchy? Well?"

"Most sore! She's go an' she's find w'ere's Frenchy. An' she's bring them word for us, w'ere we're say. She's most sore! She's do anything w'at's hurt Frenchy — an' for them ten dollar w'ich mabbe-so we're pay."

"Fine!" Lit grunted. "Fine!"

"Well? W'ere we're go, now, hah? W'at we're do?"

"Oh, everything being the way it is, I think we'll ramble out and associate with some outstanding cowthieves."

"The hell! Mabbe you're think you're *tell* somethin', because you're wiggle with them mouth? Cowthieves! She's like you're say: We're go play with them peoples w'at's live in this dam' Territory! W'at the hell!"

"I was thinking about the Howard Boys. Suppose you find your Mex' again and tell him to come to us at the Howards' place, just as soon as he finds out where Frenchy is. I'll get our horses and wait for you. I can't show around here, now. Somebody's sworn out a warrant for me — for murder!"

CHAPTER XIV
FRENCHY AND A POSSE

"I was just thinking" — thus Lit, between gasps of laughter — "how we should have brought along a few barrels of whitewash. That is, if the scheme I'm figuring works out."

"W'at will we do with them Howard boys? Kill 'em?" asked Chihuahua hopefully.

"I should say not!" cried Lit indignantly. "Frenchy and his gang may kill them, but never us! What would be the good of the whitewash if I were to kill them?"

Northwest of Gurney was the log-and-adobe stronghold of the Howard brothers. Los Alamos home ranch was south and east of the Howard place, and southwest of Los Alamos lay Wolf Montague's ranch. So King Connell had on two sides of him hard-riding, straight-shooting squatters — though the Howards and Montagues were by no means bosom friends.

Lit was gambling that the Howards had not recognized him upon that day when he joined battle with them on behalf of Sudie-May. One cowboy looks much like another. If they did recognize him today, there would be powder burned, and that was that.

"Are you safe to show yourself to the

Howards?" he asked Chihuahua.

"Me, I'm safe anyw'ere," grinned the breed cheerfully. "I'm work for King Connell, *sí!* But I'm quit him, too. An' me, I'm never take them shot for one Howard."

There was no sound about the log house as they rode up a little slope toward it. But from behind boulders on right and left Winchesters' muzzles came pushing out.

"Stop right there!" a harsh voice ordered. "Yuh' covered all-same's a short Injun with a long blanket!"

"We're stopped," Lit told the invisible one. "We rode up for a pow-wow. Come on out, we don't bite!"

Suspiciously, the Howard brothers showed themselves, a stubble-faced, sullen quartet in faded overalls, each bearing a Winchester. They studied Lit and Chihuahua. Then the oldest brother nodded curtly. Lit noted that he had a stiff-seeming shoulder. He wondered if that shoulder had stopped his lead . . .

"Light!" he grunted. "Let's have the tale."

"I understand you-all are sort of hubbing hell, with King Connell to buck," Lit said abruptly.

The youngest Howard — a slim cowboy of eighteen or so — spat contemptuously.

"Not a bit more'n he is! Even if he has

179

got Frenchy Leonard an' the rest o' them killers on his payroll. It ain't done him much good, yet!"

"My goodness!" cried Lit. "Frenchy's not what you'd call a favorite, in this neighborhood — I'd say."

"Le' me line my sights on that beavertooth' illegitimate!" the boy said. "Just gi' me one crack at him!"

"Aw, shut up, Abe!" growled the elder brother. "These fellas never rid up here just to pass the time o' day."

"We didn't!" snapped Lit. "I'm a deputy sheriff under Smoky Cole ——"

"Then you're a dam' spy for King Connell!" grunted a wide-shouldered Howard who had contented himself, heretofore, with stolid staring.

"That's a lie!" Lit said contemptuously. "Smoky Cole and I are working for *this*." He tapped the star, pulled into sight. "And nobody in this country is going to give us orders. You say that Frenchy Leonard's on the King's payroll. All right! In my pocket I've got a warrant for Frenchy for murder. And I'm going to serve that warrant. That's why we came here."

"A warrant? *For Frenchy?*"

Sheer disbelief, leaped into every Howard face.

180

"Just that! We rode out of Gurney and kept the news behind us, to find a posse Frenchy can't bluff. Now, if you-all aren't afraid of the gang, I'll swear you in and give you a chance to line your sights on him. But I'm running this show! Don't you let that slip your minds a minute!"

There were many questions to answer. But the warrant bearing Frenchy's name, re-inforced by Lit's earnest manner, proved potent. Four Howards finally consented to be sworn in as a posse. Word of the vengeful Mexican trailing Frenchy pleased them.

"That's the way to git him!" Ed Howard nodded, and Tom and Hank and the boy Abe agreed. "He's got plenty hide-outs. No use tryin' to smoke out all the holes in the dam' Territory. We better wait for that Mex'."

Two days passed, then three. In the evenings the brothers talked to Lit of their grievances. They were transplanted Missouri backwoodsmen, Ed and Tom, ex-soldiers, who had settled in the Territory because of its free land or cheap land. As they told Lit about King Connell's treatment of his neighbors, he had to agree that they were in the right.

"Connell come in, years back, same's we done," Ed explained one night. "He brought money, we brought guts. Money talks, anywhere. He dabbed his loop where he was a mind to. He put that LA iron o' his across the most an' the best o' the Territory!

"We never kicked about that. We located us this place that suited us. But because we was little fellas, ever' time we got in his way he stomped on us! He turned his gunfighters loose on us, to waylay us an' steal our stock. Naturally, we aim to shoot back an' steal *his* stuff!

"It ain't right, an' it ain't good for this country, one man hoggin' mile after mile o' land, more'n he can do a thing with. Connell an' his likes, they're shore goin' to trade their strut for a limp 'fore they git shet o' us, if ever they can!"

The Mex' came near midnight of the third day. Lit, sleeping in the lean-to, was wakened by whispering outside. When he heard Chihuahua's unmistakable throaty chuckle he got up softly.

"These fella Pedro Enriquez," Chihuahua's cat eyes had caught the blur of Lit's approaching figure, "she's find Frenchy's gang, all hole up in one old cabin north from here, by Hell Creek's end. Two days past, Frenchy, she's stick up those stage from The Points for four thousand of bullion."

"Smoky Cole know about that?"

"These Pedro, she's say Smoky's disappear. But, we will not need Smoky. I'm go wake them Howard boys!"

They rode hell-for-leather through the remaining hours of darkness, with young Abe Howard leading the way toward the old 'dobe on Hell Creek mouth. Once his tall bay stumbled and threw the boy headlong, but he hobbled back to the horse, swung up again, and quirted the animal on.

"Now, let's get organized!" grunted Lit, as well after sun-up they halted in the deep, rocky bed of Hell Creek below the 'dobe. "We'll scatter out and surround them. You fellows mind two things. These *hombres* are going to shoot to kill. That's Number One. Second: If we can take these hairpins alive, for a nice, legal hanging, that'll be twice as good as killing 'em here. So, the man who takes a shot at 'em after they stick up their hands — well! he'd better get me, first!"

When the Howards had been gone long enough to reach the brush on the 'dobe's far side, Chihuahua and Lit advanced upon the cabin. Came a shot — from the cabin or beyond it. Then, after a fleeting interval, the rattle of a fusillade. Chihuahua and Lit began to run, until they dropped down behind boulders. They surveyed the cabin.

Before the closed door, hitched to a cotton-wood log, were five rearing horses.

Chihuahua lifted his carbine. He began to shoot toward the horses. One whirled and galloped off and, as Chihuahua continued to fire flashingly, the others followed. Lit gaped. Chihuahua had cut five ropes with nine shots! Now the firing sounded, a steady battle between the Howards and the men in the cabin. Abruptly, a man appeared, coming from the direction of a pole corral on the creek bank, bent over, sprinting for the cabin. Lit forgot caution, stood up.

"Stick 'em up, Brand!" he yelled.

Brand twisted about and fired at Lit. Other lead came out of the cabin. Lit dropped down to a knee and pumped two fast shots at Brand, who staggered, then ran crookedly toward the 'dobe's door. As he ran, he yelled shrilly to Frenchy:

"Open the door! They got me!"

"Turn around an' bite 'em!" Frenchy yelled. "Don't take nothin' off them god-dam Howards!"

Brand reached the door, hammered frantically upon it. The Howards were pouring lead around him. It beat like hailstones upon the thick planks. Brand leaned upon the door and the glimpse Lit had of his side-face showed despairing terror. Obviously,

Brand's nerve had snapped under the realization of death.

And over the stuttering pound of the firing, Lit could hear the high, laughing sound of Frenchy's voice, apparently joking with his first lieutenant.

"That son of a dog!" Lit yelled to Chihuahua. "Won't open the door and risk his hide, even to help a partner!"

Then Brand went sliding down the face of the door. Firing stopped. The men outside stared. Then Brand put out a hand. It still held his pistol. He inched forward. The gun-hand came shakily up. The Colt bellowed. Where the slug went, Lit had no idea. From somewhere behind him a Winchester *whanged* — once. Brand toppled. Ed Howard's grim voice was like echo to the shot.

"I *wisht* that'd been Frenchy, instead o' his dog!"

Lit lifted his hand in signal to his side.

"Don't start the fireworks, yet awhile!" he called to the Howards. "Just keep the house covered."

Then he lifted his voice: "Frenchy! This is Lit Taylor! We've got you bottled up. We'll stay here till you-all can walk through hell on solid ice! Your only chance is to grab your ears and walk out. Surrender. This is the last chance you'll get, too!"

From the 'dobe came Frenchy's defiant yell: "Hell with you! Think I'm surrenderin' to them dam' Howards? Bring your fight over! Put it in the pot!"

"You're surrendering to me — as Smoky Cole's deputy. And I guarantee to take you down to Gurney for trial. But you can suit yourself: Grab your ears and walk out, or we'll carry you out! It's all one to me!"

"If you swear we'll get safe to Gurney, I'll risk it."

"You'll get safe to Gurney, or I won't!" Lit promised him.

The door opened. Tim Fenelon came out, sulky-faced. Hognose Ott was next. Then Frenchy and — Jed Connell! Each man's hands were lifted high. Fenelon's right arm was broken. Jed limped.

The young Abe Howard jumped forward with an oath: "Yuh lettin' him surrender? Like hell yuh will!"

His rifle swung up. Lit sensed some cause for furious hatred between Abe and Frenchy. A girl, perhaps . . . But Chihuahua tripped Abe very neatly and possessed himself of the boy's Colt and Winchester.

"Me, I'm wa'ch you now, sonny," he cautioned Abe. "You're make no more move like those, or ——"

Frenchy had watched without losing his

habitual grin. Now he turned to Lit, seemingly friendly enough.

"How d' you get this way?" he demanded. "Got a warrant?"

"Warrant enough!" Lit assured him grimly. "You're going to hang for Brownie. That's the only reason I let you-all surrender."

Frenchy laughed carelessly, but in the amber-flecked black eyes was a sinister threat as he regarded Lit. Ed Howard had been poking around inside the cabin. He came out carrying the prisoners' weapons and nodded Lit aside.

"That bullion off'n The Points stage is all in there. Now, looky here. We-uns got the name o' hard cases an' I ain't denyin' that when our stuff is stole we-uns git out an' rustle somebody else's. But in business like this-here, yuh can gamble on ary one o' us.

"Now, yuh got your hands full gittin' these *gunies* to Gurney 'thout havin' 'em taken from yuh to be lynched or else turned loose. Yuh can't saddle yo'self with this bullion. Me an' the boys'll take it back to The Points. An' if the's a reward, we'll split it with yuh-all any way yuh say."

"Fine!" Lit said. "That'll settle the puzzle. And — I'm not worried about it getting back all right."

"We're wish for to see Frenchy hang all ni-ice, no?" Chihuahua purred in Lit's ear. "Then we're go east, to them railroad in Ancho. We're put Frenchy an' them others, with them horses, on one train. We're ride for Two Squaws w'ere them railroad, she's stop. We're git off an' — she's one ni-ice, safe ride for Gurney. *'Sta bueno?*"

" *'Sta bueno!*" Lit agreed. For he had wondered about taking these prisoners south on the hostile western side of the Diablos. "We'll eat a bite, then rattle our hocks."

They herded the rawhide-hobbled prisoners into the 'dobe. The Howards, having brought up the outlaws' horses, now loaded their own with the bullion. They started for The Points, walking, leading the horses. Chihuahua went to work at the cooking fire, outside the 'dobe, while Lit stood guard over the gang.

Frenchy seemed to be unimpressed by Lit's victory. He made jokes at Lit's expense, at which Tim Fenelon and the worshipful Hognose laughed uproariously. The three of them were squatted by the side wall when Frenchy, getting up, asked for tobacco.

"Been out of smokin' since yesterday," he told Lit.

Lit fished his sack from a pocket. When

he looked up, Frenchy was advancing. Tim Fenelon, too, had got up. He stood about halfway between Lit and the wall. A brown cigarette paper was in his fingers. He was grinning. But Hognose Ott watched with eyes showing strain.

"Wait a minute," Lit said quickly. "Stay where you are. I'll chunk the sack to you. No use of you doing any more walking than's necessary."

"What the hell?" Frenchy grinned, coming on. "You might think I was goin' to chew on your ear, or somethin'. Hell, Lit! What's a li'l' row like this, between good *hombres.* You're wearin' a star an' you figger you got to play the game a certain way. I ——"

For an instant Lit wondered uncertainly if he were making a suspicious-seeming idiot of himself. Then he recalled the cold-blooded callousness of Frenchy toward Brand. He recalled poor little Brownie, who "hadn't kicked as much as a Mexican" while he died. And in him died — abruptly and forever — the last trace of boyish uncertainty. It was a Lit Taylor whom Frenchy had never seen, who half-drew his pistol.

"Get back there where I want you! You take one more step — or you, Tim! — and I'll save the hangman a job!"

His face was like a rock. Frenchy stopped short. The amber-flecked eyes were murderous as he stared at Lit. Then he shrugged and went shuffling back to the others.

"Let the son of a dog keep his dam' tobacco, then. Now, I remember, you got a sack, Hognose. We'll let him have his — an' let him smoke it in hell!"

Lit said nothing. There had been a time when what Frenchy said of him mattered. But that time was past. Super-gunman, Frenchy might be, but in any other way, he was the better man. He knew it as surely as he had ever known anything in his life.

So he watched woodenly until Chihuahua came in to announce that the cooking was finished.

"They're all right?" Chihuahua inquired. "They're not have — them notions?"

"Not now," Lit said dryly. "And if they get any more, we'll try to help 'em buck off what might get 'em hurt!"

Chapter XV
Keeping the News Behind

It was easy to see why Hognose Ott had joined Frenchy's gang, Lit thought. Conscious of inferiority to the average man, Hognose would try the weak man's trick of

190

covering up his failings by bluster. And, riding with the hard case lot behind Frenchy, Hognose would share in the gang's notoriety.

He studied them all as he and Chihuahua jogged along behind the four prisoners. Frenchy was beside Jed Connell. Tim Fenelon rode beside Hognose.

Lit began to pity Ott. He was badly scared and hardly able to conceal it. Frenchy, his idol, had come off second-best in two straight tests: he had surrendered to Lit and he had not caught Lit offguard in the 'dobe.

"Something's beginning to sort of stick with him, while he rides," Lit told Chihuahua. "He's beginning to see something dangling before his eyes, no matter how he turns his head."

"*Sí,*" Chihuahua nodded. "She's them rope with hangman's loop. Watch him. She's rub them eyes . . ."

"But he can't rub it away. Well, Frenchy's not worried, to look at him. About time for him to sing *Sam Bass* again."

And Frenchy at that moment turned in the silver-trimmed hull. He looked at Tim Fenelon's sullen face, looked at Hognose Ott. And he laughed.

"Time's gettin' shorter," he said gayly.

Then he began to sing the ballad about

the famous Texas train-robber whose reputation is out of all proportion to his meager
"earnings." The *Sam Bass* song was a
favorite of his, perhaps because he liked to
think that his own raidings made of him a
gallant, daring figure like the man who died
under Ranger Dick Ware's fire at Round
Rock.

"Sam left the Collins ranch
In the merry month of May.
With a herd of Texas cattle,
The Black Hills for to see.
Sold out in Custer City
And there got on a spree —
A tougher set of cowboys
You seldom ever see!
On their way back to Texas,
They robbed the U.P. train.
They then split up in couples
And started on again —"

"So far, so good!" Lit grunted to Chihuahua, as the song went on. "We've done what
they said couldn't be done: we've rounded
up the bunch, settled Art Brand. There they
ride — the prize hellions of the Territory,
with their hands tied to the saddle pegs . . ."
He thought of Sudie-May. She had been
so sure that Frenchy would finish him, as

soon as they met. What would she say, now, when she got the word of the fight on Hell Creek, of Frenchy's tame surrender?

He looked at Frenchy's swaggering back and his mouth hardened. Evidently, Frenchy was confident that his friends would never let him hang. But Lit was just as confident that the little outlaw's day drew near to its close. He rode on, moody of face, until they came to a house some fifteen miles from Ancho.

There was a Mexican crone here, and a boy of fourteen or so. Lit and Chihuahua loosed the rawhide whangs that bound their prisoners, let them get down and eat the meal for which Chihuahua bargained with the old woman. While they loafed outside the 'dobe, waiting for the fried beef and black beans and *tortillas,* Chihuahua came up to whisper in Lit's ear that the boy had vanished and the old woman professed ignorance of his going.

"She's trouble!" Chihuahua grunted. "Somethin', she's go pop! Well — we're watch like the hell!"

They remounted the four and themselves swung up, after eating. Now they were at the apex of an equilateral triangle, the corners of the base of which rested in the two *plazitas* of Ancho and Cherryville. Chihuahua rode with eyes narrowed grimly.

Lit watched the prisoners. Chihuahua watched the country around. "Ah!" he said at last. "Me, I'm *think* so!"

From the southeast — Cherryville-way — a dust-cloud rolled. Presently, they could make out the van of a numerous body of riders. Frenchy stared, then twisted to grin at Lit.

"Well, looks like hell's goin' to pop, right sudden. That bunch of hairpins is from Cherryville. I'm not so popular over there. Not so long ago, I downed their jailor and a Mex' he had helpin' him. Looks to me like that Mex' boy hightailed it into town to tell about us."

Lit thought that neither he nor Chihuahua was in any danger — nor, perhaps, was Jed Connell. But the other three were evidently regarded as legitimate material for a lynching-bee.

"Jailer must have been right popular!" he observed dryly. "Well, I guaranteed to get you into Gurney, to be hung all legal, so ——"

"Hell! You think them *gunies* 'll listen to you?" cried Frenchy scornfully. "Give us back our shootin' irons an' we'll make 'em sick! You goin' to keep us here with our hands tied?"

"Nope! I'm going to run you for the railroad at Ancho and keep you out of the hands of those hairpins. Come on! Dig in your persuaders!"

From the dust cloud behind them came now faint yells. It was a hard country, where if a man were downed his killer might be brought to justice or not, dependent upon circumstances and, even more, upon the personal popularity of the victim. But when punishment was decided upon, it came swiftly! The fugitives rode with chins upon shoulders. They were barely holding their own against the foremost riders.

Back to where Lit and Chihuahua rode in the post of danger, the rear, lagged Jed Connell. His raw-boned little sorrel was limping slightly. Stark fear was in Jed's brown face now. "Hell!" he groaned. "My dam' horse's goin' back on me. They'll git me!"

Lit and Chihuahua eyed each other, then Lit shrugged. Chihuahua's bowie flashed in the sunlight. Jed shrank back in the saddle. But it only slashed deftly the rawhide thongs about his wrist.

"Tell 'em you were helping me guard the prisoners!" Lit yelled. "Tell 'em your gun must have dropped out of your holster. Hell!

Tell 'em *anything* to save your worthless hide!"

Then Jed fell behind and the two spurred ahead again. They saw the pursuers mill for an instant about Jed, but when they rode on again Jed was still in the saddle, seemingly unhurt.

"Can we make it?" Lit cried anxiously.

"Quién sabe?" Chihuahua grinned. "But I'm think if we're not, them cottonwood she's sprout rotten apples . . ."

Ahead of them now loomed the station village. Lit whooped triumphantly. A train was there, motionless. A fresh outburst of yelling from the lynching party showed that they, too, saw escape threatening. Now came the first shooting of the chase. But the bullets went wide as the fugitives covered the hundred yards to the standing train.

"Off you go!" yelled Lit. "Get inside the cars!"

The horses slid to a halt and down tumbled the three prisoners. They sprang for the steps of a rickety car and scrambled up. Lit and Chihuahua brought up the procession's rear, and Lit gasped at the wide-eyed engineer:

"Deputy sheriff! Mob coming! *Give her the quirt!*"

The engineer nodded and his head disappeared. But Lit, from inside, heard a frantic burst of whooping. He stuck his head through a window in time to see a horseman slide to a stop beside the engine cab, reach in and jerk the engineer out by the collar. The mob was scattering now. Lit shot down the horse of the cowboy who had captured the engineer. But most of the hard-faced riders only laughed. The train was immovable so long as they held the engineer. They could take their time about overpowering the officers. They made no move yet to assault the car.

"What's the ruckus?" a voice inquired of Lit. He whirled nervously, to face a squat, efficient-looking individual, with behind him a lean, walrus-mustached, narrow-eyed man, the prospectors he and Chihuahua had helped against Bisbee and Wolf Montague's gang. Years ago, that seemed!

"Mob's trying to take my prisoners! They'll have to down me first!"

"Sho!" grinned the squat man. "Me an' Jake, we'll shore admire to argue a little alongside o' yuh. Take the other side, Jake!"

Chihuahua had vanished mysteriously. Lit crouched behind the sill of a window, with rifle trained upon a loud-voiced man with heavy eight-square Sharps rifle, who was inciting the others to "down that dam' sheriff an' stretch them murderers!"

At the far end of the car the squat prospector held another window. Frenchy and Hognose and Fenelon were flat on the floor in the aisle.

"First man that makes a move toward the train gets lead-poisoning!" yelled Lit. "Step right up!"

Suddenly his chin bumped upon the window-sill. For the train had lurched forward abruptly. The mob roared furiously. Lit wondered at the train's motion, for he could see the engineer, held by two cowboys, gaping amazedly, in the forefront of the men beside the train. Bullets smashed through the windows. Lit and the prospectors returned the fire.

Men leaped for cars behind that holding Lit and the prisoners. But the train was gathering way, and — someone had uncoupled those rear coaches! Bullets continued to crash into the engine and cars, but out into the open country the train shot with a whoop. It was not much of an engine, but it easily outdistanced the cow-horses pursuing.

Five or six miles they lurched along. Then, without any squealing of brakes, the train lost motion. It drew slowly to a stop. Lit looked through a window. Chihuahua came trotting back from the engine. He grinned up at Lit, twisting the spike-point of black mustache.

"Hey, Lit! She's me! I'm wa'ch them engineer many time, pull them handle one way, push him back. So, w'en we're lose them engineer, me, I'm unhitch our car from them family an' I'm slip into them engine. Hah! She's nothin' for to be them engineer. I'm pull them handle — she's go! I'm pull him back — she's stop! W'at the hell!"

Lit collapsed upon a lumpy seat and stared.

"Amor de dios!" he cried. "If I'd known it was you in that engine, I'd have hopped out at Ancho and begged 'em to kill me quick so I wouldn't risk my life! Lord! And I didn't even know how close my neck was to the axe."

He shook his head bodingly. "Well, since you've got us this far you might as well climb back into the engine and see if you can get us to Two Squaws. Likely, we can get horses there."

"Seguro! We're get them horse, easy. An' our horses — me, I'm know one fella in Ancho. She's see my sorrel an' she's say: Them dam' Chihuahua! An' she's take care of our *caballos* an' we're send for 'em *pronto."*

Chapter XVI
A Brother-Deputy

They had no trouble getting horses at Two Squaws. There was a store-keeper there who was out of the same grim rock as Halliday of Gurney. He furnished horses and saddles and before they left two of his *vaqueros* were on their way to Ancho to bring in the horses abandoned there.

Privately, he told Lit of his pleasure at seeing Frenchy and the others under arrest.

"News gets around," he said. "So we heard over here when Smoky made you a deputy. An' we kind of wondered howcome. But the boy that can loop that little devil an' drag him to jail, he's the kind of deputy Smoky ought've had a long spell back. Any time I can help you out a bit, let me know. The name's Norris!"

They rode to Gurney without any show of hostility being made. At the houses where they got food, usually the Mexican girls looked at Frenchy and sighed. *"Pobrecito!"* they called him — as if he had been a boy of ten. At first Frenchy laughed and told them what would be Lit's fate very soon. But when after a time Lit laughed, also, and in fluent Spanish told them how Frenchy had left Art Brand outside a barred door, to

200

die and described vividly the meek surrender of the gang, Frenchy turned sullen.
He began to stare at Lit as they rode and he
sang no more about Jesse James and Sam
Bass and Cole Younger.

"You know," Lit told him cheerfully on
the edge of Gurney, "if it wasn't that you're
due to hang I'd be worried about you,
Frenchy! You keep looking at me all the time
in the *meanest* way!"

"Yeh?" Frenchy snarled. "You think I'll
ever stretch a rope? Wait an' see! I'll be
ridin' the high lines when you're under the
grass roots — sonny! Talk big while you can.
You ain't got much longer, hey, Timmy?"

"Don't drag Tim into it!" Lit grinned.
"He's beginning to remember what I told
him the night I pinned a star on: You know,
Tim, I said we'd have some law west of the
Rowdy, yet!"

"To hell wi' ye!" Tim Fenelon cried —
and straightened his great body to stare at
the county seat ahead. "Sure, ye better be
rememberin' what *I* said: Over this bank o'
the Rowdy, there's but the li'l' bit o' law
we're makin' to suit ourselves!"

It seemed that word of their coming had
reached the county seat ahead of them. The
awninged sidewalks before them were
crowded. But they rode up the street with-

out meeting anyone who cared to discuss the prisoners. At the courthouse they swung down and loosed the rawhide whangs, watched the prisoners get stiffly down.

Shorty Wiggin, the deputy sheriff who served as jailor, leaned in the doorway, a sawed-off shotgun over his arm. He grinned at Lit, straightened on his crippled leg.

"Visitors, huh?" he grunted. "Hi-yah, Frenchy! Hi, Tim!"

"Hi, Shorty," Frenchy grinned. "Take a good look. We won't be around long."

They all went inside. The jail was on the second floor. A sort of watch-house commanded the stair. Here a jailor could sit in shelter and make it plain suicide for an unwelcome visitor to try climbing.

In the smaller of the two big rooms that constituted the jail, a thick section of cottonwood log was set in the 'dobe wall. Great eye-bolts were in this log. Chains and shackles dangled from them. Cots covered with webwork of rawhide thongs were near the log.

"Over you go!" Lit commanded the prisoners cheerfully. "Shorty, have you got plenty of handcuffs? I'd hate for our canaries to take a notion to leave us."

"You certainly do crowd your luck," Frenchy said softly. "Yes, sir! You are certainly crowdin' it!"

Lit grinned at him. When the trio were all manacled of hands, shackled of ankles, they could stand or sit or lie down on the cots. But none could reach another. Lit and Chihuahua went out, Shorty following and stopping to lock the room's door.

"They won't be leavin'," Shorty said grimly. "Not without I let 'em. I ain't been much as a hand, since the day my hawse decided to roll over without lettin' me git my leg out from under him. But, hell! Man don't *need* no legs, to shoot a sawed-off Greener down them stairs!"

"Any other prisoners?" Lit asked him, with jerk of head toward the door of the big room, also padlocked.

"Bunch o' them Wagon Wheel boys. They had ambitions to take the town apart an' they got so serious, the marshal rounded 'em all up. Reckon they will go to court tomorrow mornin'."

They went down the stairs. Lit and Chihuahua took the bunch of horses around to the corral behind the jail. Lit looked back at the silent ones on the sidewalks. He shook his head, frowningly.

"He's certainly got the place buffaloed!" he told Chihuahua. "They don't mean to let out any wolf-howls about the arrest."

When they had seen to the animals, they came back to the street and in an eating house sat down to belated dinner. The other customers watched them furtively. Out on the street, heading for the office of the district attorney, Lit stared frowningly up and down and shook his head.

"My Lord! This bunch beats me! They ought to be giving thanks that we've put Frenchy behind the bars. And — are they? Well, it's not what you'd call prominent to me!"

"She's this dam' Territory," Chihuahua sighed. "*Pues,* if Frenchy, she's hang, then them people w'at will not like him, they're happy. But they're think — he's not hang, yet! An' if she's not hang quick, then she's not so ni-ice, that they're show them big grin today."

They came to the district attorney's house and went in. The furtive-eyed little official looked at the warrants that Lit dropped upon his table-desk, then let his eyes shift up to Lit's almost absent expression.

"Served 'em, did you? Well, that's the kind of officer we want. I'll take care of 'em all right."

"See that you do," Lit said grimly. "Oh! Seems to me that before I pulled out — that night you remember — I heard something about a — a charge of murder, if I'm not mistaken. Against me. You happen to know anything about that?"

"Murder? Charged against you?"

The district attorney's face was a mask of surprise. Violently, he shook his head.

"Probably just one of those things," said Lit carelessly. "But I wouldn't want a warrant made out for me, you know. It'd probably hurt my feelings. Might even make me sick as hell! And when *I* get sick as hell, I cloud up and — Oh, I remember! I told you about that once. You haven't forgotten?"

"No," the district attorney admitted. "I haven't forgot a thing. But there's no charge against you, that I know about."

"Fine! Come on, Chihuahua. Let's get some air."

They loafed along the street and presently Lit, staring at the front of the Antelope Saloon, shook his head moodily.

"I am beginning to wonder how much of a notion it was, Chihuahua — leaving those warrants with the district attorney. You know, somehow I just don't altogether *trust* that gentleman!"

"No?" Chihuahua cried incredulously. "She's too bad! Me, I'm think you're *so* fond with him!"

"I swear! I'm half a mind to go back and

get 'em and keep 'em until Smoky comes back. And that reminds me: where *is* Smoky? I never thought to ask Shorty Wiggin."

"*Quién sabe?*" Chihuahua shrugged indifferently. "Smoky, she's have them twenty-one rings on them horn one dam' long time. She's need mighty few nurse. Them warrants we're git when we're want 'em, Lit. Same as you're git 'em first. Now, me, I'm think she's better if we're have them drink. W'at the hell?"

They went into the Antelope and at the bar stood enjoying the whiskey in silence. Time wore on drowsily toward supper-time. The sulky tension still seemed to grip Gurney. Lit felt it, but he could not see anyone who looked particularly responsible, found none who incited the county seat to disapproval of Frenchy's arrest. He watched the men drifting in for a pre-supper drink. The Antelope was doing a rushing business.

Then there was a bustle of movement at the street door. Lit half-turned where he leaned with one elbow on the bar. He faced men who looked vaguely nervous, uneasy, or merely strained. His eyes lifted to the door. A rasping voice came to him, clearly:

"Where's that dam' kid-deputy?" a man demanded loudly.

Chihuahua sidled noiselessly away from Lit. He achieved the effect of melting into the men standing behind him.

"Where's that dam' kid-deputy?" the voice repeated on a higher note.

Lit waited for a sight of this curious one. He appeared, now, as the loungers in the Antelope gave back and opened up a path. It was a long and lean and rawboned deputy sheriff to whom Lit had never so much as spoken. Bills was his name. He "worked the county" usually, in Smoky Cole's phrase, keeping out of the county seat most of the time.

He came swinging down the lane opened for him, to stop before Lit with thumbs hooked in crossed shell belts. From each belt sagged a Colt of extraordinarily long barrel. His squinting gray eyes flicked to Lit's waist where his .45 belt crossed to dangle black-handled Colt low on right thigh.

"Oh! So there you are!" Bills grunted belligerently, glaring at Lit. "I heard you throwed Frenchy Leonard an' Tim Fenelon an' Hognose Ott into jail."

"You — *heard* that?"

Lit's tone, his narrowing dark eyes, held puzzlement.

"That's what I said. I heard you ——"

207

"Funny!" Lit said frowningly. "Funny that you heard about it. That you had to hear about it. For I saw you standing right here in the door, looking at us when we rode up the street. And if you couldn't tell by the looks of Frenchy and the others that we'd arrested 'em and were headed for the jail right then —— Say! I'll bet they have to write you a letter at meal time!"

"Listen, you!" Bills said savagely. "Don't you start any o' your would-be funny remarks with me! I want to know who give you any authority to arrest them men. Where's the warrants? Even if you had been handed warrants to serve, you have got to hand 'em back to the sheriff or the chief deputy when you come back with prisoners. Smoky's gone somewheres. I'm chief deputy — an' I'm certainly goin' to know what's goin' on!"

"I don't mind your knowing!" Lit grinned. "And you do know. You said you did, when you came swelling in here. You know that I arrested the bunch and slammed 'em into the *calaboza*. But one thing you certainly have got wrong about being chief deputy! You dreamed that one. You're no — such — animal! If this county feels a big emptiness where a chief deputy ought to be, and has to have a chief deputy to give her the fancy touches —— Look upon him and get dazzled, Bills! Look upon him! *I'm it!*"

"Like hell you are! I'm tellin' you — right here, right now — that I'm chief deputy and I'm sayin' what'll be done! Then, I'm doin' it! I'm goin' to turn Frenchy an' the others out an' hand 'em back their hardware an' — Lord have mercy on you when I do! You'll have to kill your own snakes or git bit! There's no warrants for them boys — I ask' the district attorney. So I ain't holdin' 'em!"

"That's right," Lit said very softly. "You're not holding 'em. I'm the little stake-rope that's holding 'em. The district attorney is lying thirteen to the dozen — as usual. He got the warrants, properly returned. And he wouldn't have the guts to look me in the eye and deny it! I don't *think* he'd have the nerve to tear 'em up. I'll get 'em from him when I want 'em. Meanwhile — your little friends stay right where they are. Know why? *Por dios!* because *I* say they do!"

He knew that his hand had been forced. It was beyond his power, now, to go softly in this business until Smoky got back. He was being pushed by that one who was moving this obviously-handmade, not-too-intelligent, deputy.

He knew the danger of the situation he

faced. Given the slightest shadow of justification, the adherents of Frenchy — and of King Connell! — might decide to free the prisoners. They could always claim that Bills's denial of warrants showed that Frenchy and Fenelon and Ott were being held illegally by a "dam' kid-deputy" as Bills had twice called him. And they would be sure that, in the present condition of the county, the Territory, very little investigation would follow!

But all that was merely what he faced, in no sense an argument for changing course. He knew without thinking that he had no alternative whatever, to standing behind his guns, his smoking guns, if it came to that! He would stand between Frenchy's handcuffs and the key to those handcuffs and tell all Gurney to try putting him out of the way. And now that he had been forced to assert himself, he would play the hand out. So he watched the lank deputy grimly, one corner of hard young mouth lifted mockingly.

His elbow was still hooked over the bar's top as he leaned with every appearance of carelessness upon it. So Bills's eyes, flickering up and down Lit, could note the wide separation of gun-hand and gun-butt. Seemingly, he was emboldened by what he saw.

For his stiff-held palms twisted, closed upon the walnut butts of his own guns.

But some such move had been fairly certain, from the very beginning. Bills had not come into the Antelope just to say that Frenchy would be released. So Lit had planned his counter-move, weighed the danger against the desirability of killing this fellow outright. And it came to him that he was oddly cool about the business. He could look at a man who intended to kill him without much emotion. That coolness gave him more!

With the first twitch of Bills's hands, Lit twisted at the bar. Long body straightened. Left fist, sagging at hip-level, snapped up to jab at Bills's face. Knotted right hand hooked across from bar's top to Bills's chin.

All the force of Lit's stiffened muscles was in that blow. The sound of it was like the smack of an open hand in the quiet barroom. Bills's head snapped back. He did not stagger. He merely dropped like a sack to his knees, sagged farther, fell sideways and lay with white glint of eyeballs showing between his lids, and thick lips parted.

The men near enough to see the knockout drew a long breath in audible gasp. Lit chose to regard this as a show of concern for the sprawling deputy. He lifted a shoulder, looked around with small, one-sided grin: "Hell! He's not dead. I didn't hit him full force!" he said mendaciously.

But he was watching that crowd closely. More than half of these men, he thought, would gladly join a move to free Frenchy — and that would mean a bloody, smoky night in Gurney. He looked for Chihuahua and found him lounging with back to the rear wall of the Antelope, a grinning Bearer of the Winchester. Reassured, Lit looked down at Bills, whistled softly to himself, shook his head.

"Maybe I hit him too hard, at that — harder than he could stand," he said, as if meditating aloud. "I don't reckon he meant all he was blowing about. Probably, he was just liquored up and, being a windbag, he had to blow. Will a couple of you help me pack him over to the courthouse? We can take care of him, over there. Then I'll have a talk with him when he's feeling better."

Two men picked up the long, limp body. Lit, wondering how many steps toward the front door he could take, before the stillness of the bar-room was exploded, trailed them. His spine crawled as he saw the steady stares he got from under frowning down-drawn brows. But, there was Chihuahua at his back . . .

The men carried Bills outside and Lit stepped through the door after them. There was no more than the beginning of a rumble of talk, behind him. He thought that those pro-Frenchy men in the Antelope were waiting for a leader. And there had been nobody in the saloon who seemed to measure up to leadership.

Men on the street stared at the queer little procession. Only a couple inquired of Lit the meaning of it. He grinned at these curious ones:

"Bills is sick. We're taking him over to put him to bed."

The deputy was carried over to the courthouse. The carriers went inside, stopped and looked inquiringly at Lit. He motioned toward the stairs. They stared suspiciously.

"What's the idee o' takin' him up to the jail?" one demanded. "Say! There's somethin' funny about this — dam' funny!"

"*Pues,* she's not so dam' funny," Chihuahua suggested from the doorway behind them. "If you're not carry them Bills up, like — like them *chief* deputy she's tell you, she's not funny one bit!"

They whirled, to face the suggestive Winchester across his arm. Sullenly, they crossed to the stairs and began to climb. Shorty Wiggin came out of the little watch house at the stair head. He looked without expression at them. Lit thought that, to see Shorty eye Bills, one might think that this was the full dozen of unconscious deputies to be delivered that day.

"Going to put Bills where the little dogs can't bite him," Lit grinned. "I suppose in his way, he's all right. But in *my* way — where he seems to be getting — he's a dam' nuisance. He gets me all tangled up, Shorty."

"Such as?" Shorty inquired, but without much interest.

"He's having dreams and things. He dreamt that he's chief deputy. Of course, I know I'm chief deputy, but he might fool a pilgrim. So I'll keep him locked up until he bucks off these quaint notions of his."

"Best way," Shorty nodded gravely. "Might git some o' the weak-minded boys tangled up if he thinks he's chief dep'ty. I better take them cannon off him. One might fall out o' the holster an' mash his toe — or somethin'. Mustn't have that."

He went ahead to unlock the door of the room in which Frenchy, Fenelon and Ott were held. When Bills was carried in, the three prisoners stared frowningly at him, then looked at Lit. He grinned at Frenchy's bewildered expression. Then Shorty Wiggin took the Colts from Bills's holsters, searched him deftly for hide-outs and straightened.

"Poor fellow!" Lit drawled with mock-commiseration. "Still out! I have got to remember not to hit 'em so hard, next time."

He squatted beside Bills and took a firm grip of long hair. He lifted the deputy's head by this handle and began methodically to slap his face, right cheek, left cheek, right cheek . . . He varied the maneuver by occasionally bumping Bills's head against the floor. The method was effective — Bills regained consciousness with a hollow groan. Then, seeing Lit's sad face above him, he roared furiously and rolled over. He came scrambling to his feet.

"Better cuff his hands, first," Lit decided, standing also.

Shorty held out the manacles and Lit took them. When he stepped in closer to Bills, the deputy's hands flashed to his waist. He gaped ludicrously from one to the other of his empty holsters. Lit flicked a cuff over his right wrist while he paused, went with Bills when the deputy twisted violently, jerked him off-balance and clicked the second cuff.

"Now, now!" he said soothingly — pleasantly conscious of Frenchy's stare. "Mustn't act that way! This is really for your own good, you know. The reckless way you go helling around, you might get hurt. We're going to protect you!"

With which, he pulled viciously on the cuffs and, when the furious deputy stiffened, Lit pushed in the opposite direction and inserted a foot neatly behind Bills's ankle. Bills sat down on the floor near the wall and Lit bent to scoop up a shackle. He straightened, then, grinning down at the hobbled one.

"Now, I won't have to kill you," he told Bills pleasantly.

Chihuahua was waiting at the door. He had been looking from a front window, he said. The men were out of the Antelope, now, milling on the sidewalk under the wooden awning.

"They're not start, yet. But me, I'm think pretty soon mabbe we're have them company . . ."

Lit went to the window and looked down upon the ugly gathering at the Antelope. He whistled tunelessly under-breath. He was acting sheriff. There was no dodging the responsibility even if he had wanted to — and he knew of nothing that he wanted less! *Acting sheriff . . . Acting sheriff . . .* The words had a pleasant sound as he whispered them.

No longer was he the "Bar-B Baby," the kid-hand from the Diamond. Over here in the saltiest neighborhood between just any two points in the West, he was privileged to stand and look any man levelly in the eyes. Behind him, in the cell, were the two outstanding gunmen of time and place.

"And I put 'em in there!" Lit thought proudly. "Chihuahua and I did what nobody else wanted to do — or has wanted to try, the last couple of years."

He turned slowly at the window and looked at the two men who waited for what he would say. Lit grinned. Chihuahua was the ideal partner. As for Shorty Wiggin, a presidential order would never get as much action out of the jailor as thought of what Smoky Cole would want. For Shorty had never seen a president and he knew Smoky and worshipped him. No give-up, in those two!

"Shorty," Lit said drawlingly, "it does look something like smoke . . . You smell it? There's three of us — without dragging in any of the town people. How many Wagon Wheel boys are in the big cell?"

"Eight," said Shorty. "An' that's a notion, boy! Bein' Wagon Wheel, they naturally ain't got no love for Connell — or yet for Frenchy. Let's talk to 'em!"

He hobbled back down to the big door and unlocked it. Lit stood in the opening and grinned at the cowboys who hunkered or sprawled upon the floor, smoking, playing cards, sleeping.

"Hi!" said Lit. "Looks like they kind of metagrobolized you fellows. How're you-all fixed for guts and trouble?"

"Plenty guts!" a stocky, one-eyed man shrugged. *"No trabajo!"*

"I can fix you up with plenty! I slammed Frenchy Leonard and Tim Fenelon and Hognose Ott in, next-door. And some of the people in town don't like it — including Bills, the deputy. So I slammed Bills in with the others. Now, if you-all'd like to burn some powder in town, without getting hauled in, I'll let you-all help us hold the fort against the mob. What d' you say?"

"Lead us to it, cowboy!" the one-eyed man yelled. And the rest of the Wagon Wheel men swarmed up grinning. "Give us back our hoglegs, Shorty! We'll send Los Alamos a-howlin' home."

Shorty grinned and hobbled off to the closet in which the confiscated weapons were stacked. Lit posted the recruits on the balconies that commanded the three vulnerable walls of the courthouse. They settled down, waiting anxiously.

Coming back, he had another look at the crowd before the Antelope. It was noisier, now. Men moved on its fringes, as if trying to work into the center under the awning. Then, sudden movement made it look much like a swirling bee-swarm. Down into the street the crowd surged. Four or five men walked grimly, steadily, in the van. Someone in the mob yelled shrilly. That yell was instantly taken up by others, by all. It changed tone, became a harsh, savage, wordless roar that Lit had heard once before: in Ancho at the train. It was the blood-roar of the Mob. He did not hesitate. The sawed-off shotgun came up in his hands. He fired a barrel in air. The mob stopped, to look up at him as if his appearance were entirely unexpected.

"By God! You're certainly hungry for hell!" Lit told them almost conversationally. "Here's a dozen of us. We're going to argue with you as long as there's a shell left — and we have got plenty shells! Better buck off the notion that you're coming in. You'll be whittled down, before you ever turn Frenchy loose!"

"Hell with him!" some bold spirit yelled — from the rear.

A bullet came smacking into the 'dobe wall near Lit's head. Others followed rapidly from the men below. Lit squatted on the balcony's floor and the Wagon Wheel men, waiting for no orders, shoved their Colts forward and very blithely opened up on the mob. Men began to fall under that savage hail of lead. Others, finding the job warmer than they had expected, ran for cover.

No attempt was made to rush the wide front door of the courthouse, Lit noticed. He thought that Gurney was all too familiar with that narrow stairway and the little watchtower at its head, which one man could hold against an army. Instead, the mob split and tried the one clear side wall and the back.

Dusk was coming. The garrison answered shots from below with very accurate fire from windows and balconies. An hour passed in this long range warfare and Lit began to frown. When good dark came, it was not going to be easy to keep those determined men down there from working up close. Worst of all, the attackers had posted themselves in the second story of a building across the street from which they could hammer the Wagon Wheel men. And ammunition in the jail was melting away.

Chihuahua came loafing to find Lit. He grinned cheerfully, but lifted a shoulder in doubtful shrug.

"W'en she's dark, they're rush them front door," he said thoughtfully. "Them fella w'at's in Doolan's store, they're keep us back. They're come inside an' we're fight by them stairs. My frien', we're kill plenty. But if they're keep coming ——"

"We'll kill plenty," Lit nodded grimly. "They'll never let Frenchy out as long as I'm around to know about it! They ——"

He stiffened, staring toward the front. Outside, clear, sharp, there sounded the blast of a cavalry bugle. He and Chihuahua ran to a window. A Wagon Wheel puncher spoke over his shoulder, where he leaned to look down.

"It's Smoky Cole! An' dam' if he ain't got a slew o' soldiers with him! Now, if that ain't showin' up in style ——"

Lit stared past him. In the gray light he made out Smoky beside a rider whose bearing fairly screamed "soldier." And now a line of other soldiers were between the jail and the opposite side of the street, facing Doolan's store and the Antelope Saloon. And Smoky Cole's voice was lifting:

"Whut the hell's goin' on here? Who give yuh bar-room scum a license to shoot at my jail? By God! Yuh-all better grab yo' foot in yo' hand an' scatter out o' this! Before I make out exactly who yuh are!"

Men gave back into the shadows of the buildings over there, before that grim, stolid line of troopers. Lit ran down the stairs and outside. Smoky looked down at him.

"We've got Frenchy and Fenelon and Ott in the jail," Lit told him. "And some of their friends didn't like the notion — including Bills. They decided that my warrants had disappeared after I left 'em with the district attorney. So they had an excuse for trying to open up the jail and let Frenchy out. Shorty and Chihuahua and a bunch of Wagon Wheel hands helped me change their mind for 'em. But it was a good thing you drove up."

"Yuh done ex-act-ly right, son! I couldn't have done no more, myself, or done it different. Yuh say Bills was with the mob? I knowed he was a Connell-pup, but I never believed he'd have nerve enough to come out in the open like this! Where's he?"

"I put him in with Frenchy," Lit grinned.

"Fine! I'll want to talk to him — before I kick his rump into the street! Yuh ought've killed him, though — saved doin' it later on. Oh! This-here's Lieutenant Aire from the Governor's staff up at Faith. That's where I been. Me an' the Lieutenant, we have got some work to do here. Tell yuh about it, later on."

Lit and Lieutenant Aire shook hands. Smoky swung stiffly out of the saddle and stretched himself with a groaning yawn. But when he spoke his voice reflected very genuine pleasure.

"Put Pie into the c'ral for me, Lit, that's a good boy. I'm in a hurry. I'm *awful* anxious to go right up an' talk to Bills . . ."

Chapter XVII
"Come to the Poplar Grove!"

"Have another," Lit grunted to Chihuahua. "Then we'll slide down to that pet dance-hall of yours and handpick the battle-axes. You'd better take one more, though, so the picking won't be such a job. Now, over at Tom's Bluff, there were some pretty girls to dance with ——"

"I'm have one more with you," Chihua-hua nodded, grinning. "Then you're have one more with me an' we're think *all* them dance-ladies they're lovely."

The bar-tender shot the bottle down the length of the Antelope's bar to them. He was a red-faced and stolid soul, the bar-tender. A few hours before he had served the men who proclaimed that they would kill these two. Now, he served the intended victims. By his face, one gathered that it was all a matter of perfect indifference to him.

They finished Lit's drink. They were pouring Chihuahua's, when a stocky *vaquero* slid into the bar at Lit's elbow. He had an intelligent face, this Mexican. He looked flashingly sidelong at Lit, then stared into the bar-mirror.

"Señor," he muttered. "I bring a word for you. I cannot give it, here. Will you come — after a moment — through the back door and to the corral behind this place?"

"A word?" Lit said slowly, frowning at the man's reflected face in the glass. "And who sends this word?"

"One who has never sent you a word before — and who says that she never thought to send such a word as this."

"She?" Lit breathed incredulously. *"She!"*

"I go, now — to the corral. I will wait there for a time."

He swaggered toward the front door. Lit stared after him.

"She" could mean to him only one person. And it had not been within his wildest hopes that Sudie-May would ever send him a message. He watched the *vaquero* disappear into the night. Then he straightened, looked at Chihuahua.

"I'm going out to the corral," he told him in a low voice.

He did not wait for the breed. He loafed toward the back door, mechanically slid hand to Colt-butt, then crossed to the corral. It was moonlight and he saw the stocky figure rounding the saloon, heading in the same direction.

They stopped together beside the log walls. The *vaquero* looked stolidly up into Lit's face.

"It is well-known, everywhere, what you do in the Territory," he said evenly. "We knew upon Los Alamos. You wish to prove that the *patron* bought from Frenchy cattle belonging to your *patron,* Bar-B cattle from the Diamond. *La señorita* did not believe that her father had bought cattle with burned brands. She did not believe this — at first. Now, she says that if you will come with all the speed that your black horse can make, she will tell you of things that she has learned, concerning the cattle of the Bar-B. She will tell you what to do. She says: 'Come to the poplar grove, south of Los Alamos.' She will wait for you, there."

"She's them dam' trap!" Chihuahua grunted contemptuously.

He came around the corner of the corral,

to stop and stare at the man from Los Alamos.

"Hombre," he said softly, "you have come, not from *la señorita,* but from Jed Connell. It is of no use to try lying! That word came from Jed Connell. It is to take this man into a trap that waits for him in the poplars."

"That is not so," the *vaquero* grunted. "I bring this word from *la señorita.* It is nothing to me, if he will not come. I ride as she commands. I have ridden here. I have given him the word. What he does, now, is nothing to me."

"Wait a minute," Lit interrupted them. "I thought of that, Chihuahua. But, you know the change of heart of one other on Los Alamos. Maybe this is another, of the same kind. Maybe the two of 'em have talked things over. I — I have got to know!"

"You're know!" Chihuahua said grimly. "You're know — w'en Jed, she's slam one fi-ine slug through you! She's them dam' trap, Lit! Me, I'm smell him! You're not go."

Lit shrugged doubtfully. But all the time he knew that he would go. If there were no more than one chance in a hundred that Sudie-May had talked with old McGregor and decided, like the grim old Scot, to side against her father for once, he would go. If Jed Connell had sent this message in her

226

name, and if he were all but certain that Jed had sent it — still, he would go, taking any chance rather than the chance of disappointing her. But that did not mean that he could not cross-examine the man!

"Let's have the story again!" he grunted, to the messenger. "Tell once more what *la señorita* told you to do. Where was she, when she gave you this word for me?"

But the *vaquero* was not to be disturbed by questions, by the cross-examination in which Chihuahua joined. In the white incandescence of the moonlight, his broad face was a mask of undisturbed bronze. He would not be hurried.

Sudie-May had come from the *casaprincipal* calling for her buckskin horse and he had brought it to her, saddled. She had ordered him to get his own horse. Then they had ridden out for a mile or two. She had seemed *muy triste* — very sad. She had sat the buckskin and stared out straight ahead. He, the speaker, had trailed her respectfully, keeping silent.

Suddenly, said the *vaquero,* she had slapped gauntleted palm on saddle horn. She had turned, beckoned him up to side her. She had asked him if he knew the deputy sheriff, Taylor, at Gurney. When he had nodded, she had told him what he was to say to that deputy sheriff. She had made him repeat it until he was letter-perfect. That was all he knew.

"And where is Jed Connell?" Chihuahua asked sardonically.

"*Quíen sabe?*" the *vaquero* shrugged. "The fly upon the buffalo doesn't tell him where to go. I am but a rider of Los Alamos. *He* is the right hand of our *patron.*"

"She's them dam' trap!" Chihuahua said for the dozenth time to Lit. "You're not go!"

"Probably," Lit admitted. "But — *Hombre!* I think this thing out. I will tell you, after a while, what I will do. You will stay here until I come to find you, to ride out with you, or to send a word to *la señorita.* Come on, Chihuahua."

They went toward the Antelope's back door. Chihuahua made a snorting sound of disgust. Lit laughed harshly.

"Of course! But — I'm going, Chihuahua. Probably, it's the way you think it is. But —" he fingered the locket in his pocket and grinned suddenly "— I'm going. Will you — side me?"

"Me?" cried Chihuahua. "I'm not them dam' fool w'at's ride into one trap I can see."

"Well! She's certainly a free country, this dam' Territory! I wouldn't ask a friend of

228

mine to do a thing he didn't want to do, for me. See you some more. I've got to find Smoky."

He left Chihuahua very abruptly. He told himself that he had no right to be surprised, or hurt, because Chihuahua refused to act the idiot as he was going to do. After all, Chihuahua had no such reason as was his.

He found Smoky sitting with Lieutenant Aire in the sheriff's office on the ground floor of the courthouse. The floor was littered with Smoky's corn husk cigarette stubs. There was a quart bottle, and two tin cups flanking it, on the table. Lieutenant Aire was making notes on a sheet of paper. Smoky looked up at Lit and into his grim eyes came something like affection.

"Hello, son," he said in his almost toneless drawl. "The Army an' me, we're makin' medicine. Yuh're due to hear about it when it's ready. What's on the mind?"

"I'm sliding out of town to snoop a while," Lit shrugged.

"Don't stay out too long. There'll be plenty poppin' in Gurney, right soon. Hope yuh stumble onto somethin'."

Lit nodded to them and went out. In the corral, he got the good bay borrowed from the store-keeper Norris and put upon the tall gelding the borrowed saddle. Then, on the verge of mounting, he stopped. He left the bay in the corral and moved out to the street. He went in the shadows of the buildings as much as possible, until he could look into the Star Dance-Hall. He watched for a moment, then found Chihuahua with a hard-faced yellow-haired girl, swinging about the floor in a waltz.

"That's that!" he said to himself and turned away.

And he was queerly lonesome as he went back to the corral and his horse. It seemed strange to be riding out without that big, swaggering figure siding him.

He left the county seat very quietly, keeping away from the street, ducking into a cañon of the barren mountains. He grinned at thought of the *vaquero* waiting in Gurney for his decision. Well! he thought. Even if he did go to ram his head into what seemed a trap, he was not compelled to advertise his foolhardiness.

He rode on through the moonlit night and as the bay loped or trotted toward Los Alamos, Lit thought about the place set for his meeting. He remembered the poplar trees — slim, tall Lombardies that someone said had been planted by Sudie-May's mother. Mrs. Connell, like her husband, had been Old Country. She had wanted the poplars.

Lit recalled a motte of cottonwoods — which in the Spanish are also "alamos" — south of the Lombardies' line. He decided that the cottonwoods offered a sensible man cover, for inspection of the poplars. And he would be in the motte before dawn. And he would reach the cottonwoods through arroyos and all other shelter he could find.

"I'd feel ashamed for the rest of my life — ashamed to look her in the face," he told the bay, "if I didn't come when she asked me to. But even if she sent me that word, there's the chance that *vaquero* slipped the news to Cousin Jed Connell before he pulled out to find me . . ."

Jackrabbits and cottontails rocketed out of the trail as the bay went fast over sand or dust. The ever-present chaparral bird which Lit called *paisano* or road runner sometimes paced the gelding from the trailside. But Lit found no sign of danger anywhere in the land, met no riders, saw no silhouettes in the moonlight upon the ridges.

Coming by dry arroyos, bending low and quirting over hogbacks, riding watchfully through greasewood and mesquite and cactus on the flats, he was in the cottonwood motte in the dark hour before day. He swung out of the saddle and loosed the cinchas. He made a cigarette and scratched a match in shelter of his hat. When the first gray light showed in the eastern sky, he trained the glasses that Chihuahua had taught him to carry upon the Lombardies. There was no movement there. He expected none, yet. But when the cottonwoods above him began to rustle in the little dawn breeze and birds waked, he watched closely with lenses trained upon the far end of the poplars.

He saw a rider coming, a twinkle of movement through the slender trunks. A slim rider, not very tall . . . He straightened, then turned to the bay. He pulled tight the cinchas and swung up. Boldly, he went trotting out of the cottonwoods.

The rider was coming on, head sagging, shoulders drooping, as well as Lit could see through the trees. He remembered what the *vaquero* had said of Sudie-May — that she seemed *muy triste,* until she had made up her mind to send word to him in Gurney. He thought of Chihuahua's forebodings, too. If he had listened to the cold voice of common-sense ——

The bay slid down an arroyo's bank and men were all about Lit before his hand could move. A loop came flipping up, and another and another. His arms were jerked down to his side. He came sprawling from the saddle. A man fell across him and pinned his gun-hand. The man grunted savagely: "Git his hogleg! Then hogtie him."

Lit made no resistance. There was no use. A half-dozen of Mex' vaqueros swarmed about him and Jed Connell. He was tied deftly. Jed stood up and regarded Lit with yellow head on one side. He grinned at Lit, a slow, utterly triumphant lip-curling. "Well, we got you!" he said, then crossed the arroyo and scrambled up its side until his head was above the rim. "You can go on back to the house now, Sudie-May!" he called. "He rode right into it."

He slid down to the arroyo's floor and came back to Lit, who lay staring at him with something like nausea at his stomach's pit. There was no sign in Jed's pleased expression of any memory of the ride to Ancho. He was in no degree grateful for the saving of his life from the Cherryville mob, that day. Lit knew that, very well.

"Sudie-May said she could toll you here," Jed grunted. "I wasn't so stuck on the notion. Turned out, though, she was right."

"You're a dam' liar!" Lit said thickly. "This was your notion! your doing! Sudie-May wouldn't touch a scheme like this with a pole!"

Jed's face twisted savagely. His hand

233

jerked and the heavy lash of his quirt cut down across Lit's face.

"Goddam your soul! Don't you call me a liar! I'll beat you to death, you dam' spy!"

Lit stared at him, while the *vaqueros* watched silently, stolidly. Jed whirled upon them.

"Take him out of here! Put him back on his horse and tie his ankles under the belly. We have miles to make."

The men picked Lit up and set him in the saddle. His hands were lashed to the horn, his ankles coupled under the bay's belly by another whang. Jed Connell and the *vaqueros* mounted. They pushed in beside Lit and a man took the gelding's reins. They moved off down the arroyo, heading toward the Diablo foothills.

Chapter XVIII
"Lit — If You — Like Me —"

All day, as they rode, the land seemed empty about them. They made a long nooning, rode on again. When dusk came, the horses were plodding up the slant of the foothills.

Lit slouched sullenly in the saddle. He would still have called Jed a liar, still have said that Sudie-May would not trick him into such a place as this. But he could not forget the slim, despondent figure he had glimpsed through the poplars' trunks. It was possible, of course, that her message had been sent in good faith. Jed could have learned of it and laid the trap. But how could Jed and the *vaqueros* have hidden in that arroyo, so near the place she had set, without her knowing something about it? It seemed nearly impossible . . .

There came the sound of running water. The horses slid down into a creek, crossed it and topped out. Dark had come. A stone house loomed ghostly gray ahead. When Jed swung down before it, the *vaqueros* pulled in and grunted in satisfied tone. They got off, uncoupled Lit's ankles, took him down as if he were a bag of meal. They carried him inside and dropped him on a dirt floor. After a while he heard a fire crackling outside. There was the odor of bacon frying, coffee boiling. Time passed draggingly. Then Jed Connell came in.

"Supper time for us, bed time for you," he grunted. "No use feedin' you. Frenchy'll be along tomorrow an' then ——"

"Like hell he will! With Smoky Cole in town?"

"Whole gang'll be along tomorrow. An'

Frenchy'll spend his time comin' thinkin' about you . . ." Jed ignored Smoky in a way to worry Lit. Still chuckling, he kicked Lit and went outside again, to where the Mex' were rolling up in blankets about the fire.

Hours passed. The fire burned down and there was no moon to give light. Painfully, for his whole body seemed one great bruise and he had badly wrenched an ankle in his fall, Lit inched around the walls. He found but the one door, that before which the *vaqueros* now sprawled. There was a window in each side wall, but these were mere loopholes and set high up.

The lariat that bound Lit was of tough and pliant rawhide. With the seeming mockery of a sentient thing, it yielded to his straining only to tighten at another place. Thought of the jail-break worried Lit more than consideration of his own plight. Jed's words had seemed to hint at some plan which would remove Smoky Cole, as preface to the escape. And Lit had come to heartily like the grim, honest old man.

He was still struggling against the circling lariat when he judged midnight must have passed. The door, before which he lay, now was only a lighter square of gloom. There was no sound save the snoring of Jed Connell and the *vaqueros* when a huge, shadowy figure materialized in the doorway and, while Lit gaped, crouched and slipped inside.

"Lit!" came an almost voiceless whisper. "She's me!"

Lit answered in kind. A knife-blade slipped beneath the turns of the lariat, severing them. Then, as methodically as if outside were no light-sleeping guards, and all time waited for him, Chihuahua fell to chafing Lit's ankles and wrists. At last Lit struggled to his feet, nervous, impatient to be gone. A Colt was slipped into his hand and he limped cautiously after Chihuahua. They edged along the wall until past the blanket-swathed Mex' and Jed Connell's burlier form. Chihuahua's hand shot out to catch Lit's wrist. He led him down a rocky slope.

"Them horse for us, she's here!" breathed Chihuahua in Lit's ear. "Sudie-May, she's hold 'em. *Shh! Pues,* you're make those grunt one time more an' them fella, she's wake four-five-six!"

They went on without further words and presently saw before them, dim in the darkness, the clump-like outline of the horses.

"Who is it?" demanded a low, unsteady voice, that had, for all its tininess in this black immensity, power to thrill Lit as no other sound could have done.

"*Pues,* she's me an' Lit!" chuckled Chihuahua. "Me, I have let these young dam' fool loose. Then w'ile I'm up there, I'm let loose them horse of Jed an' those Mex', too. She will not follow soon, them fella!"

They mounted. Chihuahua, sensing Lit's stiffness, boosted him into the saddle. At Lit's involuntary groan, there came a quick gasp from the girl.

"You —— Are you hurt?"

Lit ignored the question. He was staring her way. How had she come to be with Chihuahua, tonight? he was asking himself.

"What are you doing here?" he said slowly.

"Holding horses!" she said — and laughed.

"*Amor de dios!*" Chihuahua cried exasperatedly. "She's no time for them talk! She's time for them ride! She's not hurt, Lit. You're hear of them special angel w'at *el buen dios* give them job for to look after them fella w'at's drunk or dam' fool? She's take fi-ine care for Lit — drunk or sober!"

Lit spurred the bay after them when they pushed into a trot. They rode with no more talk than occasional directions from Chihuahua, until dawn grayed the sky in the east. Lit stared at the girl through the first light. She did not look as if she had passed a sleepless night, he thought. In fact ——

238

"She looks like about everything you could sum up, spelling every letter in 'girl,' " he told himself.

"Well?" he addressed Chihuahua, who had turned in the saddle to grin back cheerfully. "What was it all about?"

"Me, I'm tell you she's them dam' trap! W'at's this dam' Territory — an' Jed Connell! — I'm know! So, I'm wait an' I'm ride out behind you. She's better, if them trap, she's not say 'crack!' on my leg, too! I'm do more. So ——"

"I knew it was like that," Lit told Sudie-May. The girl turned a little, to look at him. "I knew that either you hadn't sent the word, or that Jed had stumbled onto your sending. I — Well, I just knew it!" he finished slowly, embarrassed by the grin that twisted Chihuahua's thin mouth.

"Thank you, Mr. Taylor!" Sudie-May said lightly. But she watched him with something unreadable in face and wide, blue eyes, something like a smile hovering at red mouth corners. "I am glad that Los Alamos can produce one deed that you approve. I had almost begun to lose hope ——"

"Jed said that Frenchy was breaking jail!" Lit grunted suddenly. "I reckon our job's in Gurney."

"Do not scare!" Chihuahua grinned placidly. "Smoky, she's not born them day-before-yesterday. An' she's have them soldier with Lieutenant Aire. Frenchy's not break jail. Me, I'm sure them gang's live in them jail today. About them trap . . .

"W'en Jed, she's rope you in them arroyo, one Mex' boy w'at's look like them girl, she's ride along, hah? She's fool you plenty, w'at?"

"Plenty!" Lit nodded, watching the girl. "I — was hoping to see a girl ride along the poplars, you see. And when I saw her — thought I saw her — looking worried ——"

She stared at him curiously. He lifted a shoulder and grinned twistedly.

"When I thought I saw her, I would have charged hell with or without a bucket of water, to get to her and ask her what bothered her so!"

He pushed the bay forward, until he was knee-to-knee with her. Chihuahua stared, shook his head, whistled to himself and rode on. Sudie-May gathered up the buckskin's reins. But Lit put out his hand and caught her wrist.

"Wait a minute! I've had little enough time to talk to you! It's been *years* since I've seen you! I want to ask you some things. I want to tell you some, too!"

"I have to go!" she said in a shaky voice.

"I — Some other time, you can talk ——"

"No! This is the time and the place and — so far as I'm concerned — the girl! Listen to me! Why did you come to the cabin with Chihuahua? Did you go for him?"

She shook her head, shook it violently, looking down. Lit frowned. Then he stared at her and suddenly he leaned, so that the bay moved a step closer. Lit's arm went almost roughly around her, pulling her toward him. He caught her far shoulder with left hand, twisting her to face him.

"You mean that the two of you were out prowling, last night! And you bumped into each other! Both of you on the same trail — both coming to let me loose — Lord! What did I ever do, to make Chihuahua and you both risk your necks ——"

"It wasn't any risk!" She would not lift her eyes. "Jed wouldn't dare cross me. I would simply have told him to let you go. He would have done it — or the men would have! What I say on Los Alamos is listened to! Now — let me go!"

"Not yet! I'd like to make that permanent, honey! Like to keep on holding you, time without end . . . Why did you do this? Just because you knew that Jed had used your name?"

"What other reason could there be?" she cried.

"Oh —" Lit shrugged, staring at his sleeve "— probably none at all. But the one I'd pick out of all the others you could think of would be — because you cared a little bit about what might happen to me. But that's a lot to ask. Tell me! Suppose I'd just blundered into Jed's claws, without your name used — would you have bothered to come?"

"I — Why, how can I tell you what I might do? That wasn't the case! My name was used ——"

She kept blonde head down. She refused to meet his eyes. But suddenly Lit, seeing the rush of color in neck and cheek, grinned idiotically. He looked up, to where Chihuahua showed far ahead of them, foxtrotting steadily forward.

"You can tell me!" Lit said triumphantly. "You can tell me — yes! And it'll be the truth! You do care a little about my neck! Not so much as I want you to care, but you're beginning and you'll go on until — just maybe-so! — you'll care as much as I do about you!"

"I do not!" she flared. "I — I still think that you're the most maddening person I ever met! All you have to do is crook your

242

finger at a girl ——"

"Shoo! I never crooked any finger at you! I just saw your picture and fell in love with it. Then I came hunting you and when I found you it was ten times, a hundred times, worse with me! I told you about it — naturally! I couldn't help it. I'd have popped like a balloon if I hadn't! Why do you think I asked 'em to let me come over into the Territory? Into this bunch of killers and rustlers over here? A big coward, like me! It was because I knew I'd find you over here! That's why!"

"Coward! Chihuahua says you haven't got sense enough to be afraid! But that has nothing to do with — with the subject! You take everything for granted —"

"Some things! Because they have to be! It wouldn't be right if they didn't come about! Like — that trade I told you I'm going to make — for your locket! Look here!"

He fished inside his shirt, got out a tiny buckskin bag that hung about his neck nowadays. He opened it and probed with two fingers. A little plush-covered box came out. He opened it and showed the half of a yellow gold circlet.

She stared as if she had never in her life seen a wedding ring. Automatically, it seemed, she looked up at him. And Lit leaned, arm going tighter about her. He put his mouth hard on hers and held her moveless — and if Jed and the *vaqueros* had spurred over the hogback at the bay's very hocks, he would hardly have noticed them.

"You — you *can* kiss!" he cried at last. "*Amor de dios!* I was afraid I'd got an icicle! But ——"

He kissed her again, until she beat upon his breast with her fists and twisted her head.

"Let me go! You can't do that! I can't. You — I can't have anything to do with you. You're on the other side. You're against King. I'll not be friendly with King's enemies. I ——"

Lit laughed.

"Shoo! I'm really doing him a big favor. I'm going to show him that he can't back up the cowthieves any longer! I'm going to show him in the only way he'll understand — by hitting him dead center in his pocketbook! I ——"

"You? A boy like you, are going to show King something? You're funny! Nobody has ever beat him — and nobody ever will! He's a big man and he's stepped on a lot of feet, getting to where he is. But he does *not* encourage rustling ——"

"How about our Bar-B strays that he

bought from Frenchy?"

"They weren't Bar-B strays — to his knowledge! Frenchy says that he bought that bunch of stuff ——"

"Frenchy!" Lit said softly, scornfully.

"Listen to me! I'm not going to lie to you. I do like you — like you — very much, Lit. But you can't fight King and expect me to think about liking you. And — and there's something else. You've had all kinds of luck since you crossed the Rowdy. Well, any gambler knows that luck turns. Yours will. You — don't you see it, Lit? The more I like you, the more I think about that?"

"What are you driving at?" he demanded slowly — but already he knew . . .

"Us! You! This is hard country, Lit. You know that. I know it even better. You're going to be killed, if you keep on. Lit — if you — like me ——"

"Love you!" he corrected her. "It's not like, with me!"

"— Love me, then — you'll listen to me. Give Smoky back that tin badge! Forget the Bar-B strays! Go back to the Diamond — for a while, anyway. Tell Barbee that you're marked over here. I know that he thinks of you as a son. He'll understand. And if he wants to keep after the strays he thinks were stolen — let him send a professional detective over here, a gunman! Lit ——"

"Do you mean all that?" Lit demanded, frowningly. He sat now with hands one upon the other, resting on the saddle horn. "You want me to tell Dad Barbee that I know exactly where our stuff went, exactly who took it and received it, but that I'm afraid to go on, afraid to buck Frenchy and King Connell?"

"It's a killer's job to buck Frenchy! Lit — I've told you that I like you. I've done that for you, so why won't you do something for me?"

"If I did what you ask me to do" — Lit scowled unseeingly at the hogback's crest, over which that diplomatic person, Chihuahua, had disappeared — "I couldn't live with myself again! I'd look in the glass and see a funny kind of critter, with a cigarette paper where the backbone ought to be, accidentally walking on two legs and wearing shirt and pants and boots! I ——"

"Let me be the judge of that! Lit" — she leaned to him, now, put out her hand to catch his arm — "if I tell you that I'll consider you just as much the man — and a lot more sensible! — and that I'll want to see you when this business has, quieted ——"

It was hard for Lit to ignore the softened

face, so close to his. He knew that this was no cold-blooded trade that she offered. He *knew* that. He had only to nod, then take her. Eyes and mouth and arms awaited him. And he wanted her, more than he had ever wanted anything in his life. He had wanted her from the moment of seeing her.

His hands tightened, fell away from the saddle horn as fists. He turned to face her, hot, sulky eyes upon the loveliness of her.

"You can't do that to me!" he told her thickly. "You or any other woman. There's a thing or two that a man has to figure out for himself — if they aren't part of him without the need for figuring at all. Loyalty's one of them! I told Dad Barbee that I'd hang and rattle on this trail until I couldn't do another thing. I told Smoky Cole that I'd shoot square and straight with him."

"And you have! Nobody could say that you haven't done more than you could have been expected to do! But it's your privilege to quit any job when you want to, Lit! Don't you — want to? Don't you consider me worth that much — worth doing what I ask you?"

"The way the question really is — no! I'm not a day laborer over here. I can't get up in the morning and decide whether I'll go to work or not, or what outfit I'll work for.

No, honey! I can't do it and when you think it over, you'll see that I can't. If I had the same job, for King Connell, and quit this way ———"

"Then you're on the other side of the fence, from now on," she said evenly, after a long minute of staring. "I don't believe that King ever bought a head of rustled stock — knowingly. You, nor any other man, can come to me and say otherwise, without getting my quirt across your mouth! Remember that! Don't speak to me again! Don't expect anything from me that you wouldn't expect from King, or Jed, or — Frenchy!"

She hooked the buckskin viciously and was gone at the hard gallop. Lit had no wish to overtake her. He trailed at a long lope and, when he topped the hogback, saw her thundering down upon Chihuahua, who loafed in the saddle and smoked and waited. She passed the breed, ignoring his lifted hand.

Chihuahua stared shrewdly at Lit's grim face, twisted in the kak, and they foxtrotted forward, stirrup-to-stirrup.

"Frenchy, she's not break jail yesterday, I'm think," Chihuahua said after a long while. "But, if she's not hang very soon, me, I'm think she's git loose. She's slick. She's have frien's. Lit, I'm have them fine idee:

248

we're take Frenchy an' Hognose an' Tim from them Gurney jail. We're start for them jail in Jupiter. *Pues,* them fellas, she's try for to git away an' — *ley fuga . . .*"

Lit was staring vacantly down at the hoof-prints of Sudie-May's buckskin. It seemed to him that something had shriveled inside him. That it could never be renewed. But if he had captured his Tin Type Girl and lost her, almost in the same instant, he would not whine or sulk about it. So he forced a grin, now:

"Ah, no!" he cried lightly. "Think how dangerous that'd be. Why, Frenchy might kill us, Chihuahua. We'd better keep him in Gurney and watch those shackles he's wearing."

"W'at you're do?" Chihuahua grunted, as Lit swung off.

Lit picked up a handful of pebbles, mounted again. He set one upon gun-wrist, lifted the arm out horizontally, turned his wrist and whipped the Colt from his holster flashingly.

"Oh!" said Chihuahua. "Like them, hah?"

Chapter XIX
The Conference of the Clans

"Smoky," Chihuahua said thoughtfully, "she's hold them dam' Sunday School, w'at? An' them fella w'at's git to Gurney first, she's wear one pretty pink ribbon! W'at the hell!"

Lit made no reply, merely stared. For the phenomenon drawing Chihuahua's satirical remark engrossed him, also. Why, upon one normally-deserted five-mile stretch of trail should he see warriors of the Lazy-W, the Flying J, the Circle-56, the Dollar, and the Arrowhead outfits, brand by brand, holding themselves aloof, yet all — men of little outfits and big — pointing their horses' heads toward Gurney? It was too much for Lit.

"By Jove!" he grunted presently. "Never saw so many hard-looking two-gunmen together in all my born days."

"She's this dam' Territory!" sighed Chihuahua. "Me, I'm think you're just never see so many o' them Territory people ride together before."

They jogged on thoughtfully, with the trail before and behind them dotted with the various cliques that, heavily-armed, watchful, each taciturn toward all others, kept steady gait toward the county-seat.

"She's them new dep'ty," Chihuahua answered the unspoken question of them both. "Them Curt Thompson, w'at is from San Antonio. Me, I'm wonder w'at he's ride here for. . . ."

The new deputy, appointed by Smoky Cole up in Faith, but a day or two before Lit rode out to answer Sudie-May's summons, slid his horse to a stop and grinned upon them. He was a smallish, cat-quick youngster, about Lit's age, but with an odd maturity of violet-blue eyes. He was of that type which gives the impression of efficiency, so that one, never having seen him pull or shoot, understood that he pulled rather faster, shot rather better, than the average. His lean, not unhandsome face was darkly-tanned. His eyes were twinkling, if not always good-humoredly. All in all, he rather ornamented a deputy's star, Lit thought.

"Hi-yah!" he greeted them cheerfully. "Smoky's wantin' yuh, Lit, right sudden."

"About this?" Lit's nod at the riders was born of sudden inspiration.

"Ex-actly. Gov'nor's in Gurney. Sent soldiers a-lopin' hither an' yon, tellin' these hairpins to come in an' have a pow-wow. Gov'nor's goin' to tell 'em that they got to be good. If they will, he'll whitewash the books an' start a new deal. They're shore a-comin', now, ain't they?"

"Whole Territory, looks like," nodded Lit absently, his mind wandering to Gurney and the meaning of this Governor's Conference. "But where's King Connell and the Los Alamos crew? And John Powell of the Ladder P? Funny, neither of the Territory's big fellows are coming in . . ."

Smoky greeted them with a grunt. Curt Thompson he sent off immediately, with brief orders to "Keep 'em peaceful. Don't let 'em mill." Then he turned to Lit.

"Yuh grab your foot in your hand an' hightail it for the courthouse. Fasten yourself onto the Governor an' don't yuh git bucked off — not for nothin'. There's men in town'd as soon hang a Governor's scalp to their bridle reins as a Comanche's! I got to ride herd on 'em, with Curt Thompson an' Chihuahua helpin'."

Lit nodded and went out. A dust cloud came rolling up the street toward him. It halted, swelled, before the Antelope Saloon. There was a whooping of men and squealing of half-broken horses. Then out of the dust Lit saw King Connell and Jed moving.

Behind them were a hard-faced, well-armed, swaggering bunch of Los Alamos cowboys. Neither turned as Lit came near. They went into the saloon and Lit crossed to the courthouse.

Governor Cuthbert was tall, soldierly, yellow-haired and yellow-mustached. He wore a brigadier general's uniform. He looked curiously at Lit, then devil-may-care blue eyes lighted. He smiled and Lit smiled in return. He thought that the Governor was a good-humored man, but possibly not an easy man, regardless. He had been a famous cavalryman before retirement for wounds.

"And so you're Taylor," the Governor said. "I've heard a good deal about you from Smoky. He said that you'd be along presently. You're to sort of back Lieutenant Aire of my staff and protect my scalp, I take it?"

"I'm supposed to try," Lit nodded. "I know the ones to watch. There are plenty of hard cases in Gurney, today. Aire would hardly know them all and I've already been introduced. Wolf Montague, and four gladiators with holsters tied down and triggers tied back, just to count one average outfit . . ."

"And I asked for this job!" shrugged the Governor whimsically. "Wanted to recuperate from an old wound and write. Oh, Lord!"

Moving about watchfully, keeping always within sight of the Governor, Lit was presently approached by King Connell, whose bluff red face was all smiles.

"Sure, and it's a grand day for the Territory, my son!" cried the King. "Ah, yes! A grand day!"

"If you big fellows will let her be!" Lit nodded sourly. "The Governor's really offering all of you a last chance to cut out these grab-and-be-damned ways of yours, without having a blaze of killings in the Territory that will likely take *you* off with the little fellows. You better listen with your ears stuck up, and be damned if that's Spanish, either!

"Oh! don't forget, Connell! Whatever the Governor rigs up today, you're still owing the Bar-B for two hundred and fifty head of mixed stuff. Don't you think you won't pay the bill, either!"

"It's the same hot-headed boy!" grinned Connell, seemingly unworried. "Sure, and under his hat he packs a whole herd of beef . . . But it's a grand day, just the same!"

He rolled off, chuckling, with a lean *vaquero* trailing him. Perhaps a half hour later, this *vaquero* returned to the courthouse, where the factions were gathering slowly, tensely, bringing with them the atmosphere of a powder keg with fuse lit.

"I bring a message for His Excellency, *señor*," grinned the *vaquero*. "*Mi patron,* the *señor* Connell, expresses his deep sorrow that a message of urgency calls him back to Los Alamos. To His Excellency, he says: Go on with the conference. I will approve and abide by the action taken."

"I see . . ." nodded Lit. "Yeh, I can see plenty."

King Connell would not be bound by any direct promise now, not until he had personally conferred with Governor Cuthbert. He had come into town and so shown his willingness to aid in bringing peace to the Territory — and to assure himself that all his enemies were here. Now, he could ride out swiftly — to strike certain blows which would rid him of the near-presence of divers troublesome squatters, such as Wolf Montague and the Howards. Having burned their ranch-houses and run off their stock, he could ride in smilingly, with tracks well covered. Being supreme, he would be quite ready to bury the hatchet. Oh, he was a deep one, Connell!

The courthouse was filled, now. Lit pushed through the crowd until he stood beside the Governor. In the back of the room lounged Chihuahua, with Winchester across his arm. Against one wall leaned Smoky, narrowed, bleak blue eyes missing nothing. Curt Thompson was facing Smoky from the opposite wall and there was a dancing devil of expectancy in Curt's face.

"Speaking of arsenals!" grunted the Governor to Lit. "I should have liked to disarm these fellows before bringing them together here. But — I don't suppose I could have had the whole United States Army loaned me, for the job."

He moved to the front of the plank dais that held the desk and bench of the judge when court was in session. He put strong hands behind his back and looked slowly, deliberately, out over the grim, suspicious faces that made his audience. Lit, watching the Governor and the units of the audience with slow weave of head from side to side, saw sudden irritation come to Cuthbert's expression.

"Men!" the Governor said suddenly, explosively. "You were asked to come into Gurney for a conference with me and you must have a pretty good notion of my reason for asking you here. But, if you haven't, I'm here to explain. I'll be plain with you. I want to be sure that, when you leave here after I've finished, none of you can say that he didn't understand me!"

He took a cheroot from the inner pocket of his tunic, flicked a match head on his thumbnail and stared at them while he held the little flame to the tobacco.

"I took this job as a sort of rest," he told them — and made a grunting, disgusted noise in his throat. "Rest! A lot of rest I've had. Ever since I've been Governor of the Territory, there has been a constant state of warfare among you people. Big versus Little. Early, Original Squatter on Government Land, lying out at night to lead poison the Later Squatter. Feudist against Feudist. 'No Law West of the Rowdy!' for a battle cry."

The smoke popped from cheroot end in vicious little jets.

"You've been stealing each other's stock, poisoning water holes and tanks, bush-whacking each other, raising Hell generally. Now, I'm tired of it! This is a fine Territory. It's a big Territory. There's room here for every one of you. There's no need for any of you to put his elbows into another man's sides. No need for any of you to feel your neighbor's elbows in your sides. As for Government Land, there are laws governing its use. They are fair laws — fair to all of you."

They stared at him, with no lightening that Lit could see of tense, suspicious faces.

"I want all of you to leave here with the intent to keep those pistols and Winchesters of yours in the scabbards. I want you big cowmen to make up your minds that you have to leave the little ranchers alone. As for you men who have small holdings owned or leased, I want you to leave the big fellow's wells and fences and cattle alone."

Still they stared blankly up at him. But Lit saw one or two of them grinning covertly at this suggestion that lion and lamb lie down together. Perhaps Cuthbert saw, too . . .

"Oh, I'm not merely hoping that you'll do all this. The administration has teeth and claws, as well as a pleasant purr! I ask you to do these things — to be moderately honest; to keep your guns in slow holsters; to deal with each other as neighbors. And the men who do these things will receive from me a general amnesty for past offenses — even capital offenses! Those who don't —"

He waved the cheroot and paused impressively.

"I should say: If you don't do what I ask, of your own accord, you'll do it anyway. I'll have enough United States troops brought in here to kill off the lot of you and make room for better men! That's not a threat. It's my solemn promise! You've created conditions that are intolerable, unendurable. Those conditions are going to be changed by you or in spite of you! So when you leave here, you'd better remember that. That's all I have to say to you. I'm not an orator. I'm a soldier!"

But, it seemed, he had something more to say — if not from the platform in the courtroom. When the clans were filing out, muttering among themselves, the Governor turned to Lit. He nodded toward the stairs at the top of which sat Shorty Wiggin, forethoughtfully nursing a sawed-off riot gun, gauge twelve.

"You have a man up there that I want to talk to," he said — and smiled. "I imagine that you know more about him than almost anyone else, since you're the only one who's ever put jewelry on his wrists. I want you to escort me up to Frenchy Leonard. I have something to say to the young man."

"Going to offer him a clean bill, too?" Lit frowned. "He's charged with as cheap, low-down a murder as I can think of."

"I know how you feel," the Governor nodded. "You risked your life to put him in a cell. But I have to use extraordinary methods, sometimes, to meet abnormal conditions. I have to think of the situation as a whole, not of individuals. Let's go up."

Lit nodded sulkily and they crossed to the stairs and climbed to Shorty Wiggin. He gave Lit the cell keys and Lit opened the door of Frenchy's prison and went in. He looked sharply at the prisoners, then stood back to let the Governor past.

Frenchy was paling in the confinement of the jail. But he possessed his devil-may-care grin, just as in the days when he had ridden high, wide and handsome, up and down the Territory, feared of man and idolized of woman. He sat comfortably upon his cot, but when he saw the tall, uniformed figure of the Governor behind Lit, he stood up. Grinning, he bowed to Cuthbert.

"Yo' Excellency!" he said mockingly. "This is different from the last time I seen you, up at Faith. But you'll understand that I can't do more'n offer you a seat. Things bein' the way they are — right now . . ."

And he looked steadily, still grinning, at Lit. Lit made a grunting sound, of contempt, of amusement. Frenchy's dark eyes, with the odd, amber flecks, narrowed. But he held the grin.

"It is different, Leonard," the Governor

nodded. "And, since it is different, since you're in position to realize as you didn't realize up at Faith when I talked to you, that you aren't unbeatable, I've come to talk to you, again."

"You're company," Frenchy shrugged. "I'll — listen."

"Good! See that you do!" Cuthbert answered grimly. "Today, I offered to wipe all charges against Territorials from the books. Offered them clean sheets to start tomorrow with. Suppose I offer you the same amnesty for past crimes ——"

"What do you mean — crimes?" Frenchy interrupted. "When a man hit me, or hit at me, I hit back. That's no crime!"

"Did the ranchers from whom you stole cattle and horses hit at you?" Cuthbert demanded sternly. "The Bar-B, for instance? Don't quibble with me, Leonard! I have thought that you were pushed into the first of your murders and thefts. But that was at first. You're under indictment for two murders that I know of. You've been a law to yourself — with the help of some prominent men of the Territory."

"I don't admit that I ever seen a head o' Bar-B stuff," Frenchy grinned. But his eyes were ugly as he stared from Lit to the Governor. "But, anyhow, I don't want none

261

of your dam' amnesty. It's no good to me. The only thing worth a good-goddam to a man like me is his Colts! Take 'em off me an' some cheap glory-hunter'll bushwhack me from behind the first rock I ride past!"

"The way you killed that deputy sheriff at Arno," Lit said. "Hell! when the shoe pinches your own foot."

"Never mind, Taylor!" Cuthbert said quickly. "Keep out of this! I'm offering Leonard amnesty, for the good of the Territory as a whole. Leonard! I'm not taking your pistols out of the holsters. I'm telling you to keep them *in* the holsters."

"No good, like I said!" Frenchy cried mockingly. "When the word goes out I ain't on the shoot, I'm a dead man. You can use up a barrel o' whitewash an' make me white as a ghost. But you won't be along to cover my back. Uh-uh! Uh-uh! Nothin' doin'!"

"You don't have to stay here, where you're known. The whole country is open to you. You've talked of Mexico —"

"You're just wastin' yo' time, Cuthbert," Frenchy said carelessly. "I ain't runnin'. No reason I should hightail it out o' the Territory an' dam' if I'm goin' to. I got as much right in this country as anybody an' I'm stickin'. You're just barkin' up the wrong tree."

"Why offer him whitewash?" Lit burst out. "The good of the whole Territory, is it? What could be better than hanging him? He comes up to trial next week. We've got a cast-iron case, Governor. We'll convict him and there's a nice, new rope in the office that's just his fit!"

Cuthbert made a small head-motion. Obviously, he did not want the matter discussed. Frenchy sat down and looked steadily at Lit. Tim Fenelon and Hognose Ott, from their cots, watched Frenchy, rather than Lit. They had sprawled silently, moveless, during the talk. Only their eyes were alive.

"I'm owin' you quite a bit, now, Lit, ain't I?" Frenchy said softly. "About time we settled up . . . I don't like to owe too much, too long. So — I'm aimin' to pay you up in full, real soon. You see, I don't figure I'm goin' to be bothered by that trial . . ."

Lit grinned and reached for tobacco and papers. As upon that day in the trail when at Sudie-May's stirrup he had fished out locket and tobacco together, now the sack's strings caught the locket and it dropped to the floor. He bent quickly to recover it, but Frenchy had seen the yellow flash of the gold. He came up from the cot in a tigerish movement. For once, his set grin vanished.

He faced Lit, glaring furiously:

"Where'd you git that? Dam' yo' soul! That's mine ——"

"Why, you slinking little liar!" Lit drawled, at a venture. "You sneaked that, somewhere! Everything you ever had in your dirty hands, you stole!"

"Yeh? So that's what she told you, huh? Well, I wouldn't have got it, if she hadn't dam' well wanted me to have it. An' no matter what she says, she handed it over. You see, I know her — mighty well. She ——"

The Governor, standing with puzzled frown, looking from Lit's set face to Frenchy's sneer, now straightened and jerked up his hand. But it was too late. Frenchy had already crashed backward to his cot and off it to the floor and sprawled there, gaping up stupidly. Blood spurted from his nose and smashed mouth.

Lit caught himself with a great, slow breath. He lifted right hand to his mouth and blew upon bruised knuckles. He nodded when the Governor put hand upon his arm restrainingly.

"You're right. I'll not hurt him. But we'd better go. For he's supposed to hang — not be hammered to death . . ."

He let the Governor out, drew the door shut and had one satisfying glimpse of

Frenchy, just beginning to drag himself to a sitting position beside the cot. He grinned tightly as he turned key in lock. Then fury came up in him at recollection of Frenchy's leering face.

"Lousy little liar!" he said to himself. "As if she'd stoop to him — because of his swagger — like a Mex' floozie, or that poor little savage, Kate Quinn! I'd like to go back in there and unshackle him and beat him to death!"

He followed the Governor slowly. What he knew of Sudie-May would not let him think that she had ever been more than friendly with the little outlaw, as she might have been friendly with the other cowboys passing through Los Alamos. The idea that she had been one of Frenchy's mistresses was too absurd to consider. It was Frenchy's assumption anyone would believe his insinuation that infuriated Lit.

"I'd like to kill him," he confessed to the Governor on the stairs. "More than anything in the world, I believe that I want to kill him. He's trash! Plain trash! A sure-thing killer. I've heard about every killing he ever did. And if he ever gave a man an even break, the records don't show it. A shot from behind a rock or a 'dobe wall. That's Frenchy's notion. That big, dumb Irishman

265

in there with him is ten times the man he'll ever be. Tim wouldn't shoot a man in the back. He's a wild-eyed hellion and he likes to fight. But Frenchy is — white trash!"

"And yet, there's something about him that appeals to some of the population! He throws money to the Mexicans with a grand air. So they make a Robin Hood of him. If you try him, and convict him, I'm afraid that it's going to mean trouble . . ."

"Trouble! Good Lord! What else have we had, with Frenchy killing and stealing up and down? Suppose there is trouble when we hang him! That'll be better than trouble every day! They do say, Governor, that black powder's a sweetener of sour spots!"

Chapter XX
"I Want That Man!"

Not yet were the warriors of the clans gone from Gurney. Lit loafed around the town, listening, watching. Everywhere, the Governor's proposal, his offers and his threats, were being violently discussed. Lit found the sentiment of the Territorials divided. But it was far from an even division. There were many more to call Cuthbert a "Fool-Easterner" for trying to talk away the natural hostility of big cowman for little, than appreciated his efforts to make the statutes mean something.

It was all quite new and interesting to Lit. Law and order, property rights, had been hazy things, over on the Diamond. He had been like the average cowboy, troubling his mind over nothing more than the day's work and the night's play. But now all this discussion vitally affected him, because he was an officer of the Territory. So he studied it thoughtfully.

"The proclamation of amnesty is all right, as far as it goes," he told himself. "But it all depends on the people . . ."

Swinging long legs from the counter in Halliday's store, he listened to the group there talking, speculating.

"My notion is, the offer won't be worth a whoop," he said, "unless there are more in the Territory who want peace than want war. The Governor can't *make* these people turn to the law instead of to a buffalo gun. Not unless he locks 'em all up! And if they try the law a time or two and bump into crooked judges and district attorneys and weak-kneed grand juries and petit juries, they're going back home and oil up their six shooters! What good is it, if one of us goes out and brings in a killer or a cowthief, if he's not to get convicted in court? It seems to me that there's a lot of work to be done, if the Governor's talk is to mean action."

"Right!" Halliday cried — and grinned. "But — is this the boy that was poppin' off duck-heads not so long ago? Or is it that boy's big, grown-up brother?"

Lit grinned uncomfortably. But he was encouraged to go on. "I can see one possible good: some of the men who've been pushed out on the dodge and have had to steal and kill to get by will come in. Hard cases like Frenchy will lose some of their men. And the ones who've been on the dodge and didn't like it, they'll be sort of hard to push over the line again. That'll be to the good, anyway."

He got down off the counter and loafed to the door, hesitated there and went out.

Some good, he repeated to himself, had been accomplished. Now, if Frenchy's trial could be held without an open explosion that would fire the Territory again, he could hardly escape conviction. Hardly escape a hanging sentence, if a good jury were drawn. And if the Territory proved that it could smoothly and legally hang the most notorious outlaw within its borders, there was more prospect of peace than ever before. But — there was the district attorney to consider . . .

"There's a great big *If* in the way! *If* we can try and convict him and hang him where everybody can see the job, things will be quiet. The hard cases he's been enlisting in his gang will hunt new pastures. Maybe Dad Barbee can go to law, then, and sue the King for the price of two hundred and fifty Bar-B strays!"

Looking at the swaggering men, the pick of the Territory's warriors, along the street, with their six shooters sagging, that thought of peacefully going to law made him laugh.

Smoky Cole came up the street, then. He stopped beside Lit, who eyed the grim, silent man curiously. Smoky's lips worked upon his corn husk cigarette, pushing another inch of it out of his mouth.

"I hired two new deputies," he said at last. "Couple Dutchmen that ain't long on thinkin'. But they ain't hired to think. They're hired to do what I say — an' what I'm tellin' 'em is: To watch Frenchy an' Tim an' Hognose like they was gold-plated. They'll be guards for day an' night, now, one of 'em in the cell with them fellas all time."

"Until the hanging," Lit nodded. "If we *can* hang Frenchy."

"I got a notion I might's well order the lumber for the scaffold," Smoky said grimly.

"Governor's goin' to take a hand in that trial. I — kind o' talked to him an' it may be I let slip somethin' about our noble district attorney . . . I think Cuthbert will have a special lawyer here to sort o' take care o' the prosecution. Well — what I want o' yuh, Lit, is that yuh better head out an' scout around. Take Chihuahua. He's been drawin' deputy pay since I appointed yuh."

"You want to know why King Connell slid out so fast," Lit nodded. "And what he's been up to, while all the others were here together."

"I'd like to know," Smoky agreed grimly. "It's a two-man, eyes-open job. If one man was to stumble onto the King when he was up to some devilment ——"

"I'm glad you hired two men," Lit said, staring down the street. "You have got what I'd class as the hardest bunch between Here and Over Yonder, in town today. There's one big, green-eyed *gunie* with Wolf Montague that'll bear watching. One-eared man. I know him from the Diamond River. In fact, I have a notion that I'll tuck him away in Boot Hill one day. I certainly will if he crowds me. I hope you keep both eyes peeled and on the jail, Smoky."

"Don't worry. That's why I hired Ull an' Zorn. They got single-barrel' minds. An' double-barrel' shotguns. An' they seen trouble before. No back-up *to* 'em. Find Chihuahua an' slide out, son."

Lit nodded and moved off in search of Chihuahua. He did not find the breed in the Antelope. Nor was he in any other saloon on the street. But a Mexican youth met near Halliday's store directed Lit to a drinking place on the edge of Gurney, a square 'dobe house favored by the Mexican *vaqueros.*

Chihuahua sat in a corner with a bottle on the pine table before him. He was slouching in the chair, long legs thrust out beneath the table, shoulders drooping. He lifted his head when Lit came in. His bright blue eyes were brighter than Lit had ever seen them — glassily brilliant. His thin, hard mouth was drooping. He looked drunk.

"Feel like a ride?" Lit asked him, coming over.

"My friend," Chihuahua said — using Spanish as he rarely used it when with Lit — and speaking very slowly, very thickly, "I feel as if the bottom had fallen from the world. I have no belly. Nothing is of use. There is no color to the flowers, no taste to my whiskey."

"The Willies!" Lit grinned and banged his hand hard upon the sagging shoulders.

"Come along with me and ride it off."

"*Muy bien.* I cannot drink it away. I have tried. This is the second full bottle that I have drunk. The whiskey works upon my feet, but cannot touch my head. So — let us go. Where, is of no import to me."

Lit frowned at him. He had never seen this somber side of his friend, had never seen him anything but sardonically cheerful. But whatever it was, that made him look years older, etched grim lines on the daredevil face, was Chihuahua's private affair. He did not make the mistake of asking questions.

Chihuahua stood up, unsteadily. He braced himself with a hand upon the table and fumbled in a pocket. He got out a gold piece and dropped it ringing on the pine.

"Your whiskey, Friend Antonio," he said to the *cantinero,* "it is not good. I can feel its bite in my liver, in my stomach. But in my heart — it does not bite. But, perhaps that is not your fault. I have never found whiskey anywhere to drown the black dogs when they eat at my heart."

Antonio stared stolidly, then nodded and came over to pick up the gold. Chihuahua took Lit's arm. He rolled as they went toward the door, but — as he had said — the liquor affected only his body. He turned toward the courthouse and when they came to the corral behind it, got headstall and saddle and put them on his horse without help, working clumsily, but surely.

They went into the sheriff's office for Winchesters. When they swung into the saddles he seemed normal, except for his expression. They rode out and turned west. As the horses foxtrotted toward the end of the Diablos, Lit forgot Chihuahua's trouble in thoughts of what might lie ahead.

Hours passed as they rode toward the nearest house that Lit would inspect — the ranch of Wolf Montague, southwest of Los Alamos. It would be dark by the time they reached the Arrowhead. Chihuahua made a grunting sound and Lit looked sidelong at him. Something like his usual expression had come back to Chihuahua's eyes and mouth.

"You are a good *compañero,* Lit," Chihuahua said softly. "You do not talk when it is not the time to talk. It is another of the things I like in you. You do not ask questions. So — I finish this bad time, now, by telling you why I left the world today to go sit in the dark by myself. I do not do that often. But today, as I walked along the street watching the warriors, I passed a little white house like the house that once we owned —

my mother, my baby sister, and I — south, near Jupiter. Very like our house is this one. I have seen that many times."

He stared frowningly out upon the rolling foothill country.

"And a little girl was singing, somewhere in that house. Singing the little song about a cat, a burro and a hen, that I taught our Rosita when she was but beginning to walk. And the light went out of the street for me, when I heard her. I remembered Rosita and the day, eight years ago, when I rode back to that little *ranchita* of ours."

The thin mouth tightened, became a pale line across brown face. Lit stared fascinatedly, if covertly.

"My brown dog lay dead upon the threshold. Someone had shot him. I flung myself down and ran into the house. My mother was dead upon the floor, almost at the door. In another room Rosita, too, was dead. I was like a madman! I thought of Pablo, the boy who worked for us. I could not think that he had done these murders, simple of mind though he was. But I took out my knife and I went quietly to look for trail. It had been only because of Rosita. Nothing else of worth was in that house. Only that lovely child and she had not yet fifteen years.

"I found Pablo and my first thought was

the right thought: It was not he who killed my mother to take Rosita. For he was dying beside the corral. He had crawled there to the trough in which we watered the horses. He was a good boy, that Pablo. He could not write and so he knew that he must not die until I came and he told me what he could of the man who did those things to me."

He drew a great, slow breath, eyes lifted unseeingly to the yellow rim of the setting sun.

"I will not tell you what Pablo told me. I cannot talk of it. But he had eyes, that simple one, as well as that loyalty that one finds more often in a dog than in a man. He told me what this man was like — not so much as I wanted, because Pablo's senses went from him when he was shot and he recovered only after a long time. But enough to let me know that man when, some day, I come upon him. To know him by a certain thing. So, for eight years I have watched men. Sometimes, I have believed that he stood before me. But always it was another man."

He lapsed into brooding silence. They rode on silently until the sun was gone behind the far Soldados and the moon showed in the star-lit sky.

"Them Arrowhead, yonder!" Chihuahua grunted suddenly. "Me, I'm think she's smoke I'm smell!"

"I don't smell any," Lit answered, leaning forward. "Now I smell it!" he said fiercely after a moment. "I — expected to!"

"*Por supuesto!* W'y will King Connell slip away, but for the knife in the back of them Arrowhead an' Wagon W'eel," Chihuahua agreed. Apparently, "the black dogs" were gone and he was his usual self.

They rode cautiously up to the blackened shell that had been the Arrowhead house of Wolf Montague. Only the parts of the house which had been built of mudbrick remained. Faint wisps of smoke still rose from charred logs.

They poked about in the moonlight, but found no sign of violence to any humans about the ruins of house, corrals and sheds. Lit drew a long breath of relief at that, but he was furious, nonetheless.

They made a coffee fire and ate, then left the vicinity of the ruins to sleep in an arroyo a mile above.

"It's just a question of which one to look at first," Lit said grimly as they smoked a final cigarette that night. "He's as down on the Howards and the Wagon Wheel outfit as he ever was on Wolf Montague. He's probably making it a clean sweep."

"*Pues,* them Howards is more close," Chihuahua nodded.

They turned across trailless range, next morning. Lit was in bad humor. Connell's blows would light a fire in the Territory. All that the Governor had hoped to accomplish would be made impossible. It would be war to the knife between the outfits wiped out and the warriors of Los Alamos. And he was Smoky's deputy! He could not stay out of the thick of it.

They came over the crest of a ridge and Chihuahua, looking mechanically over the country, suddenly snatched out his glasses and focussed them upon another high point ahead. After a moment he let them down and shrugged.

"One man — Mex', I'm think — w'at's go over them ridge. Me, I'm think she's not see us. We're go look, hah?"

They rode fast until they topped that ridge over which the other had vanished. And Lit saw him perhaps an eighth of a mile away, jogging along. He grunted and Chihuahua handed over the glasses. Lit studied the tall bay horse and the slim rider upon him. He handed back the glasses and put the rowels into Midnight. All thought of the Howards had vanished.

"I want that man!" he said grimly to Chihuahua.

And down the slope he sent the black, scuttering after the lithe *vaquero* whom he had seen in Porto, riding Arch Holmes' white-faced bay gelding around Slim Hewes's store — Frenchy's spy in Porto, beyond doubt.

The *vaquero* turned at the thunder of their hoofs. And he leaned forward and rammed in the hooks. As they followed, Lit wondered at the presence here, north of Gurney, of a member of Frenchy's gang. It might mean nothing, but it might mean a great deal. Well — he consoled himself grimly — they would first catch the man, then see if he would not explain . . .

Their animals seemed fresher than the big bay. Steadily, they cut down the distance despite his spurring, his quirting the bay with rein-ends. He rode with chin on shoulder much of the time. The space between them shrank, became two hundred, a hundred and fifty, a hundred, yards. Chihuahua stopped his sorrel flashingly and was on the ground, trotting out to the side to stand motionless.

Lit understood. He continued to send Midnight pounding forward, but now he angled to the side. Looking back, he saw

Chihuahua in a slack calm, beginning deliberately to lift his carbine. Then the sound of his firing came — like the clapping of many hands. The bay ahead crashed down. Lit dug in the rowels. A moment, and he was looking down upon the man pinned beneath the dead horse. It was the *vaquero* of Porto, all right.

He flung leg over saddle fork and slid down, Winchester covering the man. He lunged and punched the wrist of the man's gun-hand, beginning to lift a Colt. Lit hooked the pistol away with his toe. He saw that the *vaquero* was bleeding from wounds in back and breast.

Chihuahua loped up and swung off. They lifted the horse from the man and pulled him to one side. He looked up at them maliciously.

"Why did you run from us?" Lit demanded. "And where had you that horse and saddle and bridle?"

The *vaquero*'s beady eyes seemed drawn by the nickeled badge on Lit's shirt. He laughed, a rattling sound that ended in a spasm of coughing.

"I am not the least of the men of Frenchy," he told them boastfully, when he could talk.

"I know you," Chihuahua nodded. "You are Juan Ortiz. I have seen you with *el francés,* who now lies in Gurney *calabozo* where my friend and I threw him. That was why I killed you — because I knew you and because all the men of *el francés* are now marked for death if they do not drop their guns."

"You think so?" Ortiz gasped painfully, mockingly. "It may be so — but I do not think so. This horse and saddle? Why, I rode upon certain business in the country north of Porto, in the country of the Diamond River. And I came upon a *vaquero* riding the bay. I liked it, and his saddle and bridle, as you know, were silver-trimmed. I liked them, so — I killed him and took them. Now, I spit upon you! I spit upon you — and die!"

His head rolled sideways, and between half-closed lids his eyes shone like beads. Chihuahua put out a hand, touched the dark forehead, nodded.

"She's dead. Now, me, I'm wonder, Lit . . . W'y will she ride here? Me, I'm think Frenchy, she's send him somew'ere, hah!"

"I think we'd better forget about the Howards, for a bit," Lit decided, staring grimly down at the murderer of that cheerful one-time rider of the Bar-B, Arch Holmes. "Even with a couple of new guards in the jail, I can't help worrying about

Frenchy. Anyway, we can tell Smoky that Connell wiped out the Arrowhead house. That's indication enough that he went on to wipe out the others."

"Frenchy, she's have them notion very strong against them hangin'," Chihuahua nodded. "We're have one look for Gurney!"

They cut across the range, riding at the mile-eating hard trot toward the Diablos. There was a pass through the mountains, by which the road to Porto might be gained. It was not the usual road, but it cut off miles.

Noon came and they let the horses breathe. They swung up. Chihuahua lifted himself in the stirrups.

"Amor de dios!" he cried. "Them whole dam' Territory, she's come for to meet us, w'at?"

"And they're riding like they can hardly wait to see us!"

CHAPTER XXI
"ANY FIGHTING MEN?"

Halliday the store-keeper was the first man Lit recognized, of the baker's dozen pouring down a slope toward them. Halliday waved his Sharps at Lit like an Indian, holding it high over head. The men behind him were store-keepers, cowboys, miscellaneous townsmen. They had one thing in common — they carried all the arms possible, rifles, shotguns, six shooters.

"Didn't yuh meet 'em?" Halliday cried when Lit and Chihuahua pulled in before the citizens. "Frenchy's gang?"

"Frenchy's gang?" Lit cried incredulously, leaning forward. "Why —— We killed one man, Juan Ortiz — Chihuahua killed him, that is! What happened?"

"Hell!" Halliday said with immense finality. "Plumb hell! They tolled one o' them new Dutchmen — Ull, it was — up close enough to 'em to grab him. An' the dam' fool was packin' the keys to their shackles an' handcuffs. They killed him with his own gun an' sneaked out an' shot Zorn, the night guard — he was still downstairs in the courtroom."

"Smoky?" Lit grunted furiously. "Where was he?"

"Asleep. Frenchy an' the others had help waitin' for 'em. Some o' them fellas that's been hangin' around keepin' so quiet an' watchin' so hawk-eyed. The bunch slid out behind the jail with ever'thing that'd shoot out o' Shorty Wiggin's closet. They never run — then. Somebody hightailed it to fetch Smoky an' Curt Thompson an' Shorty Wiggin. Frenchy an' his bunch hid in behind a corral wall an' they just shot hell out o' Smoky's bunch. Smoky an' Wiggin'll likely die. Curt Thompson's not so bad, but bad enough, with a hole in his leg an' another through his shoulder. When they'd bushwhacked Smoky, Frenchy's outfit jumped on the hawses somebody'd got for 'em. They hightailed it this way."

"I'm take them look," Chihuahua said grimly.

"Know any of the bunch that sided in with Frenchy?" Lit demanded softly. A stiffening thought had come to him: He was sheriff, now. This war had been all but dropped upon his lap. Nor was he disposed to avoid it!

"Fella they call Bisbee was one behind the wall, shootin'. An' that awful tall storekeeper, Slim Hewes from Porto. Two-three other, maybe a half-dozen, killers. My guess is they made for Porto. That's close to the Rowdy an' they know they can drop us, if once they ford the river."

"I — don't think they can," Lit disagreed, very softly. "In fact, I know damned well they won't. I'll keep after 'em clear to the Diamond — or to hell!"

Chihuahua came back at the lope. He lifted his hand in the ancient Indian summons and they rode to meet him.

"Them fellas, she's go for Porto. An' me, I'm find w'ere our Juan Ortiz, Lit, she's turn away — to ride for them hangout w'ere Smilin' Badey, she's stop. Frenchy, she's not like Badey. But if she's need help for to fight us, Smilin' Badey's good. Smilin's like for to fight them posse, any time."

"Porto!" Lit called to the others. "Let's go!"

The trail was wide, and plain, and clear, from the foothills straight toward Porto. Frenchy and his bunch — nine or ten, in all — had ridden fast, but without any attempt to cover their trail. The posse made camp that night on the dry fork of Arroyo Feo and as they sprawled around a fire, Lit had the story of the ambush in Gurney with all its details.

Curt Thompson was the hero of that fight, by Halliday's report. The young deputy had rolled over to the *acequía* — the water ditch — and despite the gaping wound in his thigh, the bullet lodged in his shoulder, had returned the outlaws' fire and kept them from coming out into the open to put pistol-muzzles to the heads of Smoky Cole and Shorty Wiggin.

"They was yellin' a lot, behind the wall," the grim storekeeper said. "I went for my

Sharps, but I had quite a ways to come. I could hear 'em yellin' to each other to jump out an' be damned certain Smoky an' Shorty went to hell. But Curt knocked some dirt into their mouths, I reckon. An' I went in with the old buffalo gun an' they decided to emigrate."

He looked thoughtfully at Lit in the fire's light.

"So — yuh' sheriff, now, Lit. An' I can say what I couldn't have said some time back: I'm dam' glad yuh are!"

"I'll try to keep you that way," Lit said absently. "It is showdown in more ways than one. There's more than Frenchy riding the high lines. Smiling Badey, for one. We have got to wipe Frenchy out. When we do, Badey and the others'll hightail it for Mexico or cooler parts."

Lit and Chihuahua talked over the situation ahead. And both agreed that Frenchy's men, plus those hard cases in Porto who would naturally join them, could make life exceedingly interesting for such a force as theirs.

"But, if we're git behind them house in Porto, before they're see us —"

"We'll try it," Lit grunted. "It means no sleep, tonight. Beyond midnight, anyhow, Halliday!"

The store-keeper listened and nodded. They sprawled for a nap, all but one sentry, but at midnight were in the saddle again. Chihuahua seemed to know this country as he knew all the Territory. He led them to a ridge before dawn and stopped.

"Porto!" he grunted. "She's down them hill. Me, I'm go see!"

And he vanished into the darkness as if his sorrel's hoofs were padded. They waited, watching the darkness thicken, then begin to turn gray. Chihuahua reappeared as from some 'dobe below them a rooster crowed.

"They're think we're come!" he said cheerfully. "They're sleep in Hewes's store. But they're not all sleep. On one roof them fella's watch. By them store, too, she's them guard."

Lit called up a picture of the village as he remembered it. Then, slowly, he divided the men.

"Halliday, behind the store there's an arroyo. The ground rises on the other side of it. If you'll take a couple over there, nobody can get out the back way. Chihuahua, if you'll take a couple to the blacksmith shop, you can cover the far side. The rest of us'll scatter out and hold the Cortina house and the saloon across the road up this way from Hewes's place. That'll leave some hard cases behind us, maybe, but it's the best I can figure, offhand."

He watched them off before leading the others softly into the southern edge of Porto. As his knot of men came quietly up to the first building a man jumped up in the gray light from where he had been squatting in the shelter of a rain barrel. He ran around the corner of the building.

Lit jumped Midnight forward. The little black spun about the corner and the man, now under the wooden awning of this little store, fired at his pursuer. Lit saw the orange flash in the dusk under the slanting roof. There was a *thut!* of slug striking saddle fork. He lifted his carbine and cocked and fired it, whipped the lever down and fired again.

The man ran out from the awning and Lit had a clear glimpse of him going toward the next house. He fired deliberately and the man sprawled in the dust. He did not move.

The others thundered around the corner, now. They looked at the fallen one, then fiercely at Lit. He waved left hand spaciously.

"Some of you to Cortina's house, yonder. Roust out the family. Three-four of you get into the saloon across the road. That's Hewes's place down there. They ought to be awake, in it!"

From the dark wall of Slim Hewes's store, there came a jet of flame and the flat, metallic *whang!* of a Winchester. A posseman swore in a surprised tone, slid sideways in the saddle, dropped his rifle and clawed weakly at the saddle horn.

Lit jumped Midnight to his side, slipped left arm about the man and lifted him clear as he roweled the black horse to one side. The others had parted, some galloping toward the Cortina 'dobe that fronted the street and presented a long, blank side wall to Hewes's store. The rest quirted and spurred across to the saloon, flung themselves down and from the ground opened on Hewes's place.

Lit saw the dust of the road spouting up under a lash of lead from the store. Something picked ever so softly at his shirt. Something else made a hissing noise all but in his ear. Then the man he supported jerked. Lit looked at him. There was a small, bluish mark upon his forehead.

He got into the shelter of Cortina's and leaned, letting the dead man gently down. From the saloon front came now a rattle of firing. It was drowned, here at Cortina's, by the pound of a log against old Cortina's door. Lit straightened, to scowl about him.

There was still no token of Halliday's arrival behind the store, or Chihuahua's garrisoning the blacksmith shop.

Suddenly, out of Cortina's, came the old man himself and behind him his fat *señora* and a troop of children and relatives and servants. They were half-dressed, for the most part. They ran close to the fronts of the buildings and pounded upon a door down the street, yelling for sanctuary.

Lit moved around to the front of Cortina's house. The great door stood open. Inside, was the noise of pounding. He went in. Some of the men were knocking loopholes in the 'dobe walls. He came out to see what the men across the road were doing. They had broken into the saloon over there and had an angling range toward the Hewes store front. And at this instant Chihuahua's men opened fire from the blacksmith shop beyond the store.

"I think this is finished, Frenchy!" Lit said grimly aloud, as if the grinning outlaw could hear through those 'dobe walls that spurted fire now. "I think this is — finish!"

But there was a battle to fight, first. Lit knew that well enough. The store in which Frenchy's men sheltered was like a fort. And it was provisioned with food and water — and whiskey! — enough for a small army.

Slim Hewes's stock included cartridges, too — of the three or four calibers the garrison's weapons would include.

Not all the hard cases were in the store . . . Lit moved along the road that was here for a brief space Porto's street, intending to cross and come up to the back of the saloon. Out of a house a shot came. The slug smashed a window that Lit was passing. He dropped flat, pushed his Winchester forward and fired as the hidden one let a second shot come his way. Two slugs, then, Lit sent into that window over there. The rifle-barrel slid back from that windowsill, with a telltale deliberateness. Lit watched grimly. No more shots came.

He got up cautiously, watching every door and window ahead of him. He stopped at the door of the house from which the shots had come. It gave to his push, creaked back and let light in upon a dirt floor. A woman's voice lifted shrilly:

"Do not shoot! Do not shoot!" she screamed in Spanish. "My man is dead."

Lit went in, moving like a cat, ready to fire or to jump aside. Under the window in the side wall lay the "mean freighter," Crowe, whom he had beat to the draw in Arno. The man's left arm was still strapped to his body, the left sleeve hanging empty. A pretty Mexican girl cowered in a corner, watching him with widened eyes.

"You need not be afraid," Lit told her. "We have not come to fight with the people of Porto. We have come to get *el francés*. But those of Porto who fight with him are our enemies. Your man was one of these."

"He was a friend of *el francés*," she nodded. "He was with him in the store until midnight when he came back to his bed with me because he did not wish to sleep on the floor. His old hurt, which you gave in Arno, was not healed. He saw you pass as he looked from the window. I begged him not to shoot, but he was sure that he could kill you. Then, he said, the others would have no stomach for fighting. It was you, he believed, who would stay until the death of *el francés* was come."

"I will put him upon a bed for you. How many are with the little devil in the store?"

"The great Teem and the little one of the loud mouth — Hognose, and a big one who walks like a bear and has but one ear. Four men I do not know came with them and with the store-keeper. Of the men here, my cousin and the brother of the store-keeper's woman joined them. Perhaps my sister's husband, Juan Ortiz, has come, bringing with him more men."

"About ten, besides Frenchy," Lit calculated. "Maybe only nine, depending on whether that one I killed when we rode in was an extra doing guard for 'em, or one of their own . . ."

He put Crowe upon the bed in a corner and went out the back door of this house and made the saloon. As he came up to that rear door, he heard the familiar report of Chihuahua's carbine from the blacksmith shop and, as for echo, the bellow of the Sharps buffalo gun from across the arroyo where Halliday watched.

The saloon garrison had two men hurt. But one could use his rifle at a window. They were sure that they had got one of Frenchy's side at a window in Hewes's. Lit told them what Crowe's woman had said.

"We're pretty even, now," he shrugged. "Don't show yourselves any more than you have to. Come dark, we'll try a lick."

He made a long round to get to Chihuahua's post. He squatted beside the breed who was watching windows and door with steel-bright eyes that shuttled to and fro ceaselessly.

"Me, I'm git one," he announced. "She's poke his face up for them shot, then she's duck. Nex' time she's poke his face up, me, I'm say *Howdy!* with them slug. I'm help

292

him to git sick, *por dios!*"

"I count about eight in there, now. If the men in the saloon really dropped one as they claim they did. One thing's sure, Chihuahua, they'll be in there when we want 'em! But it may take a long while to smoke 'em out. And if the like of Smiling Badey or some of the other hard cases come down on us, we're apt to be the ones taking it on the run."

"An' so?" Chihuahua grinned, looking flashingly at him. "We're do — w'at?"

"Run 'em out!" Lit said grimly. "Keep 'em busy. I'm going to get to work."

He worked around to Halliday and found that gentleman comfortable behind a boulder with the Sharps on a tripod of three sticks. Halliday could report no casualties. They might have hit somebody, but he could not be sure. To him, Lit repeated what he had said to Chihuahua. Then he went back to one of the stores. There were men crowded there, watching the battle. Lit could not tell from their guarded expressions what side they favored. They watched him with inscrutable eyes, the whites and the Mexicans both. He looked around.

"Any fighting men?" he asked. Nobody answered. "I can use a few more."

"We ain't takin' sides," a grizzled man

answered. "It might wipe out Frenchy, but — we got livin's to make, here."

Lit nodded. He could understand their point of view. There were still hard cases riding up and down the Territory. There would be hard cases — for all the Governor and the peace officers might do — for a long while yet. But, he did wish for a half dozen more of the Halliday kind — men who realized that the long sight was the sight to take, when dealing with such as Frenchy Leonard!

"Well," he said slowly, grimly, "we are going to wipe Frenchy out. Don't make any mistake about that. It's just a question of how best to do it."

One of the hard-faced Americans laughed shortly:

"Yeh," he said sardonically, "that's been the way with Frenchy an' everybody who bucked him, ever since he come up from Old Mexico!"

Lit grinned and asked the store-keeper for kerosene. Every face turned his way at the word. The store-keeper hesitated. Lit moved a little closer to him.

"I said — kerosene. So I *hope* you haven't run out of it?"

The store-keeper shrugged. He seemed to have made a decision:

"All right," he nodded resignedly. "I reckon you got men enough to take it off me, if I never handed it over to you."

Lit took the big can when it was filled for him. At the door, he turned slowly, to look from face to face at that quiet group.

"In Porto, today," he drawled, "I can see just two kinds of men: one kind is for me, and the other kind is against me. Is that plain to everybody?"

Slowly, they nodded. Lit grinned one-sidely, turned and went on out. As he walked toward Cortina's, he studied the weak point, the most exposed point, of his besieging line. That was the saloon diagonally opposite Hewes's store.

As he reached the Cortina house, a man came to the corner of the saloon, sheltered by the side wall from Frenchy's fire. He gestured significantly — with a sweeping motion toward the ground, a lift of two fingers. Then he indicated himself with pointing fore-finger.

Lit understood, and waved the man back toward his post. He was the only one left to fight, there. The other two were gone. Frenchy was taking toll of the attackers! He would bite into them more deeply still, Lit feared, before he was smoked out of the Hewes store.

"Well," he thought, as he stepped into the Cortina door, to put the kerosene down, "it's a price we'll have to pay, I reckon! It's a matter of getting through the day with as few down as we can manage. When it's dark, I'll try to show Frenchy a few with this coal oil!"

He came back out, after a word with his garrison in the house. They had no losses, nor serious hurts. He went by roundabout course, to cross the street and enter the saloon from the back. The man who had signaled him was at the front window. He grinned at Lit over rifle-stock.

"Rance an' Chucky passed in their chips. Reckon Rance went happy — he always said he wanted to die in a saloon!"

CHAPTER XXII
"SO WE COME FOGGIN' IT!"

Noon came and Lit sent by the man with him food to Chihuahua and to Halliday. The man came back. Halliday had lost a man, killed. Chihuahua had been a little luckier. One of his men had taken a slug through the thigh and another across the scalp.

"I helped him around an' turned him over to Cortina," said the messenger. "Well — do'no' what we're doin' to him, Taylor, but

Frenchy's certainly playin' the wolf with us!"

"We'll finish him!" Lit said grimly. "As soon as it's dark, I'm going to coal oil him out into the open. And if he comes out shooting, he'll go down the same way! But my idea is that he'll grab his ears. Frenchy likes a wall to fight behind. I've been up and down his tally and I never yet have found a place where he smoked it with a good man, in the open!"

"He's a tough kid," the cowboy said doubtfully. "I been in the Territory a long time. Frenchy an' Smilin' Badey, they are both plenty tough. Do'no' where I'd put my money, in a war between them two."

"Not going to be any war between 'em!" Lit told him angrily. "This war is Frenchy's last. And it's between Frenchy and us. You put your money on us and you won't have to copper."

He lowered across at the front of Hewes's store. He saw a shadow rising above the sill of a smashed window. Furtively, he shifted aim. It was a man's elbow. The head appeared . . . Lit squeezed trigger and with the flat, vicious report, a man jumped up, at that window. The cowboy's Winchester *whanged!* Lit saw dust jump out of the man's shirt with that second shot. Then the man fell across the sill, half-in, half-out, of the store.

"Know him?" Lit asked the cowboy.

"Seen him around the saloons in Gurney, that's all. I reckon if we scalp him, we'll have to chop his scalp in two. We both hit him. Looky! He ain't dead! He's movin'!"

Lit pushed up the carbine, then let it down.

"They're pulling him back into the store, that's all. Listen to Halliday! They couldn't be trying to get out the back ——"

He inched back, stood up and listened to the staccato blaze of firing from across the arroyo behind Hewes's place. It was answered from the store — and from somewhere along the street . . .

"I'm going to see what's happening! That sounds like help for Frenchy. You'll have to handle this by yourself!"

He ran down the saloon and out. He ran along the backs of two houses, then up a wall to the street. He stopped there, listening, trying to locate that new point of fire. It was somewhere opposite him, at the back of the houses across the street. He had thought that Chihuahua had stopped Juan Ortiz before he had carried Frenchy's message. But there was the possibility that Ortiz had been on his way back when killed. If that were true, this might be Smiling Badey, second only to Frenchy as a gunman.

He ran across the street and between two houses. There were three rifles talking, somewhere on his right. He thought that they were in a corral forty yards behind the houses and in a line with Halliday's position. Then a noise at the street-end of the narrow tunnel in which he stood jerked his head about. A big man stood there. His pistol was lifting.

Lit dropped and heard the Colt bellow. He wriggled around the corner of the house as the man continued to shoot at him. Something seared across back and shoulder blade like a white-hot iron. Then he was around the corner and scuttling for the only shelter he saw — a hole from which had come the mud for the 'dobe bricks of this house. He rolled into it and all but turned a somersault to turn his Winchester on the pistolman.

But that worthy was sheltered by the house-corner. And now a man in the corral opened on Lit. He dropped flat in the bottom of the yard-deep hole. Lead was nicking its lips. But the thing that infuriated him was his isolation. He was completely out of the battle, held here by that cross-fire.

The firing stopped. He listened, then

stiffened and began to crouch. For he heard
horses coming at the pounding gallop, coming up the road from Gurney-way. He
ventured to look cautiously over the edge of
the hole and drew no fire. He could not yet
see the horsemen, but his turning head let
him catch a glimpse of that big man who
had driven him out of the tunnel. The pistolman was staring around the corner of the
house, staring in the direction from which
came the pound of hoofs.

Lit flicked up the Winchester and fired.
The man disappeared, but whether hit or
merely taking shelter, Lit could not say. And
three riders rocketed around a house. Lit
stared, then grinned ferociously. They were
the Howards, Ed, Tom and young Abe. He
yelled at them — yelled his name. Then he
shoved Winchester over the edge of the hole
covering the corral.

He saw a rifle come out between the
cottonwood logs. He fired instantly, more in
the hope of disturbing that one's aim than
with any expectation of hitting him. The
Howards flung themselves from their horses
and from the ground opened on the corral.
Lit continued to pound the cracks between
the logs of that shelter. He heard the Howards yelling and drew down his empty
carbine. They jumped up and began to run

toward the corner of the corral. Lit looked thoughtfully over his shoulder, saw nothing of the man behind him, and scrambled out of the hole.

When he neared the corral, he saw a rider topping a ridge a hundred yards away, bending low, quirting his horse furiously. Ed Howard turned — Tom and Abe were trotting toward the corral. He grinned at Lit:

"Smilin' Badey," he grunted. "Totin' off a plumb bellyful o' fight! We-uns was out lookin' for them Connell skunks that burned us out. Met a fella that told us yuh-all had hit for Porto on Frenchy's trail. So we come foggin' it!"

"And you landed like something the doctor ordered! Frenchy sent a word to Badey. I reckon he gathered up three men and came to help smoke us up. Oh! There was one in between the houses, back yonder. Three of 'em in the corral ——"

"Between us, we finished two in the corral," young Abe yelled. "No wonder Smilin' dogged it! He's like Frenchy: he likes a gang with him an' somethin' to skulk behind!"

They moved cautiously toward the space between the houses. The man was gone and there was a trail of blood to mark where he had gone along the tunnel to a horse in the street. *He* had not stopped in Porto!

Lit went to where he could yell to Halliday. That grim gentleman answered in a bellow. He was by himself, now. One of the Badey rifles from the corral had broken his second man's arm.

"Can you hold out by yourself?" Lit asked. "The Howards are here and one of 'em will side you."

"Send one over. He can load for me, anyhow. I'm shootin' three guns an' that's hard on a fat man!"

Tom Howard crossed the arroyo to join him when Lit called. Ed and young Abe and Lit went to the saloon. The cowboy grinned at them. He said he had not fired a shot since Lit's going.

"Reckon they was all at the back tryin' to see what the shootin' was about," he shrugged. "So yuh run Badey, huh? Well, that was a good job, runnin' him an' wipin' out his bunch. Reckon he only had one or two handy when the word got to him. For he usually travels with a dozen to twenty."

"Abe," said Lit, "will you slide over to the blacksmith shop and back up Chihuahua, till dark? Ed and us two are enough here. Come dark — there's going to be fireworks and a parade! or I miss my guess, plenty."

Abe nodded and disappeared. Ed and the cowboy and Lit watched the front of the

302

store. Lit wondered who was left in there. Frenchy was still alive. He was pretty sure of that. For he thought that the others would surrender, if left alone. They had enough men to keep up firing on four sides. Ed Howard had his shirt ripped by a slug when he exposed himself.

"But I think I got the fella," he grunted, retiring calmly. "Looked like a Mex'. Frenchy got some Mex' in there?"

Lit told him what Crowe's woman had said about the garrison. Ed nodded, chewing his Star.

"Juan Ortiz, an' a couple o' Badey's killers, an' that fella Crowe, an' two-three hard cases out o' Gurney saloons, would be a tol'able clean-up by itself. An' we'll settle some more before it's over. I wish King Connell was in Hewes's with Frenchy, though! I'd like to line my sights on him! But he'll keep out o' sight, like always, until he thinks the smoke's blowed away."

Lit looked uncomfortably at the grim, set face. He had all but forgotten the blows Connell had struck at his enemies. But they would not forget! As soon as this business here was finished, the Howards would be riding a vengeance trail against Los Alamos. He thought of Sudie-May and so vivid was the picture he called up that Ed spoke twice to him before he heard.

"Dark'll be soon," Ed said tonelessly. "An' that coal oil yuh got'll be mighty handy to make a light . . ."

He got up, stretched, leaned a little to look at the store. Lit, seeing him stiffen, moved to stare, too. But in the graying light the smashed front of Hewes's place was not clear. Then a heavy burst of firing sounded, from the rear.

"They're monkeyin' with that dam' front door!" Ed Howard grunted. "I seen it move. If they're goin' to try a break ——"

The door opened flashingly. Lit, Ed Howard, the cowboy at their side, shoved Winchesters forward and poured lead into the dark opening. A big figure leaped out, made the corner in two great strides. Then lead from Halliday's position or Chihuahua's struck him and Tim Fenelon fell like a tree cut down. Lit stared frowningly. He shook his head somberly and looked at the door again. A man lay over the threshold, now.

"Frenchy's yellin' somethin'," Ed Howard called without turning. "Ah! He wants him out o' the way, so's they can shut that door ag'in. Reckon he never counted on more'n one man over this side. The's the door. We'll burn 'em out yet, Lit."

Sullen silence gripped the street, with

failure of that attempt. Lit and Ed went out and across to Cortina's. The town was like a place deserted. The houses were shuttered, doors closed. Even that store where he had got the kerosene was no longer the post of idlers. The dusk was thickening. Lit brought the kerosene out. He called to the men holding the house:

"Pound hell out of the wall, but don't put any buttonholes in *my* clothes! I'm going across to the corner. I'll be out of their range, there."

"Me, too," Ed Howard grunted. "I got a tin cup. Come on!"

He took one side of the can's bale and they raced across the space between house and store, covered by shooting. They squatted at the corner. At their backs, the rifles in Cortina's rattled.

From the store's windows in this wall that firing was answered. Lit looked sidelong at Ed's grim face. He laughed. This was the end of Frenchy in the Territory, he thought triumphantly. He moved the big can of kerosene. Ed gathered himself. They worked around the corner and Ed held the tin cup under the can. Lit poured it full. Ed's long arm moved. He splashed the kerosene on the heavy door, refilled the cup, splashed a window . . .

They worked fast, throwing the oil over the store front, then came back to the side wall, crawled along it in the growing dusk, treated the back wall and for climax Lit swung the can and sent it up to the flat roof to spill the remnant there. Ed at the front corner, Lit at the back, scratched matches and hurled them. Flames burst up, ran in a sheet up the end walls.

Lit yelled from shelter of Cortina's, yelling for the surrender of Frenchy's garrison. From the store defiant yells answered the demand. And firing burst out. Apparently, Frenchy's men lined every wall. But the kerosene on the roof caught, now. A pillar of smoke-edged flame shot up. And out of the store's front door, with a yell that they gave up, Hognose Ott and another man stumbled, flames licking at them as they jumped out.

Their hands were up. Lit yelled at them — to cross to the saloon and surrender to the men there. Out of the store came shots — into the backs of the two. Hognose Ott spun around with a strangled cry, fell flat. The man with him — a stranger to Lit — put his head down as if facing wind, began to run. Then his knees wobbled. He fell headfirst and clawed at the ground. Defiantly, the shooting continued in the store.

Lit grunted to Ed Howard, watching with Winchester ready for the dash Frenchy and the others must make:

"He's a cold-blooded little devil. But he'll have to come out — to surrender or die — or stay in there and burn!"

"Who, yuh reckon, is still in the'?"

"Could be Bisbee, and Frenchy, and Hewes — maybe a couple more. *Frenchy!*" he yelled, against the crackle of the flames at roof and front. "Better come out — and have the rope fitted!"

The firing inside swelled to a very thunder. Lit scowled. More men were in there — must be in there! — than he had believed possible. That terrific burst of firing proved it.

There was a rumbling crash. Someone, somewhere, yelled that the roof had fallen in. Then Lit, watching from the front of Cortina's, saw two men, carrying a third between them, lurch from the store. They put down the limp one they carried, in the street. Their hands lifted.

"Come on over!" Lit yelled, watching the door. For these were unimportant privates of Frenchy's force — a Mexican, a hard-case cowboy. Unless that one on the ground were the little outlaw . . . He called to them as they bent and picked up the wounded man again. The cowboy answered:

"Side-pardner o' mine. Shot through both hips."

In the Cortina house the cowboy grinned defiantly at Lit.

"Well, sir! I reckon y' win — but we gethered a few tail feathers off y' bunch! An' we certainly ———"

Lit was in no humor for polite compliments, between victor and vanquished. His dark eyes were very narrow as he rammed his face across and stooped a little to face the cowboy very closely.

"Ne' mind the talk! You can gabble after while! Where is Frenchy? And Bisbee? And Slim Hewes? Talk up, you!"

"In Hell, I reckon," the cowboy said sulkily. "Y' don't need to be so dam' fierce about it! I seen 'em at the back windows. They was bettin' on which one'd kill Halliday across the arroyo. Then the roof come down. Looked like ever' dam' thing in the store blazed up when it fell. It shut Frenchy an' Slim an' Bisbee off from me an' that Mex' that was the only ones left in the front. So we picked up my pardner an' got out. That's all I know about it. If Frenchy an' the others never come out the back door, they're fried to a frizzle!"

Lit went out and to the corner of the Cortina house, looked at the blackened 'dobe walls that held the flames of the wooden part of Hewes's store as a furnace might hold charcoal. He went down the side wall of Cortina's house, with arm up to shield his face from the terrific heat that came from the store. At the back, he looked at the inferno seething inside, visible through back door, back windows. He shook dark head grimly.

"If they were not dead when the roof fell, they are certainly dead now! *Halliday!*" he lifted his voice. *"Halliday!"*

"Comin' up!" the store-keeper answered from the arroyo. "Chihuahua's comin' from the blacksmith shop, too. What happened — to them inside?"

"We have got one floating cowboy, one Mexican from Porto, here, and another cowboy shot through the hips."

Briefly, he told Halliday of Tim Fenelon's death, and of Frenchy's murder of Hognose Ott and that other, nameless, man. Halliday nodded, looking at the fire in the store.

"Then that's that! We was coverin' the back door. Nobody got out, I'll swear to that. Won't you, Tom?"

Tom Howard spat and nodded, staring at the flames.

"Frenchy an' them others got a fore-taste

o' hellfire!" he contributed. "Many o' the posse cash in?"

"Four," said Lit. "And four hurt more or less. I reckon our play is to bury the ones who cashed in and see about the ones that are hurt. Probably, it'll be better to leave them here until they're able to ride. Cortina'll take care of 'em — with Frenchy gone and Smiling Badey out of the running . . ."

He left Halliday and Chihuahua, who had come around from the blacksmith shop with young Abe Howard and the other of his party, moving about. He walked draggingly, staring moodily at what lay ahead of him without consciously seeing anything.

It was not that his iron body was weary. The long day had not brought anything to touch an ordinary day of riding and working on the range, and any cowboy was able to "do his sleeping in the winter-time." But the strain of past weeks had seemed to come to a final tension here. All the hatred he had held for Frenchy had blazed up. All the watchfulness he had been forced to practice, to try to beat the little outlaw once and for all had been increased, here. Now — the strain was slacked.

He had done what he had intended, promised, to do. He had come into the Territory the rawest of youngsters. He saw that now, looking back as over years upon himself as he had been when riding over from the Diamond. He felt terrifically mature. And yet, that was not all that dragged upon him, slouched his big shoulders.

"There's King Connell yet to settle with," he thought. "That's not like bucking Frenchy, of course. But with Smoky out of it, I'll be the one to make Connell knuckle under and settle up for the damage he's done the little fellows. And, of course, he's still owing the Bar-B for those strays! When I've done that, I'll turn over my star to somebody and ——"

That was the trouble! He would turn his back on the Territory and all it held. He would ride back to the Diamond to take up the regular round of work. Some day, he would own the Bar-B. For he knew that old Barbee thought of him as son and heir. But there was no attraction in that prospect.

Standing in the shadows by a house, watching dark, soft-footed people go by furtively as Porto's folk came from barred and shuttered houses with the battle's end, he thought of Sudie-May and because of the distance between them, his picture was paradoxically clearer . . .

The picture that came was of that moment

311

on the trail, when he had shown her the little plush-covered box with its wedding ring — that hung now in buckskin sack from cord about his neck . . .

He could all but feel the pliant body in the circle of his arm, pressing close against him, the soft warmth of parted mouth lifted, clinging to his, could see again the pulse hammering in smooth temple and the quick rise and fall of round young breasts.

"Dios!" he breathed huskily, and shook his head fiercely, as if that would rid him of the pictures before inner eye, the dryness of his mouth. "I lost her — that day! When I had to choose between being a lover or a man . . ."

"Lit!" Chihuahua said softly from his very elbow. "You're better to come with me. We're not finish Frenchy — yet!"

Slowly, almost stupidly, Lit dragged himself back across the space between the place of his remembering and Porto, here, with its bullet-riddled doors and windows, its patches of red dust, its still figures.

"Not finished — Frenchy — yet? What do you mean?"

"Three men's slip from them store. Under them wall, into one *acequía. Sí!* She's make them tunnel to them ditch. She's crawl by them ditch w'ile Halliday, she's watch for them door. *Pues,* me, I'm find one fi-ine trail through them arroyo, to w'ere she's git horses . . . She's ride off like the hell!"

Chapter XXIII
"Will He Head for Connell's?"

Lit had no interest in the trail that Chihuahua had found. If Chihuahua had cut the trace of three men leaving the store by a tunnel under the wall, crawling down Hewes's water ditch to the arroyo and going along that dry water course to the place where horses were stabled, that was enough.

He ran beside the breed, back to where Halliday and others were making ready to bury the dead in Porto's little Boot Hill. He told the grim store-keeper what they knew must be the truth — that the three most dangerous men in Hewes's place had escaped. Halliday swore furiously. Lit checked him.

"We'll get 'em!" he said impatiently. "Now — here's the way I see it: Chihuahua, Ed Howard — if you'll go, Ed — and I are enough to handle 'em. And we can go faster. We're all on good horses. You take charge, here, Halliday. Come back to Gurney when you're ready. If we lose their trail, we'll make up a posse, or a series of posses, in Gurney. For the little son of a dog's hit back for the Territory. Probably feels safer there. More people to help cover him. Come on, Chihuahua, Ed!"

They got their horses saddled, rammed food into saddle pockets, swung up. Chihuahua had followed the trail of the three for distance enough to show that Frenchy had led the way back along the trail he had used, coming to Porto.

As they followed, at a steady lope, Lit thought grimly of Frenchy — and thought straight, as well. He considered all that he knew of that little egotist, and the people — Mexicans, Anglos, of the Territory.

Frenchy would regard this terrific beating he had taken, in Porto, as no more than a temporary check. You couldn't make him understand that he had been bested. So, he would ride back into the land that knew him. And cowboys, sheepherders, ranchers and Mexican farmers, all would feed him, give him horses and weapons and ammunition under more or less compulsion, even lie to officers about his whereabouts.

There were fifty places he could take cover. Girls of the *peon* class considered it an honor to lie in his arms. They would influence the men of their families to aid him. So, what seemed a foolish turnabout, when ahead lay the wilderness between Porto and the Diamond, became the logical turnabout.

"Will he head for Connell's?" Lit asked Chihuahua abruptly. "At first, I mean?"

"Me, I'm not have one big surprise, if she's do that," Chihuahua nodded. "King, she's owe Frenchy money. An' she's scared for Frenchy, too. *Por supuesto!* She's one fi-ine place for Frenchy an' them other, Los Alamos."

During the night they halted occasionally, to let Chihuahua get down and scratch matches and inspect the trail. Always, the hoofprints pointed to the south, the tracks of three horses. Steadily and fast the trio rode, by testimony of the trail. Lit grinned one-sidedly. Frenchy would expect him to believe what for a time he had believed — that the blazing roof had buried them, the flaming store been their funeral pyre.

"Is he due for a surprise?" he thought and his shoulders shook gently as he laughed.

With day they found a 'dobe house off the trail a little way. The trail of the fugitives led up to it. But the Mexican girl who was its only occupant now faced them defiantly. She would say nothing of Frenchy. Lit laughed and put hand under her chin. She clawed at him like an angry cat.

"Do not touch me! I know you! The man who tricked *el francés* and like a coward threw him into the jail at Gurney. Keep your hands from me. *I* have lain in his arms. Such as you ——"

She spat eloquently. Lit grinned at her.

"When I have killed him, you may come to see him. You will find there — if they care to come — twenty others, to whom he said what he said to you."

They ate the food unwillingly given them by her. The horses rested with *cinchas* loosened. For an hour, they loafed before the store and smoked and talked disjointedly. Then Lit got up, scratched Midnight's nose and tightened *latigos.*

"Good-bye, Beautiful!" he grinned at the girl. "When I have killed Frenchy, I will send you a Man!"

"Hijo de la perra!" she screamed at him. *"El francés* will give me your hair for a braided chain!"

"What he does to the women!" Lit told Chihuahua with helpless grin. Then thought of another woman, who had once taken Frenchy's part, sobered him. He could not believe that Frenchy's fascination, that so affected the like of that savage girl back there, would also affect Sudie-May. But no more than vague connection between the two was sufficient to make him lower at the trail ahead and answer with sullen grunts the occasional remark of Ed Howard and Chihuahua.

Near noon, the trail vanished in a welter of rocky ridges and shallow arroyos. And Ed Howard's horse went lame in the sharp thorns of bayonet weed. Chihuahua cast about like a great hound, but finally acknowledged defeat with a shrug.

"We'll forget his trail," Lit decided. "We'll cut across to Los Alamos. You come along, Ed, as fast as you can. If he didn't head straight for Connell's, we'll have to hunt for his hole-up."

He and Chihuahua left Ed and the lame horse and went at steady hard trot across the open range. The afternoon passed. Dusk came, and darkness. And, looking down from a hogback at last, they saw below them the yellow squares that were lighted windows in the *casa principal* of Los Alamos.

Staring at the lights, Lit found the prospect of seeing Sudie-May within a few minutes disturbing, yet oddly pleasant. He shrank from it, yet he would not have turned away, he knew, for anything.

They went quietly for a half-mile, then

swung off the horses in a little motte of cottonwood trees near the main *acequía* that brought water to the house-yard. They scouted the corrals afoot but could not locate horses that were surely those of the three they hunted.

From the low houses of laborers and *vaqueros,* there came the murmur of voices, with the jangle of guitars. From the great house of King Connell no sounds came. Chihuahua thought that the outlaws would hardly be in the *casa grande.* He went scouting the bunkhouse and the rows of 'dobes. He came back to where Lit moved around the great bulk of the house. Neither sign nor word of Frenchy had there been, among the riders getting ready for sleep down there.

"Let's see if King's home, then," said Lit.

They went noiselessly up to look at a high-set barred window in the house-wall. As they stared up at it, listening to the faint mutter of voices within, suddenly there came to them out of the window a rasping, high-pitched, cackle of laughter. Lit stiffened and glared furiously upward.

"Bisbee!" he breathed, turning. But Chihuahua had vanished without a sound.

Lit looked around for him, decided that he was moving on his own account, and went down the wall toward the entrance of the patio around which the big house was built. He could have made no mistake — he had heard that queer laugh of Bisbee's several times, in Tom's Bluff. And if Bisbee were here, so were Frenchy and Slim Hewes. Doubtless, they were talking with King Connell inside.

He went into the patio entrance and noiselessly across the tiled pavement of this tunnel-like passage. Chihuahua would be somewhere near at the needed moment. And Lit felt that now, in cover of night, was the proper time to surprise Frenchy. In daylight, with all Los Alamos hostile to him, taking the little killer unaware was all but impossible.

He went soundlessly out under the roof that encircled the patio, under which doors opened to many rooms. He worked around in the darkness, listening, looking for light under doors, trying to locate that room out of which Bisbee's spine-rasping cackle had come.

He heard a shuffle of feet somewhere ahead. There was a door half-open, almost at his elbow. Lit stepped into that black opening. The feet came closer, paused at the door. Lit shrank farther inside and flattened himself against the wall there. Probably, that was some servant going through the patio.

Then the doorway was blocked by a body. A grim voice spoke, in a low voice:

"Who's that in there? Answer up, or ——"

Lit had not drawn his pistol. He did not take time, now, to try covering Slim Hewes. For without doubt the tall store-keeper was menacing the room with Colt-muzzle.

Lit struck out and his fist caught Hewes. There was the metallic rattle of pistol dropping to tiles. Then the store-keeper's long arms came out, caught Lit's shoulder. The grip was like nothing he had ever met, before. He had always known that Slim Hewes was credited with enormous strength. But he had considered himself a match for anyone he might meet. Now — he had to wonder!

He whipped up a clawing hand, caught Hewes's arm and jerked. Hewes staggered into the room. There was the slam of the door — as if he had caught it and pulled it shut. They were in total darkness, darkness so thick that to Lit it seemed something to feel, like a heavy black blanket that shrouded them.

Not in the least had the gaunt store-keeper relaxed vise-like grip on Lit's shoulder. As they staggered across the room, each holding the other, Lit lashing out furiously with left fist, Hewes's fumbling hand caught Lit's left arm above the elbow. He fell against Lit, who instantly banged the top of hard head into the store-keeper's chin and was rewarded by a pained grunt. But Hewes lunged backward, then forward. They crashed to the tiled floor with Lit underneath and he saved himself from stunning impact only by jerking head upward so that his shoulders met the tiles.

Surge as he might, he could not get out from underneath. Hewes was like an anaconda, curling long legs about Lit's legs, bracing elbows out and down. Lit jerked head forward and banged Hewes in the face again. But release of his left arm, the convulsive twitch of the store-keeper's hand belt-ward, warned him that Hewes was trying for a weapon with which to end the struggle. Hewes had dropped his pistol. It must be a knife — and Lit had the average man's cold dread of slicing steel.

He was tired, gasping from the strain of the tug-of-war with the gigantic store-keeper. But if Hewes got a knife out, he had no chance of escaping injury.

He hooked out savagely, felt fist impact upon flesh, then rolled desperately and dislodged Hewes from above him. He came to his knees — Lit — then lunged at the invisible bulk of the store-keeper. His hand struck Hewes's hand. He caught the wrist, twisted it, bore the hand down. Hewes groaned softly. Lying flat upon Hewes, Lit heard an odd bubbling sound that seemed to be Hewes's breathing . . .

He dared not get up, slack the hold that he had snatched on the wrist and on Hewes's other arm. Then something sticky seeped upon the left hand that pressed against Hewes's chest. He drew in air in great gasps, wondering. Cautiously, he gathered himself, let go his grip on Hewes and slid backward, fumbling for Colt-grip as he moved. There was no sound except that bubbling noise.

Pointing the pistol at the sound, he fumbled in his pockets until he found a match. He struck it and stared tensely as he leaned forward. Hewes's hand had fallen away from the hilt of the bowie knife that was buried to the guard in his breast. Lit got shakily to his feet and moved over to look more closely. Hewes was dead.

"Por dios!" Lit thought wonderingly. "If ever you'd got hold of Frenchy, he wouldn't have been kingpin for long!"

Chapter XXIV
"— Why, He's Faster'n Me!"

Listening at the door, Lit could hear no sound from the patio to indicate that the battle had been heard outside this room. That was hardly surprising in this house of yard-thick walls of plastered mud brick. He reholstered his pistol and worked stiffened arms reflectively before he ventured to open the door cautiously and put face into the crack.

The patio was dark and silent. But across it, glimpsed between flowers and shrubs that surrounded a fountain in its center, he saw now a yellow thread of light under a door. He stared that way and nodded slightly. That should be the room from which Bisbee's spine-rasping cackle had sounded. He slipped outside and went across the patio, straight for that door.

Coming to it, he heard a mutter of voices. He thought that King's was one of them. He put ear against the heavy oak, but still the voices were only a murmur. Then King Connell's booming voice lifted, plain enough to be understood as to words:

"No! Ye want too much. Ye're unreasonable, my lad. If ye want a couple hundreds, I'll advance that much. Not because I'm owing ye a cent, mind! But for ould times' sake and, it may be, because of favors ye can be doing me in times to come. But when ye come talking thousands — ye have got your sights too lifted! Talk sense and — remember ye're talking to King Connell!"

Very softly, Lit fumbled with the hand-made iron latch and pushed on the door. Frenchy's voice came to him, with the door's opening. Light of tone, careless, still it held a sinister note, Lit thought.

"I'm not forgettin' a thing, King. Not a — thing. Most of all, I ain't forgettin' who's doin' the talkin'."

Lit slid inside. It was a sort of office, this room, lighted by one lamp hanging from the ceiling, corners enshadowed. There was a huge iron-banded oaken desk of size to fit King Connell, who loafed behind it. Sudie-May perched upon a corner of its flat top near her father. She was staring at Frenchy, who half-sat, half-leaned, upon the arm of a huge chair, a shabby, dirty figure with the soil of Porto-fighting still marking him.

Nobody seemed to hear the door as it opened and closed behind Lit. There was tension in this group. Lit found it in the King's red face, in Sudie-May's bearing,

even in Frenchy, who had a surface light-
ness of manner. Bisbee sat in the deep
embrasure of the window, leaning against
the iron bars, head a little back, eyes closed.
Lit flattened himself against the wall. Somehow, he felt oddly very much at ease.
Frenchy's side-face was toward him, but
Frenchy was grinning at Connell, apparently gripped by his own thoughts to the
exclusion of everything else.

"A couple thousands, King," he said easily. "Or — say, three thousands. Call it a —
weddin' present . . ."

"What are ye talkin' about?" King Connell
boomed at him. But Lit, watching from the
shadows by the door the red face plain
under a hanging oil lamp, saw a sudden
twinkle of perspiration on Connell's forehead, cheeks. Sudie-May stiffened, turned a
little, stared at Frenchy.

"About us!" Frenchy cried, laughing.
"Take it easy, King. You know, it's right
funny! King Connell, Big Auger o' the Territory, settin' in his *casa grande* with fifty
men o' his outside . . . An' me, I'm the Big
Auger! I tell him what to do an' I back it up
with one finger — an' King Connell does
it . . ."

"Ye talk like a damned fool!" King Connell
said, but there was uneasiness plain in his

voice. "Ye get into trouble and ye come to Los Alamos. Ye ask help and yet ——"

"I ain't askin' help from nobody! I dam' well take what I want. Nobody's stopped me yet, neither! Money or horses or cows or women — Frenchy Leonard takes his pick! I never come here for help. I come here to collect some money you been owin' me plenty long. An' while I'm here, I'm takin' the gal I been aimin' to take all along."

Bisbee suddenly moved a little in the window and the slight movement seemed to catch Frenchy's eyes. He looked that way and laughed. Lit watched them as if they were figures in a play. Most of all he stared somberly at the slim girl in frilly négligée who sat with legs twisted sideways, the cameo-clear profile lighted by the lamp's glow.

"Hey, Bisbee?" Frenchy cried. "I been aimin' to take her a long time, ain't I? An' you never said a word to me, about havin' the same notion — but lackin' the guts to back it up. You see, King, Bisbee wanted to make a play for Sudie-May, ever since that time he worked for you. But *he* was scared o' you. When he found out I was comin' here, he thought that was fine. I'd get her, then he'd find a chance to put one in my back. That'd leave him with her! But it won't work, Bisbee! It — won't — work!"

"You're crazy!" Bisbee said from the window. "I ain't figurin' on no such thing!"

"No? The hell you say! But — ne' mind! It won't work!"

He moved a step nearer the desk, coming straight with a catlike twist. He seemed to be watching the huge figure of King Connell as he stopped before the moveless girl. Lit stiffened, as Sudie-May had stiffened. He felt a pulse hammering in his throat. He swallowed as he saw the quick rise and fall of her breasts, under the silk of the négligée.

"It's Old Mexico for us, hon'!" Frenchy told her. "With a few head o' Pa's cows to blow in down there! We'll leave that purty boy-deputy o' yours to find out I never got burned to death in Porto — an' to look at you in that locket . . . Me, I'll have lots better than a picture, hon'. I ——"

"I wouldn't touch you — except with a quirt!" the girl said huskily. "And before I'd let you touch me ——"

"Be still, King!" Frenchy snarled, as the huge Connell began to prop himself up behind the desk, red face twisting furiously. "You make a move an' I'll cut you in two!"

He looked sidelong at Sudie-May. And his face was reddened, Lit saw curiously.

"Wouldn't touch me, huh?" he said very softly to her. "You will change your mind about that. You'll come along — an' willin' — if you know what's good for King! An' after a while, when I'm through with you ——"

"That'll be all!" Lit said in flat voice. "Plenty!"

There was the heavy creaking of Connell's chair, the rustle as Bisbee shifted position in the window, the scuff of Frenchy's heel on the polished oak floor. But to Lit Sudie-May's gasp as she whirled on the desk and leaned to stare incredulously was loudest sound of them all. He moved a step toward Frenchy who stood staring, amber-flecked eyes narrow, shoulders drooping a little, right hand crooked of fingers like a claw.

"I didn't think you were burned to death in the store — not for long," Lit said evenly. "Knowing you by your back-trail, it was easy to see how you'd left the others to save their own skins, while — as usual — you sneaked off. I watched you at the stone house on Hell Creek, you know — when you let Art Brand be killed because you were afraid to open the door for him. Yeh, I know you from the back, Frenchy — and I don't know a thing about you that's straight, or white!"

"Well!" Frenchy cried, grinning. "The Boy-Deputy! Actually figured somethin' out for hisself, yes, sir! An' now he comes wanderin' up, just in time to say good-bye to me an' my gal an' see us off. Or, maybe, he come up for a lesson: come to see a li'l' draw I do!"

His shoulders slouched a little more. He shook his head in jerky motion to right and left, to clear the amber-flecked eyes of the lank black locks hanging down his forehead.

"It goes like — this!" Frenchy cried. "Tell Old Devil!"

Lit heard the thin sound of Sudie-May's scream. Out of eye-corner he glimpsed King Connell, rising, scooping Sudie-May to him across the great desk, dropping her in its shelter. But that was seen almost unconsciously. For Frenchy was drawing the deadly Colt with which he was supposed to have no equal. And Lit was focussed on the task of matching that draw, even besting it . . .

He ignored the flash of Frenchy's hand to gun-butt that — he knew from watching the outlaw shoot in Tom's Bluff — was like nothing in the world except the dart of a striking snake's head. He was going through the movements of the draw with all the smooth, mechanically swift twitch perfected during hour after weary hour of daily practice.

He did not think of Frenchy beating him, Frenchy killing him with gun undrawn. His hand slapped the smooth butt of his Colt, his thumb-joint drew back the hammer and the gun slid from tied-down holster, leveled on Frenchy, roared and belched flame as the hammer dropped.

Almost blending with the report was the bellow of Frenchy's gun. A tiny hand seemed to pluck at the blouse of his shirt. He thumbed back the hammer, fired again, saw Frenchy spin about, come down to one knee and prop himself with gun-hand on floor.

"Why — why, he's faster'n me!" Frenchy gasped amazedly.

Lit twitched smoking Colt up and covered Bisbee. It seemed to him that he had seen the green-eyed man drop hand to gun, while he and Frenchy were slapping leather. But now Bisbee came *sagging* from the embrasure, to collapse upon the floor. Lit stared, but King Connell stood up, behind his desk, with Sudie-May's limp body across a thick arm.

"Le' me be getting her outside!" Connell panted. "Praise God! She fainted when his hand slapped his pistol!"

He ran across the room, jerked open the door, and vanished outside. Lit stared grimly down at the still bodies on the floor. The door was pushed back, Chihuahua slipped in, pistol in left hand, bloody knife in right. He glared at Bisbee, crossed to him like a stalking cat, stooped.

"It was you!" Lit grunted, with glance at the window.

"*Por supuesto?* W'en I'm hear him laugh, w'en we're outside, then I'm know! *I'm know!* In all these world, Lit, she's only one fella w'at's laugh like that . . . Pablo, them boy w'at's work for me, she's always make them same noise like everything she's hear — dog, cat, *man!* Before Pablo, she's die, she's show me how them man w'at's kill my mother, sister, laugh. She's show me many time before she's die. Tonight, w'en I'm hear him, I'm find me one ladder. I'm kill him with my knife, through them bars."

He put out sinewy brown hand, lifted the long hair that hid Bisbee's gotched ear.

"Pablo, she's tell me that, too! *Amor de dios!* In them saloon in Gurney, me, I'm stand before him, an' not know! W'at the hell!"

"I want to see Connell," Lit grunted suddenly, bringing himself back to thought of his own problems.

He went out into the patio. On his left an open door was a yellow square in the house wall. As he looked that way, a woman passed the door, crossing that room. There were servants in the patio, now. Evidently, the shots had roused the place. Lit went around the patio and stopped in the doorway. Connell was down on his knees before a great couch on which Sudie-May was stretched. A Mexican woman stood by her, holding a glass of water. Lit stepped into the room and called Connell's name.

"Don't be bothering me now," King Connell grunted, without turning. "She fainted at the very first. I think she's taken no harm. But ——"

Lit came unwillingly over to tap his shoulder imperatively.

"I have to talk to you, Connell!" he said grimly. "Right away. Before we leave. I'm acting sheriff of the county — as you know. As Frenchy may have told you, my posse just about wiped out the worst cutthroats of the Territory. But there's a thing or two left to settle — what you owe the Bar-B for the stuff Frenchy rustled and you bought from him. And you're going to pay up for the damage you did to the Howards and all the others! I'll take your word for it. Pass your word and I'll be on my way. Refuse and —

by God! I'll take you out of this through all your hard-case cowboys. I'll slam you in Gurney jail and *you* won't break out! Law's come west of the Rowdy today!"

Men were crowding around the door, outside. But Chihuahua, he saw with a side-glance, was inside, watching them. He lifted his voice a little — Lit:

"I'll be running the county for a while, Smoky being laid up. Tomorrow, I'm going to gather in that cousin-foreman of yours who was so thick with Frenchy. I can put enough charges against Jed Connell to pack him away for a few years, too! I'm going to round up every last one that sided with Frenchy!"

Inwardly, he grinned. For Jed Connell's face had vanished from those about the door. Lit rather fancied that the Territory would not be troubled long with Jed's presence.

Connell got lumberingly to his feet. He looked steadily at Lit for a long moment. Then he grinned and put out his huge hand. Lit ignored it, but met his eyes grimly.

"My son! I owe ye plenty!" Connell said huskily. "That little divil meant every word he said — but one! And that one was about leavin' me alive. But it's not my own neck I'm thanking ye for. I've lived hard and in nature I've tramped plenty of toes to climb to where I am — and stick in the saddle. It's for ——"

"Don't thank me!" Lit said flatly. "I came to get Frenchy. I got him. It — just happened that I landed in the room at a time when getting him helped you. I don't want your thanks. I want your word that you'll settle for the damage you've done, when I tell you how much it is."

"You'd better — give in," a low voice counseled the King, from the couch behind him. "I — know Mr. Taylor. He's a stubborn man . . . He means every word he says and — I have to agree with him that you owe for a lot of things. I've been watching a good deal. I've roped cows on the range and puzzled out the original brands. Give him your word to foot the bill."

"All right!" Connell said with shrug of great shoulders. "I'll pay Barbee's bill and I'll pay for the fun we had raising hell with Montague and Howard and the others. Is that all?"

"So far as I'm concerned," Lit nodded, face a mask.

"Good! I'll not be telling ye I'm sorry for anything. No man ever spun his loop over a range like mine, in this Territory — or anywhere else, it may be! — without making his own Law, many's the time. It's been eat or be eat! Ye came in, preachin' that Law'd come west of the Rowdy. But ye can't blame me that I laid back to see what happened. Ye did more than any one of us believed ye could do — aye! Smoky Cole or anyone else! Now ——"

"Trot!" Sudie-May said to him quickly. "I know what you're about to say. You can say it later. But, right now ——"

Connell stared at her, nodded, and like an overgrown boy slouched toward the door. Lit turned with him. But at the door, last of the little procession, a word halted him. He turned, frowning. Sudie-May sat upon the couch, looking steadily at him.

"Shut the door. Then come here," she said evenly.

He hesitated. She lifted her hand, and thumb and forefinger snapped explosively. He hooked the door with his toe, slammed it, came over to lower down at her.

"Sit down," she commanded. "Now! That's better. I wanted to talk to you."

"Nothing to talk about," Lit said in careless tone.

"Is *that* so?" she countered acidly. "I can't agree with you. There's a lot to talk about. I know that by all the rules laid down in the novels, a sweet young girl like me should be prostrated because Frenchy is dead down yonder. But, somehow — I can't seem to put any enthusiasm into thinking about him. I was almost raised with him. I thought I knew him — as a happy-go-lucky, dare-devil sort of cowboy, a little on the rustle, of course, but more good than bad. Then you showed him up as a coward — at Hell Creek. And tonight, he showed his real self. So — let's forget him! As quickly as we can. The important thing is ———"

"What?" Lit said angrily, staring at her.

"You," she said calmly. "And, of course, me. You're going back to Gurney, aren't you? Going to turn over the star as quickly as possible to somebody. Then you're going back to the Diamond and ———"

"— And break in at managing the Bar-B," he nodded.

"That's what I thought . . . And — I don't like it, Lit! I don't like it a little bit!"

Suddenly, calmness vanished, that almost mannish calm she had held. She looked up at him with little head tilted, caught his shirt-sleeve, shook it gently. She leaned to him and tilted face farther back. There was nothing mannish about her, now! She was utterly feminine in that clinging négligée.

"Do you want me? Still want me?"

"You said ———" he began thickly.

336

"And *you* said ——" she stopped him. "So we're even. You haven't told me, though, what I asked you. Do you — want me?"

Lit turned, caught her, and silk ripped under hard hand. He held her close against him, found her mouth coming up to meet his as upon the trail — but with no drawing back at all, now. So, for breathless minutes.

A discreet knock sounded upon the door. Lit lifted his head. In angry voice Sudie-May addressed the knocking one: "Go away!"

Minutes later, the knocking sounded again. She lifted her head from his shoulder, smiled at him, straightened, looked at the wide sleeve of the négligée.

"If my father sees this and reacts traditionally, young man, you know what he'll do? He'll make you marry me!"

"Let's show him, then," Lit grinned.

"He wants to offer you the management of Los Alamos. He and the Governor are going to write a book on *The Horse.* He thinks it's a big secret. But I have heard him talk about you — and swear at you . . . I knew what was in his transparent mind. Let's let him in!"

She called and King stumped in. He looked up at the ceiling, cleared his throat. "It's like this, Lit," he began, then stared as

Sudie-May laughed. "Ye little divil! Ye told him — though how ye knew ——"

"I'll run things my way!" Lit warned him. "Letting the little fellows live in peace, having Los Alamos men and money undo the damage you've done!"

"It's a free hand I'm givin' ye!" Connell grinned. "I'll take the rest I'm due. Uh — ye need me for anything else?"

He grinned at the double-headshake and went out. They were sitting quietly, her head on his shoulder, when from the patio came a discreet voice: "Oh, Lit! She's me!"

Chihuahua came in, grinning.

"Me, I'm think mabbe-so you're shoot at them door. So I'm holloa first. I'm ride off, now, pretty soon."

"Where?" Lit demanded, frowning.

"*Quién sabe?* Me, I'm have them foot w'at's itch. She must be scratch against them new trail."

"But — but you'll come back, *amigo?*" Lit cried.

"*Segur' Miguel!* Me, I'm come back one day, an' " — he grinned at Sudie-May — "w'en I'm come into them patio, I'm mabbe see one fi-ine little girl, with them yellow hair like — like her mother. An' she's look at me, them little girl. She's say:

" 'She's them dam' Uncle Chihuahua! W'at the hell!' "